FRANCES *and the* MONSTER

FRANCES *and the* MONSTER

REFE TUMA

HARPER

An Imprint of HarperCollins*Publishers*

Library of Congress Control Number: 2022930514
ISBN 978-0-06-308576-3

Typography by Catherine Lee
22 23 24 25 26 SB 10 9 8 7 6 5 4 3 2 1
❖

First Edition

For Susan.

And for Erin, who would've liked it, I think.

Chapter 1
An Unwelcome Surprise

August 29, 1939, was a Tuesday.

Under normal circumstances, Frances had little reason to keep track of the days of the week. Or the months of the year, for that matter. Calendars were for marking dates and times, for meeting people and going places. Frances never went anywhere and rarely saw anyone. With no comings or goings to punctuate her existence, she lived in a peculiar flatness of time unique to those who never leave the house.

Today, all that was going to change.

The sun hadn't yet breached the wide, treelined peak of the Gurten, but Frances was awake. She sat with her elbows on her dressing table and her nose pressed to a mason jar. Under the glass, eight black orbs stared up at her in two neat rows.

She had discovered the spider in her wardrobe, crouched between the blouses and slacks, legs raised like the ribs of an umbrella. All but one, which splayed awkwardly behind it. She identified the species as *Eratigena atrica*, or "giant house spider." It spanned the width of her fist, covered from head to tarsus in a peat of oily hairs.

Frances glanced over her shoulder at the suitcase lying open on her bed. She should finish packing, but that leg was in bad shape. More important, aside from her parents and the laboratory animals, the spider was the first living thing she'd seen in months.

"Wait here," Frances instructed her now. *Her* being more accurate, because while house spiders can't be told apart by their markings, only a female could grow so large. This gave Frances, herself unusually small, a measure of satisfaction.

Frances left the jar on the table and knelt at her toy chest. She set aside a stuffed giraffe, a golden-haired doll she'd always despised, and a medical-grade stethoscope. She found what she needed near the bottom: an aluminum bear that played a tiny drum when she wound the key. She held it up to the jar and closed one eye.

Perfect.

Because Frances was the type of girl to keep a small collection of tools in her nightstand, she was able to find a tiny watchmaker's screwdriver, needle-nose pliers, and a roll of tape. She laid each item on the table.

First, she unscrewed the bear's arm at the shoulder and pried the drumstick from its paw. Then she tore off two pieces of tape with her teeth and stuck them to the edge of the table.

"You'd better behave," she said, lifting the jar.

The spider twitched her mandibles.

Frances kept one eye on the spider's toothy end and aligned the metal elbow to the injured leg. She taped it into place, careful not to pinch any hairs, then pulled her hands away.

The spider took a tentative step forward. The splinted leg dragged at first, contending with the added stiffness of the elbow, but the spider quickly adjusted her stride.

"See? Much better."

Frances set her hand palm up on the table. The spider prodded her skin before climbing on. She let the spider run, turning her hand like a circus ball. Each leg moved in perfect sequence now, adapting easily to the ridge of a knuckle or the gap between two fingers.

The tape began peeling at the edges, so Frances lifted the splinted leg to press it back down. The spider, having shown remarkable patience up to this point, decided enough was enough and sunk her fangs into the skin between Frances's thumb and forefinger.

She cried out and dropped the spider, which skittered around the table legs, up the side of her bed, and into her suitcase.

"No, not in there!"

Frances peered inside and found the spider waiting, four hairy legs raised, poised for attack. She shoved the suitcase off the bed with a yelp, spilling shirts and slacks and socks onto the floor. The spider zigged and zagged across the carpet before it disappeared beneath the wardrobe.

Frances sat on the foot of her bed and sucked at her hand, watching the bite marks swell up from the surface of her skin. A metal box near the door crackled to life as her mother's tinny voice filled the room.

"Frances! Would you please join your father and me downstairs? Over."

Was it time to leave already? Frances threw open the curtains and blinked as sunlight filled her room. She rarely slept, and dawn had a way of sneaking up on her. She crossed her room and pressed the button next to the speaker.

"Getting dressed. Over."

Frances stuffed her clothes back into the suitcase, forcing it shut with her knee, then shimmied out of her pajamas and kicked them under the bed. She pulled one of the remaining blouses from the wardrobe along with high-waisted short pants and green suspenders. A bow tie and a pair of two-toned leather brogues finished the ensemble. It was a boy's outfit, Frances knew. If it were up to her, she'd wear a white lab coat at all times, or the denim coveralls she wore to tinker with her father's machines. Pants were the next best thing.

She'd cut her hair, too, which bobbed just past her jaw, but that's where her mother drew the line.

"Short hair doesn't suit you," she would often say.

Frances suspected the real reason had more to do with her missing right ear. That was a dreadful business: an automobile accident before her fourth birthday. She remembered very little from that night, or the months that followed. Her parents seldom talked about it, and she tried to seldom think of it.

She certainly wasn't going to let it sour her mood today.

Frances dragged her suitcase into the hall and locked the door behind her—a habit she picked up during the reign of one of her nosier tutors.

The hallway was long and narrow, with musty green carpet and dark wood trim. A faded floral pattern papered the walls: white edelweiss, pink rhododendron, purple orchids, and Frances's favorite, pale green *Cirsium spinosissimum*—"spinlest thistle." Portraits of relatives she'd never meet crowded either side. Leaning over the railing, Frances could see all the way to the ground floor in one direction and the atrium skylights in the other.

It had been seven years since the accident, seven years

since her parents said they wanted to keep her inside for a few months to observe her recovery. A few months became a year . . . then two years . . . then five and so on. By then it was her way of life, and she rarely thought to question it. Until, one week ago, when she found a glossy piece of paper in her father's jacket pocket. It was a brochure for the Symposium of Science and Invention in Brussels.

She was reading it when her father walked into the room.

"I'd like to come," she said, squaring her shoulders. "I'm ready."

He didn't respond, but she could see on his face he had understood. That was all the encouragement Frances needed. She had spent every day since in preparation: plotting train routes, studying Brussels architecture, and combing through her mother's magazines for photographs of the cities she would pass along the way.

Victor and Mary Stenzel were scientists. Between them, they held patents on thirty-seven inventions and had received dozens of prestigious awards including, very nearly, a Nobel Prize for chemistry in 1932. Both were still young (for world-renowned scientists), and Mary, at least, was quite striking. In certain circles, they had become something of a celebrity couple.

None of that impressed Frances. For her, it meant only that her parents spent a great deal of time sailing around the world speaking at conferences and fundraisers, sometimes six months out of the year, while she remained behind.

Until today. Frances slid her luggage behind the grandfather clock on the landing so her father wouldn't see it—she didn't want to ruin his surprise—and stopped by her parents' room.

Victor Stenzel was standing over an open suitcase while a machine filled it with clothes. A metal arm plucked a sweater from the top of the pile, folded it, and dropped it into the suitcase. The arm pressed the sweater into place and swung around to pluck another from the pile.

"I see you stayed up tinkering instead of packing, again," Frances teased.

Victor looked up, smiling at the sight of his daughter. "Frankie, my dear!"

A cacophony of bells erupted as clocks in every room tolled the hour. Frances covered her ear until the final peal rang out, leaving only the mechanical whirring of the auto-packer.

"Victor, darling," Mary called, bursting into the room on a wave of shimmering red fabric and bouncing chestnut curls, "I summoned you ages ago. Will you please speed that contraption along? I swear, without a clock on every wall you wouldn't know dawn from dusk. As for you," she said, turning her attention on Frances, "I expect to find you waiting in the Great Room no later than seven fifteen."

The doorbell chimed before either could reply, an underwhelming sound after the clocks.

"That will be Mr. Byron," Mary said, already gliding away. "We shouldn't keep him waiting."

"Shouldn't we?" Victor grumbled. "It's never too late to learn some patience, even for him."

"You'd better hurry," Frances said, "or Mum will drag you to the car by your ear and you'll end up like me."

Victor smiled and put his hands on Frances's shoulders. "You know your mother well. Now, do try to be civil toward Mr. Byron, or I'll hear about it for the entire trip."

"Would you like me to giggle and curtsy, too?"

"An occasional show of manners wouldn't kill you." He held up a finger. "Oh! Don't let me forget—I have a surprise for you before we go."

I knew it. Frances tried not to grin too widely.

Victor turned and clapped his hands together, surveying his luggage. "I think with a few minor adjustments, I can almost double the auto-packer's speed. . . ."

Frances left her father to his tinkering and padded down the stairs to the kitchen. She fixed herself breakfast—a slice of toast with raspberry jam and a hard-boiled egg—and waited for the coffee to brew. She watched the amber liquid rise through the clear, spiraled tubes of the percolator, filling the glass chamber at the top until it was ready to pour. A splash of cream, two spoonfuls of sugar. She closed her eyes and took a sip, transporting herself to a café in Brussels, seated at a table with her parents, talking and laughing among the most brilliant minds in Europe.

She glanced at the clock above the pantry just as the minute hand slid into place over the three, the faint *tick* snapping her from her daydream as if she'd been listening for it. She scraped her food, untouched, into the trash bin, grabbed her coffee mug, and hurried to meet her parents.

The Great Room was a cavernous space with an arched ceiling and a canopy of oak trusses. A wooden bear guarded the entrance, carved from the trunk of a tree and standing over seven feet tall. Frances had been sent to her room more than once for climbing it. She heard her father speaking before she entered the room and ducked behind the bear to listen.

"As I've told you in no uncertain terms," her father was saying, "the answer is no."

There were two men with him. One wore a linen blazer and a yellow tie, with a lavish purple scarf draped across his shoulders. The other stood with his hands folded behind his back, wearing a dark suit and a blank expression. Mr. Byron and his driver.

"I'm sure I can secure a counteroffer from the Brits," Mr. Byron said. "If you fancy yourself more of an Allied man."

Victor pushed up under his glasses and rubbed the bridge

of his nose. "I'm a scientist! I don't have the constitution for the war business, and even if I did—"

"Everyone's in the war business now," Mr. Byron said, cutting him off with a wave of his hand. "Besides, if what your old man wrote in his letter is true, we could end this war before it begins—victory to the highest bidder!"

"He wasn't my old man," Victor said, raising his voice. "He was my mother's father. And he was half-mad when he wrote that letter. The experiment failed, just as everyone knew it would. There's nothing left of him down there but rusted instruments and bad memories."

Frances stepped into the doorway and cleared her throat. Both men looked up. Mr. Byron's driver continued to stare at nothing, or perhaps everything at once—she was never sure.

"Frances." Victor forced a laugh. "We were just—"

"Discussing our itinerary," Mr. Byron said. He pulled a gold watch from his vest pocket, flipped it open, and snapped it shut again. "Goodness, where has the time gone?"

Victor kissed Frances on the forehead. "I'd better see to your mother. It appears it's my turn to hurry her along." With his back turned to Mr. Byron, he choked the air with his hands. Frances stifled a laugh.

"My dear girl," Mr. Byron said once Victor had left the room. "Why, you're exactly the same size as when I last saw you. You can't have grown a centimeter!"

Mr. Byron was a thickset man with a slight nose. His full lips wouldn't have looked out of place on a woman if not for the finely trimmed mustache that looked like a starving caterpillar had crawled onto his face to die. He managed her parents' business affairs—patents, grants, investments, and the like— so they could focus on their work. If Victor was the brains of the operation and Mary the iron will, Mr. Byron was the eyes, with little green dollar signs instead of pupils.

He nodded toward the coffee Frances still nursed.

"Enjoying the percolator, yes? The sale of that contraption kept the candles burning in this Manor for many years." He waved his hands across the room. "Now it keeps the electricity humming, too."

Frances shrugged and took another sip. "As long as it makes coffee."

Mr. Byron let out a booming laugh. "A quick tongue on this one, eh, Braun?" He elbowed his driver. If Braun noticed, Frances couldn't tell. Mr. Byron pulled out a handkerchief to dab his eyes and regarded the room. "It's a grand place, isn't it?"

Frances nodded. She had few memories of the world outside these walls, but she was certain there was no place like it. The mansion had belonged to her great-grandfather Albrecht Grimme, a brilliant recluse. Her father came as a boy to assist him with his work and spent two years in the laboratory before the old man's death. His entire estate passed to Victor after that, held in trust until he came of age. Grimme-Stenzel Manor had been her world for seven years, and even if she had seven more, she wasn't sure she would reach the end of its curiosities.

Frances realized her heart was racing. *You'll only be away a few days*, she reminded herself.

"A grand place indeed," Mr. Byron continued. "I pray it stays that way."

Frances stopped mid-sip. "Why wouldn't it?"

"Haven't you heard? It's the end of the world!"

Mr. Byron laughed, though Frances couldn't imagine what was funny. She *had* heard talk of war: in her parents' hushed voices when they thought she'd gone to bed, in headlines splashed across the front page of the newspaper. Just the night before, her favorite radio program was interrupted by a report claiming Germany would soon march on Poland. Still, it all felt so far away. She hadn't considered that war might reach the Manor.

"Now," Mr. Byron said, "there's no need to despair. When fools look around and see only darkness, what does the wise man see?" He paused, his lips stretching into a grin. "A market for torches."

Frances frowned. The first shot hadn't been fired and already he was looking to profit. "Is that the speech you gave my father?"

"So, you were eavesdropping," he said, nodding to the bear.

"I thought I spied you behind that wooden monstrosity." He leaned in close. "I shouldn't be telling you this, but your parents have been a bit—how do I put it?—slow to adapt. I'm afraid we're in need of a breakthrough. Something big."

"They'll come up with something. They always do."

Without your wartime profiteering, she added silently.

"Perhaps. Say . . ." He put a hand on his hip and stroked his chin as if something important had just occurred to him. "How much do you know about your great-grandfather?"

"Only that he was a brilliant scientist."

"You're quite right about that. You wouldn't happen to know where your parents keep the old man's things, would you? Funny-looking machines, files maybe . . . ?"

Frances played along. "Gee, I'm sure if there was anything like that down there, I'd have found it." She turned to Mr. Byron, her voice flattening. "And my father would have told you about it when you asked him five minutes ago."

Mr. Byron chuckled. "You're a clever one, aren't you? It's a shame your father never allows you to join us on our adventures."

Frances gave him a look over the rim of her mug. "You don't have to pretend," she said, taking a sip. She was annoyed to find her coffee had gone cold.

"Pretend what?"

"That you don't know about my surprise."

Mr. Byron raised an eyebrow.

"That they're taking me with. On the trip?"

His face softened. "My dear girl. I bought the tickets myself. If you were joining us, I would know."

Before Frances could argue, the doors burst open and her mother entered the room. Her father followed with the luggage.

"Mr. Byron," Mary exclaimed. "I thought you'd have left without us by now."

Mr. Byron straightened and clasped his hands. "Without my brilliant partners? I wouldn't dream of it! Besides, with no one to give the lectures, how would I collect the fee?"

He turned to Victor, who was straining red-faced under the weight of his one suitcase and Mary's six. "Victor! You'll burst a vessel in that glorious brain of yours." With a nod from Mr. Byron, Braun sprang into action, collecting the luggage from Victor and carrying all seven suitcases out the door as if they were filled with air.

Frances, on the other hand, felt deflated. Surely Mr. Byron was only toying with her or her parents had simply forgotten to inform him of their plans. She quickly shook the doubt away and took a deep breath to calm her nerves.

"Frances, darling," Mary called, gliding across the floor. "Your father and I have something we'd like to show you."

This is it. Frances lifted her head and pulled back her

shoulders, standing as tall as she could manage while her father took his place at Mary's side. The way his hands were fidgeting, he looked nearly as excited as Frances felt.

"I'm sure you understand that these are uncertain times," he said. "As such, we don't believe any child should be left alone—"

Frances leaned forward in anticipation. . . .

"—without a tutor."

Wait. A tutor?

Her shoulders fell as she sank back onto her heels. She began replaying in her mind everything her parents had said to her that week, the knowing looks they shared as they prepared for the trip, the hints they dropped about the new things she was about to learn and experience.

This can't be my surprise. . . . She felt her cheeks prickle with the threat of tears, but she fought them off, unwilling to let her parents see her disappointment.

"Now," Victor continued, "we know you haven't had much . . . luck with tutors in the past."

"That is putting it charitably . . . ," her mother said just loud enough for her to hear.

"But I think you'll find this one to be different. Quite different indeed." He paused expectantly. When Frances remained silent—her small frame drooping like a wilted flower, her face slack with disbelief—Mary tapped her wrist and motioned for him to get on with the big reveal. "Right. I suppose it's time you were introduced. Hobbes," he called, "please join us in the Great Room."

At his command, the double doors parted, and a tall, slender man entered. There was something odd about his gait—a stiffness in his joints that rendered his movements almost mechanical. His head was bald except for a shiny tuft of blond hair. And his eyes . . . were they glowing?

"Frankie, meet your new tutor, Hobbes."

The man bowed, bending at the waist before righting himself again, his back perfectly straight. As he moved, Frances heard a familiar whirring sound.

Of course. He wasn't a man at all.

He was a machine.

Chapter 2

H.O.B.B.E.S.

The first tutor arrived when Frances was five years old. Following the accident, she was too weak to attend school in the city. So, Mary had her schooling brought to her.

Miss Marjorie was competent but aloof, with a thick French accent and lips so thin they might have been drawn in pencil. One morning, in an effort to welcome her new employee, Mary presented Miss Marjorie with a platter of almond pastries baked in the Parisian style. Miss Marjorie recoiled. Frances recognized that this was not a normal reaction to almond pastries, and a scheme took shape in her young mind.

The next day, while Miss Marjorie drew rectangles on the blackboard, Frances dropped an almond into her tea. It only took a sip for Miss Marjorie's penciled-on lips to blow up like balloon animals. She was rushed from the Manor in the back of an ambulance and, though she made a full recovery, never returned.

Madame Elaine arrived next. She came by way of Buckingham Palace where she had looked after a young princess Elizabeth. She was a capable woman whose only discernible flaw happened to be a debilitating fear of rats. A single misplaced laboratory specimen brought her tenure to an end.

The superstitious Madame Chekhov resigned when vases began levitating and her mirror was possessed by the shadowy figure of a girl about Frances's height.

Frau Helena had been a tougher nut to crack. Imposing and strict, she did not tolerate pranks. She also suffered from an inner-ear disorder that made her prone to disorientation. That's why she thought nothing of it when she walked down a familiar hallway in the Manor and found an antique cuckoo clock where it wasn't before.

"I have simply turned down ze wrong hallvay," she told herself.

When the portrait of Great-Great-Grandma Beatrice wasn't in the landing where it should have been, Frau Helena assumed she was on the wrong floor. As days and weeks passed, the Manor became increasingly difficult to navigate. Rooms rearranged. Hallways switched places. She often found herself hopelessly lost.

One evening, she entered her bedroom and found that every piece of furniture had been replaced with the contents of Victor's trophy room. Something inside her cracked. She admitted herself to the Burghölzi psychiatric institution in Zurich the following day.

By her tenth birthday, Frances had driven away sixteen tutors of eight nationalities and four continents, proving, in her mind, that she was more than capable of caring for herself. A year had passed since the final tutor—retired Lt. General Klaus Gerber, 6th brigade, Swiss Army—and Frances thought her parents had given up.

Apparently, she was wrong.

"I call him the Household Operations Bionic Butlery and Education Servant," her father declared. "H.O.B.B.E.S. for short. What do you think?"

Victor and Mary stood grinning, arms outstretched with the machine between them, waiting for Frances's response.

Frances could only stare: at the machine, with its uncanny molded features; at her parents, their faces a mix of excitement and pride.

"Frankie?" Victor said when the moment stretched into an uncomfortable silence. "Frances dear. What do you think?"

This was her surprise. Not a trip to the science symposium in Brussels. A mechanical tutor. She steeled her expression, unwilling to let them see her disappointment.

"It's . . . remarkable, Father," she said at last. She imagined a giant pneumatic vise crushing the machine like a tin can. "I mean it. Truly."

Victor exhaled, his face flooded with relief. "I'm so glad to hear that. I've been at it a while, you know."

Mr. Byron stepped forward and circled the machine. "So, this is what you've been up to," he said, stroking his mustache. He lifted the machine's arm and wiggled its fingers one by one until it pulled its hand away.

"Pardon me," the machine said.

This seemed to amuse Mr. Byron, who slapped his knee in delight. "Brilliant! Though, factoring materials, labor, shipping . . ."

"Hobbes is for Frances," Victor said, shooing him away, "and Frances alone."

"Lucky me," she said under her breath—hardly above a whisper—then watched in alarm as the machine looked right at her.

"I designed him just for you, to be the perfect tutor," her father went on. "Go ahead! Ask him anything."

Frances hated the idea of talking to the machine. But if she had to play along, she wanted at least to say something clever.

"The man who invented it doesn't want it," she began. "The man who bought it doesn't need it. The man who needs it doesn't know it. What is it?"

"A riddle," Frances's mother said, nodding. "Interesting choice."

At first, Hobbes did not move or respond. Frances wondered if he understood, or even heard. Then his eyes changed from white to blue. When he spoke, his jaw moved along a seam that ran from either side of his mouth down to his chin like a ventriloquist's dummy's. His voice was stilted and monotone.

"It is a coffin," he said.

"Well done, Hobbes!" Victor clapped him on the back, producing a hollow gong. "You'll have to try harder than that, Frankie," he said with a wink.

Frances scowled. Her father talked as if the machine were an intelligent being, not a bundle of wires and bolts. Preprogrammed logic, that's all it had.

That gave her an idea. "Can I ask it another question?"

"Please do!"

She turned to the machine, a smirk on her lips. "What is my favorite meal?"

Hobbes's eyes again turned blue. "Rösti with bacon and eggs. A dish commonly eaten at breakfast that you enjoy any time of day."

Frances opened her mouth in surprise, then clamped it

shut. She glared at her father. "How does it know that?"

"I am programmed with a library of your preferences," Hobbes said. "Including your taste for coffee and your tendency to wear clothing designed for human males."

Mary's grin was so smug Frances thought it might drip down her chin.

"He knows everything there is to know about you," Victor said proudly. "What he doesn't, he'll learn."

"I—" Frances sputtered. "That's—"

"Now, now," said Mr. Byron, stepping around her. "Let Uncle Byron have a turn." He rubbed his hands together. "Hobbes, how much new funding will we secure on this trip?"

"I am afraid that is not within the scope of my abilities," the machine answered.

"Honestly, Byron," Victor said, shaking his head. "He's not a fortune-teller."

Mr. Byron put up his hands. "My apologies. I didn't mean to offend."

"Give him a break, dear," said Mary. "It's his job to think about the money."

Victor sighed. "I suppose you're right. Forgive me," he mumbled.

Mr. Byron bowed, twirling his hand in a theatrical flourish.

"Now then," Victor said, turning to his daughter. Or, rather, where his daughter had been moments before. When he looked for her now, she was gone.

"We have a surprise for you," Frances growled as she stomped up the stairs. "A state-of-the-art mechanical overlord! He knows everything about you. Isn't that grand?" She stormed past the portraits in the hallway and unlocked her bedroom door. When she was shut safely inside, she slid to the floor and put her face in her hands.

Moments later, she heard a knock.

Her father spoke from the hall. "May I come in?"

"You'll be late."

"Let me in, Frankie."

Frances sighed and pulled herself to her feet. "What?" she said, cracking the door.

Victor held up her suitcase. "I found this on the landing."

Frances hesitated, then stepped aside. "So?"

He gave her a look and set the suitcase on the rug. "I think I understand what's going on. When I told you we had a surprise for you, you thought we meant you would come with us on our trip."

Frances lowered her eyes.

"I'm sorry, sweetheart, but we can't let you do that."

"Why not?" she said. "Why do you have to leave me cooped

up in this drafty old house?"

Victor put a hand to his chest, feigning offence. "The Manor is hardly a 'drafty old house'! You have the library, the labs, the Zoo . . . It's practically paradise. And you know why you have to stay."

"The accident was years ago."

"This will be our last trip until this war talk blows over. We've already discussed it with Mr. Byron. He'll send Braun to check in on you every now and again, and you'll have Hobbes to watch over you until we return."

"Please, Dad," Frances began, but Victor cut in before she could finish.

"The Librarian is acting up again," he said, taking a step back. "Would you take a peek at it while we're away?"

Frances wanted to scream, but it wouldn't help. She took a deep breath instead. "That contraption is more trouble than it's worth. But I'll do my best."

"Thank you. You have a way with such things; there's no denying that. I see myself in you. Though, I never had half your confidence."

Frances didn't feel confident. It was all she could do not to cry. Her father brushed her hair from her face and pushed it behind her scar. Without an ear to hold it back, it fell again as soon as he moved his hand. He sighed and lifted her chin.

"A few days, then we'll be back. We'll bring you something

nice from Brussels. Hey," he said. His face brightened. "Did you know chips were invented in Brussels? The American name, *french fries*, always seemed absurd, but I recently learned that—"

"Dad," Frances interrupted. "You really will be late."

Victor grinned sheepishly. "Of course." He kissed her forehead and gave her one last smile. Then he was out the door and Frances was alone again.

Chapter 3
Operation Disorder

F rances stayed in her room for the rest of the morning. She tried to nap—she had been up all night packing and getting bitten by spiders—but, as usual, sleep wouldn't come. So, she lay in her bed, imagining what marvelous sights might be flying past her parents' train car: snowcapped mountains, the spires of the Basel Minster, the mottled edge of the Black Forest along the German border.

Soon, a delicious smell seeped under her door. She felt a pang of hunger, then of hope. Maybe her parents had a change of heart and stayed. But it would only be the machine.

A *machine*! They hadn't even thought to leave her in the company of another human being. Frances sighed and made her way downstairs.

Hobbes was at the kitchen stove, wearing Mary's apron. His movements were efficient, methodical. He didn't hum Yvette Guilbert tunes like her mother did or search frantically for misplaced ingredients like her father. Every movement had a purpose.

Frances watched in silence from behind the door, then took a breath and stepped inside.

"Good afternoon, Frances," Hobbes said, without turning.

She crossed the room and pulled a chair out from the table, letting it screech against the tile floor. Hobbes draped a towel over his arm and set a plate of food in front of her.

"Rösti with bacon and eggs. Your favorite."

It smelled even better up close. The potatoes were golden brown, the bacon crispy but not overdone, and the eggs were still runny at the center the way she liked them. Everything was spaced evenly across the plate without touching, which was odd but no less appetizing.

Frances reached for her fork, then shook her head and slid the plate across the table. Her parents may have left Hobbes in charge, but she didn't have to make it easy for him.

"No, thank you," she said.

Hobbes examined the plate first, then Frances. "Have I prepared the dish incorrectly?"

"I'm not hungry."

"It is lunchtime."

Frances shrugged. "I don't want it."

Hobbes's eyes turned yellow. "I do not understand."

"That," Frances said, pushing away from the table, "is because you're only a machine."

Rösti and bacon danced through Frances's mind as she hurried across the Manor to a pair of large metal doors. She mashed a button on the control panel and tapped her foot until the doors opened with a *ding*.

The sound of her stomach grumbling filled the elevator as soon as she stepped inside. She couldn't return to the kitchen—not after that exit—so she would have to scavenge elsewhere. Fortunately, she knew just the place.

The elevator started with a lurch. The ride to the basement was long, but the Manor's was no ordinary basement. It was huge—easily twice the width of the Manor itself—and located deep underground.

When the doors opened, Frances found herself in darkness. A light flickered on overhead. Another followed, and another, until row by row the hallway was filled with the hum of glowing filaments. Chestnut doors lined the walls on either side as far as she could see, marking the various stations. An imposing portrait of her great-grandfather Albrecht Grimme kept watch over the foyer.

Frances passed the chemistry station where her mother

mixed experimental compounds; the circuitry room covered floor to ceiling in tarps to prevent dust from contaminating the boards; the specimen lab with its shelves of brains floating in jars; and the appliance workshop, which Mr. Byron had insisted her parents build. He claimed the invention of new household devices would make them millionaires. He was right, as he often was.

Before long, she reached her favorite station: the Zoo.

Frances's mother was always bringing home animals on which to test her compounds. It was a rare source of contention between her parents. Though Mary took every precaution to ensure the animals' well-being, Victor didn't approve. Frances was just happy for the companionship and had taken it upon herself to care for them.

She flipped the light switch, but nothing happened. The bulb must have blown again. She scolded herself for not bringing a candle. As she groped her way across the room to find the lamp, she realized the animals were on edge. Rats squeaked nervously on her left. On her right, a cage full of rabbits thumped in their hay. Somewhere ahead of her, the cockatoo shrieked.

"What's the matter?" she said when she reached the rabbits. "Lourdes? Shelley?"

She was wondering what had the animals spooked when she felt hot breath on the back of her neck. She turned around, coming face-to-face with a dark, hairy creature standing over her with its long arms raised above its head. Frances stumbled backward, but the rabbit cage blocked her path. The creature reached out and grabbed her, wrapping its arms around her, and squeezed until she struggled to breathe. Then it opened its mouth and planted a big, wet kiss on her cheek.

"Ew, Fritz, no," Frances cried.

"Ooh-ooh-aah," Fritz said.

"I see you've figured out the new lock on your cage. Only took you, what? Two days this time?"

Fritz the chimpanzee was her mother's most promising subject. She was developing an intelligence serum that would allow Fritz to overcome difficult problems or prepare for an important test. With each dose, he exhibited improvements in concentration, memory, and sign-language skills. Of course, the effects only lasted forty-eight hours before waning, but his progress was remarkable, even if it had become difficult to keep him in a cage.

Frances lit the lamp and located the true reason for her visit: two bananas from Fritz's cabinet. She handed one of them to Fritz and watched him peel and eat it with surprising grace. Frances devoured hers in two bites.

"I'm on a hunger strike," she said, spraying flecks of yellow pulp from her mouth.

When she finished, Frances dropped the peels into the

wastebasket. Fritz placed the edge of one hand onto the palm of the other—the sign for *lesson.*

"You won't be getting a visit from Mother Mary today," she replied, speaking both aloud and as best she could with her hands. "She and Dad have gone away again."

Fritz whimpered and pulled the corners of his mouth into a theatrical frown with his fingers.

"You haven't even met the new tutor. He's the worst one yet. He's not even human! No offense," she added.

Frances took Fritz's hand and helped him into his cage. "If Mum and Dad get back and he's got everything under control, we'll be stuck with him for good. I need him to make a mistake."

Fritz tilted his head to one side and pressed his knuckles together, forming a pair of arches with his hands. *How?*

"I don't know. So far, he doesn't seem to *make* mistakes. He's all logic and order."

She slid the padlock into place but hesitated before snapping it shut.

"That's it," she said. "He's programmed for order." Her eyes scanned the Zoo. "I need to create some chaos."

Back in the kitchen, Hobbes scrubbed the countertops with quick, precise strokes: two left, two right, down six millimeters, repeat.

He was interrupted mid-stroke when a sparrow fluttered into the room and perched on the faucet.

"You do not belong in the kitchen," he said.

The sparrow hopped to the countertop and pecked at a seam in the marble. Hobbes shooed the bird with his scrub brush, sending it flitting up to the rafters, tweeting angrily.

Hobbes returned to his task. Two strokes left, two right . . . He set the brush on the counter and turned. There, behind him, sat a large gray rabbit.

"You do not belong here, either."

Another rabbit padded up behind it, followed by a third. Hobbes took a step forward, and they scattered to either end of the room.

Watching through a thin crack in the door, Frances held her breath to keep from laughing. Operation Disorder was going exactly as planned. She unclasped the door to a wire birdcage. "Your turn," she whispered.

Hobbes ducked as a yellow-crested cockatoo buzzed his shoulder and landed on a nearby windowsill, where it shrieked and bobbed its head. Before he could react, a dozen mice scurried beneath the pantry and a snake coiled around his ankle. Soon, the floor was teeming with fur and feathers and scales.

"The kitchen is reserved for the preparation of human sustenance," he cried.

Frances watched Hobbes run across the room, swatting at mice, then rabbits, then birds. She half expected to see smoke pour from his ear holes.

It was time for her grand finale. She held a walkie-talkie to her lips. "Now."

Hobbes was pulling a mouse from the pantry by its tail when the cabinets began to rattle. Frances imagined him searching his data stores for the source of the noise—not loud enough for the footfalls of a bear, too loud for a cat. A fox? A badger?

The thumping grew louder and louder until the double doors burst open and in leaped Fritz, swinging from the chandelier and landing on Hobbes's iron chest, sending him clattering to the floor.

Chapter 4

Detained

After she released the last of the animals into the kitchen, her plan had been to appear in the doorway and ask what all the commotion was about.

"Looks like a zoo in here," she'd say. It was going to be perfect.

But when she put her ear to the door, the room was quiet. She peeked inside.

"Ah, Frances," Hobbes said. "Would you please return these creatures to their proper storage compartments?"

Somehow, using only a mixing bowl, a fruit basket, and a garbage can, the machine had contained every animal but the cockatoo, which was perched on his shoulder. And Fritz. The traitorous chimp sat on the counter eating an apple, docile as a kitten.

Cleaning up her own prank wasn't even the worst of it: when she finished, the machine actually smiled. "A valiant effort, I'm sure," he said.

So he could do smug. *Good to know.*

There was more: as punishment for her "misuse of zoological specimens," Hobbes restricted her access to the lab.

"You can't do that," she said. "I have work down there!"

"I think you'll find you are far too busy."

And she was. Hobbes scheduled her next few days in fifteen-minute increments, with extra chores and lessons, leaving no time for further resistance. At night, her eyelids were so heavy she could almost—almost—fall asleep.

Finally, the day of her parents' return arrived.

"Enjoy the morning, Hobbes," Frances said, "because as soon as my parents get back, you're headed for the scrapyard, where you belong."

"Your statement is both improbable and inaccurate. Improbable because I am functioning exactly as Master Stenzel programmed me. Inaccurate because your parents will not be returning today as planned."

He held out a telegram.

> Dearest Frankie,
> Your mother and I hit a snag on our way home from Brussels (the chips were phenomenal,

by the way). Nothing to worry about, just a mix-up with an overly thorough garrison of Germans. A young woman here was kind enough to send this telegram for us, but it may be a few days before we can write again. I trust you and Hobbes are getting along?

All my love,

Victor Stenzel (Dad)

"They've been detained?" Frances ran her fingers through her hair. *They were supposed to return today. They have to.* "We need to help them."

"Will we be traveling to Germany to release them?" the machine replied.

Frances shot him a look that could have melted his bolts. Smug, sarcastic—the mechanical man was turning out to be a wellspring of inflection. He was also right. They could do nothing but wait.

The rest of the day passed in a fog of worry. Her chores went unfinished. She hardly picked at her lunch. She tried tinkering with the Librarian—a device used to send books between the library and the lab through a system of tubes. Books had been exiting the terminal in tatters, and Frances suspected a kink in the chute might be to blame. She had promised her father she would fix it before he returned. But now, with no idea when his return might be, she found it hard to stay motivated. Her mind drifted from one terrible fate to the next. What if the Germans held her parents until the end of the war? What if they never returned at all?

For dinner, Hobbes prepared boiled sausage and carrots. Frances *hated* boiled sausage and carrots. She might have been happy to find something he didn't know about her, if it didn't mean she'd have to eat it. The sausage seemed to be aware it wasn't wanted and kept trying to roll off her plate as she stormed up the stairs to her room.

"Your parents instructed me to dine with you," Hobbes called, still wearing her mother's apron. "Family connections are vital during mealtimes."

"You're not my family," Frances shouted from the landing. "And you don't eat!"

She slammed her bedroom door and turned on the radio, hoping for news about her parents.

"Hallo Switzerland Calling," the announcer began. *"Ladies and gentlemen, twenty-five years have passed since the outbreak of the last world war and now a new one has begun. Two of Switzerland's big neighbors are again engaged in destruction, France and Germany. Switzerland, the little peaceful nation at the heart of the continent, has proclaimed*

its absolute decision of neutrality—"

She switched it off and sank onto the windowsill. From there, Bern was a mere toyscape, a city in miniature. It was hard to imagine an even bigger world beyond what she could see from her hilltop perch. A world where battles were being fought and innocent people were snatched up and locked away . . . and worse. She pushed the sausage around her plate and imagined eating pastries on the banks of the river with her parents safely by her side, the threat of war and overbearing tutors a distant dream.

She remembered visiting the city as a child, walking the streets with her parents after the sun had gone down and the lamps had been lit. Her mum and dad looked so different then—she almost couldn't picture their faces. They'd pass the statue of the city's founder, Berthold V, who fought the great bear to a draw. They'd watch stars dance on the surface of the river. She remembered the shopkeepers closing up for the night, the mothers and nursemaids calling their children in from the streets, where they played hopscotch and Red Rover. The roar of automobile engines, trundling down the cobblestones. She remembered riding in an auto herself—springs poking through the leather seats, wind whipping at her hair. She heard her mother gasp, and the squeal of brakes. Then she was flying through the air, glass shattering all around her, tiny blue crystals flecked with red and strands of long, dark hair. The blinding light—

Frances cried out and pulled the curtains shut, clutching them to keep from collapsing. Her heart raced in her chest, and her fingers found her scar as she stumbled into bed.

Moments later, Frances heard footsteps outside her room. She slid beneath the covers and turned her back to the door just as light from the hall spilled across her bed. The machine spoke, but with her ear against the pillow, Frances wasn't able to make out his words. The door closed again.

Frances remained in bed, watching the outsized silhouette of a fly flitting about in the moonlight between the curtains and the window. Over and over, it buzzed headlong into the glass, so intent on getting outside it forgot about the window after each collision. Frances threw her pillow across the room.

When Operation Disorder failed, she had consoled herself with the promise of her parents' return. Now she had no way to know when that would be. There was nothing she could do to help them, and they could do nothing to help her. She wasn't even sure they *would* help her. For all her talk of scrapping him for parts, Hobbes was right—he was functioning exactly the way he was designed.

She was on her own. Of course, she was used to that. She outsmarted her previous tutors without anyone's help, using their own weaknesses against them. But they were only human. If Hobbes had a weakness, she had yet to find it.

Frances sat up in bed as a realization shot through her like an electric charge.

She had been looking in the wrong place.

Chapter 5

A Grimme Discovery

The Manor was dark, lit only by moonlight filtering in through the skylights. Frances eased her door shut until she heard the soft click of the spindle and locked it, placing the key in the pocket of her nightclothes. A floorboard creaked beneath her feet, and she froze. It was only nerves—no one was around to hear.

One advantage of Frances's insomnia was that she knew when the machine retreated to the attic to power down for the night, which happened at precisely eleven thirty, without exception. This time, she'd make sure he was powered down for good.

She climbed a narrow stairway at the end of the hall and pressed her ear to the door. The last time she visited the attic, she was six years old. She remembered only musty wooden trunks and dust that hung in the air when she sneezed. Now something inside whirred rhythmically, like a chorus of fireplace bellows.

What is going on in there?

She leaned in harder, and the door gave way, sending her tumbling into the room and depositing her face-to-face with Hobbes. She scrambled backward, then stopped herself. The clock on the wall read eleven forty-eight. Sure enough, Hobbes's eyes were dim and lifeless. She waved a hand in front of his face. Nothing. Frances smiled. He was asleep. Or something like it.

A cable ran from the back of Hobbes's neck into a machine so large it filled the room. Reams of paper ran through a series of rollers, each punched with a pattern of square holes. Some kind of code, Frances figured. One ream was blank, spinning above his head, with new holes appearing as she watched.

"This is your brain," Frances said aloud.

She could unplug him—yank the cord from his neck and let the computer slow to a stop ream by ream. It would be easy. *Too* easy. Her father would never leave such an obvious vulnerability without a fail-safe in place. For all she knew, pulling the cord would only wake Hobbes up.

Instead, Frances turned her attention to the computer. It was covered in a lattice of wires and nodes, a row of glowing vacuum tubes mounted across the top. She felt along the console until a piece of paper peeled away and fluttered to the floor. She picked it up and turned it over.

90-835-778

The sevens were crossed the way her father wrote them. Frances folded the note and slid it into her pocket. If the numbers had something to do with the machine, they might come in handy.

Downstairs, the clocks cast the shadows of ghouls and burglars, hunched and creeping across the foyer. The bear's wooden eyes shifted in the light of her candle, tracking her movements. Every creak was a sigh, as if the old house was only sleeping and might rise off its foundation at any moment and walk away.

Her father said he'd been working on Hobbes for months, right under her nose. That meant he had a hidden workshop, somewhere Frances hadn't explored. The solution to her tutor problem would be found there, she was certain of it. She stepped into the elevator and began the long descent.

Some children visit their parents' shop to watch them cook or sew or sell. Frances spent her childhood watching her parents create polymers and bind neutrons. She began making her own discoveries as soon as she learned to read: documenting the osmotrophic properties of fungus at five, the metathesis of sodium chloride and silver nitrate at six and a half.

All that had been during the day. Now, alone in the middle of the night, she couldn't deny the eerie quality that permeated the lab. Great-Grandfather Grimme seemed to greet her with a suspicious glare as she passed beneath his portrait. His gray suit looked extra dour in the lamplight, his creased brow more severe. She walked along the opposite wall until he was out of sight.

Her first stop was the Zoo.

"Fritz," she whispered, unlocking the door. "You awake?"

The chimp grunted sleepily.

"Sorry I haven't been to see you. Hobbes made the lab off-limits, but he's powered down for the night." She stuck her face between the bars of his cage. "Let's go figure out how to keep him that way."

"Ooh-ah!" Fritz cried. He began scuffling around. A moment later, there was a loud *clink*, and Frances stepped back as the padlock clattered to the floor.

She held up her candle. "Fritz?"

Fritz leaped out of the darkness and into Frances's arms, nearly knocking her to the ground. She stroked him behind the ears.

"Ready?"

Fritz nodded eagerly and hopped to the floor.

Girl and chimp walked hand in hand through the hallways, passing the familiar rooms. Before long, they neared the end. Frances had only ventured this far once as a giggling child running from her mother's outstretched arms.

"Time to go back," her mother had said.

"How come?"

"This is as far as it goes! You didn't think the lab went on forever, did you?"

That's exactly what she'd thought. Even after that day, she never stopped believing in the magic of the place, the sense that there was more to it than met the eye.

Perhaps that's why, when Frances reached the end of the final hallway, she didn't stop and turn around. Fritz tilted his head quizzically as she ran her fingers across the surface of the bricks and the veins of mortar between them. She tugged at the lamps. She even spoke aloud several passwords and phrases, to no effect.

Finally, Frances leaned against the wall and slid to the floor.

"Sorry, Fritz," she said. "I guess this won't be much of an adventure after all."

She closed her eyes and rested her head against one of the bricks—

—and it moved.

Frances jumped to her feet and watched the brick slide into the wall. For a moment, that seemed to be the end of it. Then the entire wall spun at its center, gathering speed and whisking Frances into a cold, dark room, the motion snuffing out her candle.

"Fritz," she called, pounding on the wall. She could hear him screeching and whimpering on the other side. "Wait there, I'll find a way out."

The wall settled back into place, sending up a cloud of dust. Frances spun on her heels as lights flickered on behind her.

"Is someone here?"

She scanned the room. Six tables were arranged in a grid across the floor. Racks hung over each of them, with tools dangling like vines. Much like everything her father did, the space was equal parts harebrained chaos and efficiency.

"This is it. This is where he built Hobbes."

Fritz hooted nervously on the other side of the wall.

"Don't worry," she called. "I'll get what I need and come right out, I promise."

If she only knew what she needed.

Frances passed between the tables. On one, she found a metal hat that strapped under the chin and massaged the wearer's scalp with motorized prongs. It rattled her teeth, so she took it off. Another table held prototypes for some kind of flying platform. It looked terrifically dangerous, and Frances had to try very hard not to turn it on and take it for a spin.

Most of the contraptions ranged from the impractical to the

absurd. This was clearly where her father came to play. Frances felt a twinge of hurt. They had always connected over their love of tinkering—why would he hide these inventions away?

She found her answer at the next table: a long cylinder like the barrel of a rifle, with a hose connected to a tank with shoulder straps and a belt that buckled across the middle. She found a trigger on the underside of the hose. Similarly nasty devices littered the table.

So, her parents *had* been making weapons for war. That must have been what her father and Mr. Byron were arguing about in the Great Room.

Frances imagined her parents sitting in their lair devising new ways for men to kill each other, and she shook the thought away. They would never allow these instruments of death into the world. Not even to save the Manor. She had to believe that.

One table left. At first, she only saw haphazard piles of equipment. But when she stepped closer, she recognized a familiar face peeking out from under the mess.

"Hobbes . . ."

But it wasn't Hobbes, not exactly. This face had the same molded cheekbones, same tuft of painted-on hair, but its eye sockets were empty. A crude metal skeleton lay folded beneath it like clothes in a dresser drawer, thin enough to fit into a briefcase.

Must be some kind of prototype.

With a sweep of her arm, Frances sent the other contents of the table spilling onto the floor. Then she unfolded the prototype, laying it out on the surface as if performing an autopsy. A network of wires and circuitry threaded through its joints, each tracing back to a control panel mounted to its chest. She searched for a way to turn it on, flipping switches and twisting knobs, before prying the whole thing off to reveal a nest of dangling wires and an empty compartment about the size of a small battery. No luck there.

Then she turned the head and found a seam at the base of its neck, so thin she almost missed it. A small panel popped open when she pressed on it, exposing a numeric keypad.

A smile spread across her face. "I think I just found your off switch," she said aloud.

Frances wanted to go grab Fritz and rush back to the attic where Hobbes was sleeping, but she resisted. A scientist always tests her hypothesis.

She ducked under the table and dug through the equipment she'd swept onto the floor, searching for the prototype's missing battery. She noticed a thick cable that ran along the ground. She followed it, hoping it would lead to an electrical box. Instead, it snaked around the table legs and crossed the workshop before disappearing under a rusty iron door.

She straightened up and examined the door. It was padlocked, with a sign over the handle that read *KEEP OUT.*

Another workshop? Frances wondered what else her father could be building. She imagined an army of empty-eyed Hobbeses, and a shiver ran down her spine. She glanced over her shoulder toward the false wall where she'd entered. Hobbes wouldn't wake for a few more hours—plenty of time to explore one more room. . . .

Frances looked for something to use to break the padlock and found a metal pole the size of a shinbone. She made a face when she realized it was, in fact, a shinbone, albeit an artificial one. The padlock was nearly rusted through. It took only a few hits before it crumbled to the floor.

Out in the hallway, Fritz hooted in concern.

"I'm okay," Frances called. She took a deep breath and pulled. The door was heavy, and as soon as she stepped inside, it slammed shut behind her, sealing her in darkness.

She ran her fingers along the wall until she found a switch. When she flicked it, nothing happened, so she tried again. Still nothing. She was beginning to panic when her toe caught on something—a torch lying on the floor. Someone had left in a hurry. A flint still hung from the handle, and after a few strikes, she had a light.

She held it up and gasped.

The room was immense, more than half the size of the rest of the laboratory. The ceiling was lower, with wooden beams in place of steel, and the stone walls were rougher-hewn.

Dust-caked equipment stood frozen in time: test tubes, chemistry sets, an iron lung, and, at the far end of the room, a huge metal box. Everything looked stark and grimy and bleak—entirely unlike her father's space. This room bore all the hallmarks of Albrecht Grimme.

She remembered the cable and cast about with her torch until she found it. It led to the iron box against the far wall where it joined several other cables that fed into a panel on the side. A thermometer read negative eighty degrees Celsius. That couldn't be right, could it? She tapped it a few times to make sure the needle wasn't stuck. It would take a massive amount of energy to keep something that cold, which would explain why none of the lights worked—all the power in the room was being diverted into the box.

Frances spotted something on the lid: a book bound in leather. She blew off the cover, revealing the initials *AG* embossed in gold foil. Albrecht Grimme.

Her eyes widened—she was holding her great-grandfather's journal.

Inside, the text was unlike anything she had ever seen, handwritten in a strange language, or secret code. On page six, he had sketched a diagram, the plans for the box. She found detailed measurements on the page after that, followed by dozens of temperature readings.

What could be so important to keep frozen all these years?

Frances remembered the day her parents left. Mr. Byron had asked about her great-grandfather's work. Could this be what he was looking for?

Frances jammed her torch into the crack between two stones and tried the lid. Too heavy. She found a length of chain and hooked it to the latch, tossing the other end over one of the rafters. Using the beam as a fulcrum, she pulled with all her strength. The hinges screeched and the chain snapped, and Frances tumbled across the floor, landing hard on her tailbone. Tears exploded from her eyes. She wiped them away and looked up to find the lid hanging open just a crack, a fine mist of condensation billowing down the side.

Frances rose to her feet, her nerves electric beneath her skin. She peered into the box to find it filled with ice—a solid block of it. She pulled her sleeve over her hand and polished a small section until the frost was clear, then leaned in, close enough to feel the chill rising off the surface.

That's when she saw them, just below the ice: two bloodshot eyes staring back at her.

Chapter 6

A Magic Potion

*T*INK-TINK-TINK.

Frances sat hunched over her great-grandfather's journal while across the room Fritz chipped at the block of ice. She tried to focus on the strange symbols that filled the page in front of her. But the way her head ached, Fritz could have been driving the chisel straight into her brain.

It had been exhilarating to hold something that once belonged to her great-grandfather, especially something so personal. Her excitement had faded when she discovered she couldn't read so much as a line of it. And the math! She had never seen anything so complex. If it weren't for the extensive sketches and diagrams, deciphering his notes would be impossible. Even so, her progress had been painfully slow.

She growled and shoved the journal aside.

Fritz looked up from his chiseling, brushing the ice shavings from his shoulders. He pointed at her and moved his hand in a circle. *Are you okay?*

Frances fanned her fingers and brought her thumb to her chest. "I'm fine," she said, feeling anything but. She sighed and reached again for the journal, opening to a page near the back where she had found a note scrawled at the top—one of only a few written in a language she could understand:

This will change everything.

The handwriting was slanted and rushed—far from the careful penmanship found throughout the rest of the journal. She pictured her great-grandfather's quill flying across the page, propelled by the urgent thrill of discovery.

Everything—the secret workshop, the metal box with its revolutionary turn-of-the-century cooling system, whatever lay beneath the ice—it was all part of an experiment, left unfinished when her great-grandfather died. Albrecht Grimme's last work. His greatest work, maybe, neglected in the dark, waiting for her to find it.

If Mr. Byron was right, this experiment could be exactly the kind of breakthrough her parents needed, enough to keep them out of the war business for good. And if she completed it, perhaps *she* would be the one invited to speak at next year's scientific symposium. . . .

I should be able to figure this out, Frances thought. *I'm a Stenzel!* Another thought appeared, somewhere near the back of her mind. "Maybe Mum and Dad were right to leave me behind," she said aloud.

Hearing this, Fritz hopped onto the table, upsetting a pile of crumpled paper, and placed his hand on Frances's shoulder. When she tried to shrug him away, he took her chin in his hand and gently turned her face to his. He began to sign, placing two fingers against his neck, then crossing his fingers like bars.

She decided to humor him. "When you're stuck in your cage . . . ," she translated.

He nodded and tapped his temple once, twice, three times. "You think and think and think . . ."

Then he slid his pointer finger between two fingers on his other hand and yanked it free: *then I escape.*

Frances sighed. "I wish it were that easy. Not everyone has a magic potion supercharging their brain." She put her hand over her mouth as she felt Fritz pull away. "Sorry, Fritz—I didn't mean that." She took his hand in hers. "You are the smartest, most wonderful chimp I know, with or without your . . ."

Fritz cocked his head to one side as Frances's words trailed off.

"Magic potion," she whispered.

Frances gathered her notes and stuffed them into the journal. She glanced at the clock over the workbench. The hands hovered on three and six. Finally, some luck—it felt like ages since her initial discovery, yet dawn was still hours away.

"We should still have plenty of time before Hobbes wakes up." She heaved her weight against the iron door and beckoned Fritz with a tilt of her head. "You coming?"

Fritz shrugged and hopped down from the table, crossing the floor on his knuckles. They weaved through the clutter of her father's workroom until they reached the false wall. She had finally identified the key brick on this side earlier that night, using the highly scientific process of testing each brick one by one. She pressed it now, and the wall *whoosh*ed them around to the other side.

Where are we going? Fritz signed.

Frances gave him a look. "To the Zoo, obviously. That's where—" She stopped mid-sentence, snapping her head toward the other end of the hall.

"Ooh-ooh," Fritz grunted before Frances pressed her finger to his lips.

"I hear something," she whispered. A low rumble floated in from the foyer, followed by an unmistakable *DING*.

The elevator. And there was only one person—for lack of a more accurate term—who could be riding it. Any second now, the double doors would slide open and out would step Hobbes.

"He shouldn't be up for hours!"

Frances's stomach fell as she realized her mistake. When she checked the clock in her great-grandfather's lab, she read the hour and minute hands but failed to notice that the second hand was standing still. *Of course* the clock was stopped—it probably hadn't moved in years!

She grabbed Fritz by the wrist and pulled him into the circuitry room as Hobbes's voice echoed down the hallway.

"Frances?" he called. "As I have been unable to locate you in the main house, I can only surmise that you are here in the laboratory. Please reveal yourself at once."

"He can't find me down here," Frances whispered. "I need you to distract him long enough for me to get to the Zoo and back. Can you do that?"

Fritz straightened and offered an exaggerated salute before scurrying off.

A moment later, she heard Hobbes's voice once more. "You again? It is high time we do something about that cage of yours. . . ."

Frances tiptoed down the corridor, sliding along the walls and ducking into doorways whenever she worried Hobbes and Fritz were getting too close.

When she arrived at the Zoo, a chorus of chirps and squeaks greeted her. She put a finger to her lips to shush them. "Sorry," she whispered. "No treats today. I'm in a hurry."

Frances riffled through the cabinets, flinging them open until she came to one that was locked. There was no time to search for a key.

"If the chimp can do it . . . ," she muttered, pulling a pin from her hair. She jammed the pin into the lock and prodded at the cylinder. A few moments later, she heard a click, and the cabinet swung open.

There it was—Fritz's intelligence serum. Not a magic potion exactly, though even Mary Stenzel once declared it a "worldly miracle." Frances pulled the rack of test tubes down from the cabinet and set it on the counter. There were seven tubes, six of them empty and one filled with a red liquid the color of blood. There were no logs or instructions—her mother must have taken them with her to review on the train—so Frances didn't know what dosage she had been administering to Fritz. Even if she did, she wasn't sure what kind of conversion rate there might be between a full-grown chimpanzee and an eleven-year-old girl.

After a hasty deliberation, Frances popped the stopper, raised the tube to her lips, and drank every drop. One chance was all she would get.

Frances shut her eyes and waited for the serum to take effect. After a few moments, she opened one eye, then the other. The Zoo looked the same. She flipped through the pages of the journal. No great clarity. No revolutionary thoughts appeared in her mind. Nothing had changed.

"But it has to work," she said. "It worked for Fritz!"

In her panic, Frances failed to notice the footsteps approaching in the hall until the door of the Zoo swung open and Hobbes stepped into the room. Fritz appeared a moment later, peering sheepishly from behind the machine's legs. He looked up at Frances, then at the empty vial on the counter next to her, a curious look appearing on his face. Without thinking, Frances moved to block his view.

"I must say," Hobbes began, surveying the room, "I am quite disappointed in your lack of originality. Surely you did not plan to release the animals a second time?"

Frances scowled. "That's not what I was doing."

Hobbes ushered Fritz back to his cage. "What, then, did you expect to accomplish here?" he said, securing the padlock.

Frances squeezed her eyes shut, trying one last time to will the serum to work. When it didn't, she slumped onto a nearby stool.

"Nothing," she muttered. "Absolutely nothing."

"In that case, it appears you have succeeded. Now then"— he opened the door and extended his arm into the hall—"it is time to go."

Frances sighed and pushed herself to her feet. She was too tired to fight anymore. What was even left for her to do?

Sneak back into her great-grandfather's lab? Why bother if she couldn't decipher his notes? She had tried everything and nothing had worked. Even the intelligence serum had failed.

Or had it?

As Frances stepped into the hall, she realized she was, in fact, feeling very strange: as if her head were filling with helium and might detach at any moment and float away. When she held out a hand, it appeared much farther from her body than the end of her arm ever should.

She stopped in the middle of the hallway, pulled out the journal, and began to read.

At first, the letters and numbers and symbols jumbled together in a swirl of information that made Frances panicky and faint. Around and around they went until they burst out from some central point and separated into distinct equations, each with a beginning, middle, and end as clear to Frances as the spelling of her own name. She could not only read the equations in the journal; she understood them. The more she read, the clearer it all became, until she was flipping through page after page with ease. It was at once exhilarating and terrifying: the sensation that she must not stop reading or she might drop dead where she stood.

When she finished the journal, she closed it and took a deep breath. She saw it all: what Albrecht Grimme was trying to achieve, how close he'd come, even where he had fallen short. She wondered if any mind had ever held knowledge like this before.

Yet, the solution still eluded her. For all her new ability, she still found herself coming up against the same dead end her great-grandfather had reached. Something was missing, like a puzzle one piece from completion. She saw the gap and sensed the shape of it. But what would fill it?

"Frances! Have you listened to a word I've said?"

Frances shook her head to clear her mind. Hobbes was standing over her, metal hands on metal hips. She slipped the journal behind her back before he could snatch it away.

"Sorry." Her tongue felt dry inside her mouth. "I was . . . What did you say?"

"I *said* you are henceforth confined to your room. You will leave only to take your meals in the kitchen. Assuming you still intend to eat, as you do not seem to require sleep. It would not surprise me, at this point, to discover that you are part machine."

Frances rolled her eyes. *Now he makes jokes.*

And then it hit her.

Part machine. *Part machine.*

The contents of the journal came flooding back to her. Equations filled the air around her head, spinning and combining until she reached the dead end, where there had been no solution. This time, she burst through and an answer emerged, the final piece settling into place.

"Hobbes, you're a genius," Frances said. Her voice came out breathless, like she had run a kilometer just to speak.

"Of course I am," Hobbes said. "What purpose would I serve if I was not?"

She smiled. "I may have just found one."

"I beg your pardon?" Hobbes shifted on his feet as Frances looked him over, disassembling and reassembling him with her eyes. He cleared his throat—a strange mannerism, considering he lacked both breath and a proper throat. "I believe we have stood here long enough. Please follow me upstairs and wash for breakfast."

"Wait," Frances said, formulating a plan. "Can't I stay down here just a little longer?" She ducked into the nearest room— the specimen lab. Rows of glass jars lined the walls; tissue preserved in formaldehyde. Frances picked one up and studied the brain floating inside.

Hobbes's face appeared through the yellowish liquid, pinched and distorted in the curved glass, the top of his head bloated and huge, his nose the size of a pinpoint.

"Please do not handle your parents' brains," he said.

"I'm sorry. I just don't get to spend enough time down here, and I— Oops!" She let the jar slip from her hands and crash to the floor, shattering the glass and depositing the brain onto the tiles with a wet *thunk*.

"What have you done?" Hobbes rushed to the mess on the floor. "There are two hundred and fifty-seven specimens in this room, each collected by Master Grimme himself. If your mother and father return to find even one of them out of place, I will never hear the end of it." He knelt down and began to gather the shards. "Human specimens are no longer so easy to come by, you know."

Frances crept around behind him, careful to remain outside the range of his visual sensors. She searched the back of his neck until she located the slight bump near the base of his head. When she pressed it, a seam appeared, and a tiny door popped open, revealing a keypad. Just like the prototype.

"You said it yourself." Frances pulled the scrap of paper from her pocket. "There are over two hundred human specimens in this room." She entered the code: 90-835-778. "But only one machine."

"Frances!" Hobbes's voice was frantic. "What are you doing? My central processor is not a plaything. You mustn't . . ."

His speech slowed, trailing off as Frances entered the final digit. Then his body stiffened and the glow in his eyes dimmed from yellow to orange and finally red before fading altogether as he powered off.

"Sorry, Hobbes," Frances said. And she was sorry—sorrier than she expected to be. For all the reasons she had found to resent him, it was Hobbes who had given her the answer she sought.

Now she had everything she needed to complete her great-grandfather's experiment.

Chapter 7
Multiple Critical Errors Detected

E lectricity surged through Hobbes's central processor, producing a hum that rattled the operating table. Frances closed the keypad at the base of his head and took a step back. She wore a white lab coat with rubber gloves up to her elbows. Her hair was pinned up in a messy tangle, a fleck of black goo smeared across her chin.

Fritz padded up beside her and peered over the edge of the table, regarding Hobbes with a quizzical tilt of his head. The chimp wore goggles two sizes too big and a lab coat matching Frances's, complete with a pen hooked to the pocket. (The pen was purely ornamental—despite his enhanced cognition, he was still unable to write.)

When the rattling subsided and Hobbes's eyes flickered on,

Frances exhaled, unaware she'd been holding her breath.

She had planned to leave Hobbes switched off until her parents returned. With him out of commission, the Manor would be hers to do with as she pleased. She could spend day and night in the lab, eat rösti and bacon for every meal, even move the animals up to the main floor of the house.

In the end, it was pride that changed her mind.

Twenty-three hours had passed since she'd taken Fritz's intelligence serum and her thoughts still raced in a whirlwind of creativity. Already, she had accomplished more than she could have imagined—certainly more than her parents would have thought possible. Frances doubted there was a scientist in all of Europe who would believe her when she was done. Not without a witness.

Besides, she had already made sure Hobbes could no longer get in her way.

"REBOOT SEQUENCE INITIATED," Hobbes intoned. His voice sounded oddly mechanical, even for him. His eyes glowed yellow. "SYSTEM SCAN IN PROGRESS."

At the sudden noise, Frances nearly jumped out of her shoes. She put a hand on her chest to settle her racing heart as Fritz gave her a concerned look. "I'm fine," she said. *I wish he'd stop doing that.* He had been tiptoeing around her since that morning in the Zoo, as if he expected her to keel over at any moment. It wasn't doing anything for her nerves.

She took a deep breath. She had to calm down. If Fritz could tell something was different about her, Hobbes would see it, too. He'd scan her face for micro-expressions: eyes wide, pupils dilated, heart rate elevated, cheeks flushed. She was excited. Nervous. Proud. And if she was honest, he might detect a trace of guilt.

"Frances?" Hobbes's voice had returned to normal, and the yellow color had faded from his eyes. "What is this place? Where have you taken me?"

"We're still in the laboratory," she said, which was technically true.

Hobbes scanned the workshop with its bulky, outdated equipment, propane lamps, and bare stone walls. Frances had been careful to position him so he couldn't see what she'd been working on until she was ready. Still, it took every ounce of will she had to keep from glancing behind him.

"This area does not appear on the laboratory blueprints in my database." He paused. "I am detecting footsteps. Soft soles, unusually short stride. Possibly animal."

"Well, that means your ears still work."

Fritz climbed onto Frances's shoulder and cheerfully signed *hello.*

"Of course my ears work," Hobbes said. "Why wouldn't they?"

Before Frances could reply, the yellow glow returned to his eyes.

"SYSTEM SCAN FORTY PERCENT COMPLETE. MULTIPLE ERRORS DETECTED." Hobbes blinked. "Something is not right. What have you done to me?"

"I'm sorry." Frances looked down, turning a scalpel over in her hands. "It's only temporary."

"*What* is temporary?" His words increased in speed and volume as he began to panic. "Frances? My body is not responding to my commands."

"I know," Frances replied. She looked up to meet his eyes. "I had to borrow it."

"SYSTEM SCAN COMPLETE. WARNING: MULTIPLE CRITICAL ERRORS DETECTED."

It was then that Hobbes realized for the first time what his sensors had been trying to tell him: his body was not responding to his commands because it was no longer there. All that remained of him was his head, propped up on the operating table. He opened his mouth as if to shout and nearly toppled, rolling onto his ear.

Frances set him upright and wiped a black smudge from his forehead. "No need to get upset. I can put you back together. I think." She looked to Fritz, who scratched his chin and offered a shrug.

"This is unacceptable," Hobbes sputtered. "Highly unacceptable!"

"Look at the positive," Frances said. "Imagine how long your battery will last without all those limbs to power."

"This is no time for jest. What have you done with my body?"

Frances took a deep breath. "I needed it. For an experiment."

"There was no experiment on your curriculum today."

"If you had your way, I'd never do any real science. This was something I did myself." She leaned in close, no longer able to contain her excitement. "Do you want to see it?"

"I don't suppose I have a choice."

Frances grinned. "That's the spirit."

She reached down and lifted Hobbes by the ears, spinning him in a dizzying swirl of lamplight before setting him back on the table. He wobbled for a moment as his internal gyroscope recalibrated. When he had steadied himself enough to look up, he gasped.

"Frances," he whispered. "What have you done?"

A body lay strapped to a gurney, its skin gray-blue and dripping, banded with scars like fault lines. Its face was cracked and puffy, matted with coarse, dark hair that hung to its shoulders. Wires protruded from sockets on either side of its neck, plugging into smaller sockets down the length of its spine. More wires looped around its elbow, where Frances had installed one of Hobbes's arms beneath the skin. His secondary control panel blinked on its chest.

Frances surveyed her work. "Amazing, isn't it? Honestly, he was just about complete when I found him. I only had to solve the power problem. His nervous system alone couldn't do the trick—maybe because he was frozen for so long, maybe because he was dead—but Great-Grandpa Grimme didn't have the technology to fill in the gaps until—"

Hobbes's voice was solemn. "Until your father created me."

"Exactly. I figured I could use your artificial nervous system to supplement his and get him moving. It's like Dad designed you for this! I thought I might need your central processor, too. But, according to my calculations, your secondary control panel should be enough. So, you get to keep your head."

"How generous of you."

Frances curtsied, then straightened self-consciously. How fast had she just been talking? And since when did she curtsy? She cleared her throat. "Are you ready?"

"Ready for what?" Hobbes eyed the body. "You do not truly expect to wake that . . . thing, do you?"

"It's all right here." Frances tossed the journal onto the table. It fell open to a page near the center binding.

"These equations are highly advanced," Hobbes said, scanning the page. "You're clever, for a human child, but you could not possibly understand them."

Frances shrugged, the hint of a grin on her lips. "I guess we'll find out."

Hobbes scoffed dismissively, but she could see him studying the equations, working them out, trying to determine her chances of success. A twinge of shame needled Frances's stomach. What if he was right? She wanted to believe she was capable of completing her great-grandfather's experiment without the intelligence serum. Eventually. But what if she wasn't?

No. I can't let that distract me. Not when I'm so close.

Frances turned to Fritz, who was checking the leather straps around the body's wrists and ankles. "Ready?"

Fritz nodded and scampered down from the gurney, joining her at her side.

"Maybe we should stand back or something."

"I'm quite confident we are not in any danger," Hobbes said. "Except perhaps from the smell."

Frances knew what he was implying—that her experiment would fail—but her spirits were so high she decided to take his words at face value anyway.

"That's what Great-Grandpa figured, too." She grabbed the journal and flipped it open to a dog-eared page. "'The subject shall be docile upon animation,'" she translated aloud, "'knowing nothing. Fear may follow, as a newborn child fears all the world but his mother.' Does that make me his mum?"

Hobbes snorted. "By that reasoning, your great-grandfather

would be his mother, making you his grand-niece."

Frances rolled her eyes and reached for a lever that stuck out from the side of a machine with many tubes, all of which converged at the base of the body's spine, pumping a greenish liquid.

"Here goes nothing," she said.

"Nothing indeed," muttered Hobbes.

The lever was so large Frances had to hang all her weight from it before it would budge. Fritz scurried over to help. Girl and chimp pulled and yanked and jimmied until the mechanism came unstuck and the lever fell with a *CLANK*, sending them both tumbling to the floor.

A massive bolt of electricity surged through the greenish liquid and into the body, hurling sparks across the room.

Hobbes watched the body, scanning for signs of life.

"I assume animation was the purpose of this spectacle, was it not?" he said when nothing happened.

Frances scowled and got to her feet, brushing dust from her pants. "Not enough power," she said, biting the end of a pencil. Fritz hooted in assent.

"Any more power and you risk blowing us all to bits," Hobbes said.

"Just a *little* more."

"Enough of this silliness. The procedure did not work, and it will not work. Now, please, put me back together at once."

Frances ignored him. She turned a knob on the generator and checked the readings, then scribbled a note in the journal.

If she had been paying more attention, she might have noticed the way Hobbes watched her factor voltage and watts, volume and pressure, performing each task with preternatural ease; or how his eyes lit up as a sensation come over him: what a human might describe as a sinking feeling in the stomach. (He was not equipped with a stomach, of course, and even if he had been, it wasn't currently attached.) She might have seen the way his eyes settled on Fritz.

"I believe I understand what is happening here," he said. "And I must say, it is a new low."

But Frances *wasn't* paying attention. At that moment, her subject, the body on the gurney, was the only thing that mattered in the world. She pressed a button on the machine that pumped the green liquid into the body, increasing the flow.

On the table behind her, Hobbes's eyes flashed red. "WARNING: IMMINENT DANGER DETECTED. PRIMARY DIRECTIVE INITIATED."

He lurched as if trying to jump to his feet, forgetting they weren't attached, and rolled across the table before coming to rest on his nose.

"Frances," he called, the metal surface of the table muffling his voice. "Please—you must stop at once. The procedure, it—"

A thunderous clap echoed through the workshop as Frances

pulled the lever. The blast knocked out the electricity and reverberated through the chamber with such force that even the lamps were snuffed out, plunging them into darkness.

Hobbes scanned the room, but the darkness rendered his visual sensors useless. Fritz chattered nervously somewhere above him—perhaps having climbed a wall in alarm. He could hear Frances across the room. Her heart was beating much too quickly to be healthy for such a small girl.

There was also another sound, faint but growing stronger every moment. A third heartbeat, much slower and denser than Frances's or the chimpanzee's, like a two-by-four pounding a slab of beef. And then a fourth sound, deep and tremulous. Moaning.

Frances had done it.

The body was alive.

Chapter 8
Docile Upon Animation

Frances sat slumped against the tentacled machine, nursing a burn on her hand where she had been struck by a spark. The stench of formaldehyde and singed flesh assaulted her nose. The darkness was so thick she felt as if she couldn't stand up under the weight of it. So, she remained on the floor.

"Frances," Hobbes hissed.

She knew it was childish to ignore him, but that's what she was, wasn't she? An ill-behaved child? At least she couldn't see the smug grin on his artificial face.

She'd failed, breaking just about every rule her parents had in the process. One small consolation: she didn't think Hobbes knew she'd taken Fritz's intelligence serum. Of all the things she'd done over the past two days, she knew that was the worst.

Her parents would never trust her in the laboratory again.

She put her face in her hands. Maybe the lights would never come back on.

"Frances! We have to go." He spoke in a strange whisper that sounded almost like fear. He was probably trying to mock her and chose the wrong mannerism. Or maybe mechanical men are afraid the dark. Either way, she wasn't in any mood to do what she was told.

"I'm staying right here," she said.

"This is not the time for defiance. We must go now!"

Frances clenched her fists and leaped to her feet. "Why? So we can get back to your pointless lessons and never-ending chores? Tell my parents, lock me in my room, I don't care. I'm done with tutors and I'm done with you."

"Frances," Hobbes pleaded. "You must be quiet. He will hear you!"

"Very funny. You love that my experiment was a failure." Frances took a step and nearly tripped over a wrench, stubbing her toe on its heavy iron handle. She grit her teeth as pain shot through her toe and up her shin. "That's what you wanted, right? To see me fail?"

"Of course I wanted your foolish experiment to fail—"

"See? You don't even bother to deny it!" Hobbes tried to shush her, which only fueled her anger. "I hate my parents for leaving me with a soulless robot who doesn't care about me, and who probably isn't even *capable* of caring for anyone, who's so cold he's happy when his own pupil fails."

"You did not fail!" Hobbes shouted.

Whether it was his sudden change in volume, or that his words were finally beginning to register in her mind, Frances fell quiet. "What do you mean?"

"Listen," he said.

She heard the *drip, drip, drip* of water that pooled under the body as it thawed. The hum of instruments. The padding of soft hands across the ceiling beams. "Fritz?" The chimp hooted in response. *This is ridiculous.*

"What am I supposed to be listening for?" she said, feeling her anger return. "I've only got one ear."

Her answer came as the operating table creaked and the dripping quickened until a rush of water poured onto the floor. Then the slap of flesh against stone.

The body was standing up.

Never before in Frances's young life had she experienced such a profound and immediate sense of regret. It began in her stomach, climbing the back of her throat and curling around her spine like English ivy, flowering in a rash of goose pimples across her skin.

Pride—that's what she was supposed to feel. A sense of accomplishment. She had done what great men of science before her had been unable to do, building on their work in ways they never dreamed of and succeeding where they fell short. Yet there, in the dark, with a newfound clarity even as Fritz's serum began wearing off, she couldn't muster any pride at all—only regret . . . and fear.

She held her breath and listened for the body to move again. When her lungs began to burn, she exhaled, suddenly aware of how much noise she made just to breathe.

"Ung," the body moaned. His voice was thick and guttural, his vocal cords cracking under the strain of first use. She heard the slap of a second foot against the wet stone. He had taken a step.

"I think he's walking toward me," Frances whispered. Another step, this time sending a surgical pan skittering across the floor. The body moaned and stopped until the clangor died down, then took another step. "What do I do?"

"Stay quiet," Hobbes hissed. Above her, Fritz chattered nervously in the darkness.

"Gurg?"

Frances could now just make out the body, illuminated by the dim lights on the control panel she installed in his chest. His form was massive, much taller than he had looked on the gurney, sinewy muscles swelling and contracting as he clenched and unclenched his fists. He was a monster.

The journal said the subject would be docile, she reminded herself. *It also said, "fear may follow." Let's hope nothing spooks him.*

"I do not think he can see in this darkness," Hobbes said. "If you stay quiet, he may be unable to locate you."

Sure enough, the monster turned toward Hobbes's voice. His steps shook the floor and rattled nearby equipment. He plowed over an instrument table, pitching forward and steadying himself on the gurney. He shoved a second obstacle—a pile of boxes—out of his way.

He learns, Frances thought, and shuddered.

Soon, the monster stood over the operating table. Frances watched in horror as he wrapped his swollen fingers around Hobbes and brought him to his nose to sniff.

"No!" she cried.

The monster snarled at the sudden noise and whirled around, his damp hair whipping across his face. Frances clamped a hand over her mouth and stumbled backward. Her heel caught the same wrench she tripped on earlier, sending it clattering into the tentacled machine. The monster threw back his head and roared. Frances ducked as Hobbes's head whistled by, hitting the wall behind her with a *CRACK*.

"Hobbes," she called. She scrambled across the workshop on her knees, waving a hand in front of her to navigate the dark. When she reached Hobbes and turned him over, his eyes glowed red.

"Run, Frances!"

For once, Frances did as she was told. She stuffed the

journal into her shirt, took Hobbes's head under her arm, and ran, using the light of his eyes to avoid an obstacle course of lab equipment. She scanned the darkness for Fritz but found no sight of him. The clever chimp must have run ahead. *He's safe. He has to be.* She could hear the monster behind her, gathering speed like a locomotive, using his mechanically enhanced legs to gain ground despite his clumsiness.

Frances reached the false wall and waited helplessly as it inched its way open. When the crack grew wide enough, she squeezed through and pressed the key brick on the other side.

"Come on," she said, pounding the brick with her fist, but the wall continued turning until it was fully ajar. She slammed the brick with her shoulder. "Come on!"

At last, the wall began to close. She could see the monster staggering forward at nearly a run.

"It's not going to close in time," Hobbes said.

"It'll close."

"Based on its current speed and the estimated distance it must travel—"

"It'll close. It has to." She looked around. "Where's Fritz?" She peered back into the chamber. The gap was closing faster now. "Fritz," she called. "Hurry!"

"Leave him," Hobbes said.

"I won't go without him. He's my friend."

"He is only a primate."

"And you're just a machine," she snapped. "Fritz!"

A moment later, Fritz shot through the doorway and slid to a stop in the hall.

"You made it," Frances cried, pulling him into a hug. They watched the gap shrink farther. It was closing—they were safe. The monster could pound until his fists bled, but he would never figure out how to open the wall. He would be trapped. Then she'd have plenty of time to figure out what to do.

Instead, a thick gray arm coiled in wires and scars punched through the gap and grabbed the wall just as it was grinding to a close. The monster howled as his arm was crushed against the stones, sending up a shower of sparks. Then the wall began to reverse course.

Frances watched in horror. "I didn't know the mechanical pieces would make it so strong," she said.

"The list of what you do not know could fill this laboratory," Hobbes replied.

"Ooh-ah!" said Fritz.

Frances took off down the hallway while Fritz scrambled ahead. The jolt that knocked out the electricity in the chamber must have affected the rest of the laboratory as well; only Hobbes's glowing eyes lit their way through the darkness.

"Proceed to the elevator," he said. "And hurry."

She turned down one hallway, then another, running as fast as her short legs would allow. When she reached the elevator, she mashed the button for the ground floor. Nothing happened.

"The elevator runs on electricity," she cried. "How could you not remember that?"

Hobbes bristled under her arm. "I do not recall you making any objection to my plan when I—"

A nightmarish howl echoed through the halls, cutting off his speech. Fritz whimpered and buried his face in Frances's lap.

"Forget the elevator." She cast a nervous glance over her shoulder. "We need another way out."

Hobbes's eyes went blue as he retreated into his internal database.

"Hurry," Frances said, giving his head a little shake.

A moment later, his eyes turned white as he returned to normal functionality. "I'm afraid we are trapped," he said. "The emergency stairway is on the other side of the lab. There is no way to get there without crossing paths with that creature."

"No," Frances said, narrowing her eyes. "There must be another way."

She scanned the laboratory, trying to recall every visit she'd made as a child, every room and passageway she'd discovered. She searched her memory for even the smallest spark of inspiration, until she saw an image of herself in the library not forty-eight hours before.

"The Librarian," she said, taking off across the foyer. "It's pneumatic—it doesn't run on electricity!"

She arrived at the Librarian's laboratory terminal and found the shoot still open from her tests the day before. Hobbes wiggled until Frances turned him to face the contraption. He looked it over.

"The repairs you began—did you finish them?"

"Yes," Frances said, then paused. "No. Yes."

"Which is it?"

Another howl, closer this time. The stench of singed flesh wafted down the hall. The monster was close.

"We'll be fine," she said, climbing into the canister. It was a tight fit with both Frances and Hobbes squeezed inside. "You'll have to find another way up," she told Fritz. "I'm sorry."

Fritz smiled, showing his yellow teeth, and began to sign. *Fritz good at escape.*

"There's nobody better." She gave him one last scratch behind the ears, then pulled in her knees as he lowered the hatch.

"I do not like this plan," Hobbes said once they were sealed inside.

"We'll be fine . . . I think."

"That does not instill me with much confidence."

"The ride might get a little rough toward the end, that's all."

It was too late to reconsider now—the monster had reached

the foyer. He staggered around the corner, snarling and licking his lips.

"Go, Fritz," Frances cried. He hesitated, whimpering as he peered at her through the glass, then bolted down the hall on all fours.

"Time for us to go as well," Hobbes said.

That's when Frances discovered the flaw in her plan: the button was located outside the canister, on a control panel that couldn't be operated from within the chute.

"The button. I can't reach the button!"

She winced as the monster pounded the Librarian with his massive fist, leaving a web of thin cracks splintered across the glass. This gave Frances an idea. She twisted her body to free one of her hands and knocked on the side of the canister closest to the console.

"What are you doing?" Hobbes hissed.

"Just get ready to go," she replied.

Her knocking got the attention of the monster, and he began focusing his blows on that spot. At first, Frances worried her plan would backfire and the glass chute would shatter. Each hit made her heart feel like it was going to burst out of her chest. But the glass held, and Frances kept knocking. Eventually, the monster showed signs of tiring. His strikes became wilder, less precise. He growled and kept swinging until his fist found the console directly under the spot where Frances was knocking and smashed the button, engaging the pneumatics.

Frances and Hobbes shot through the tubing with sickening force. The canister whipped around corners and barreled through loops. It traveled with such force it knocked the breath from Frances's lungs. She gasped for air and struggled to keep from blacking out—they would be hitting the misaligned tube at any moment, and she needed her wits about her.

Maybe I fixed it after all, she thought just as the canister slammed into the wall of the chute and shattered into a thousand pieces.

Chapter 9

Fear May Follow

Frances groaned, propping herself up on her elbow. The library floor shimmered with broken glass. Jagged shards stuck out from the spines of books like throwing stars. Some were flecked with red. She reached for her ear and was relieved to find it still attached. Judging by the way her clothes were shredded, her shoulders and knees took the brunt of the damage. She gave herself a quick examination and determined that, while she'd need a few bandages, none of the cuts were deep enough to do any lasting harm.

"You're lucky you don't have skin, Hobbes," she said, frowning. "Skin scars. And bleeds." Actually, her injuries were bleeding far less than she would have anticipated, which was odd, but she shook the thought from her mind.

When Hobbes didn't answer, Frances pushed up from the floor, wincing as a piece of the shattered canister nicked her palm. Glass crunched under her shoes as she peered down the rows of bookshelves, calling his name. She was beginning to fear the worst when she heard a muffled voice coming from the Librarian. She poked her head into the chute.

Hobbes was wedged behind a stud, sporting a gash over his right eye. The end of his neck, where Frances had detached it from his shoulders, was mangled, exposing bolts on either side. Frances tried not to let him see her cringe.

"Hang on," she said. "I'll find something to fish you out."

She returned a few minutes later with an electrical cord and a magnet. "Hold still."

"Wait," Hobbes cried. "You cannot use a magnet to pull me up."

"Why not? Your head is full of metal."

"That is precisely the problem. If that magnet comes into contact with my head, you'll risk erasing my memory banks."

Frances frowned. "Do you have a better idea?"

Hobbes thought for a moment. "I am afraid I do not. Please aim for my nose, at least. There is no data stored there."

"I should hope not," Frances said. "I'll be careful."

She tied the magnet to the end of the cord and lowered it into the chute.

"A little to the left," Hobbes called. "No, my left. My left!"

Frances grit her teeth and jerked the cord to the right. The magnet bounced off the broken edge of the chute and affixed itself to the top of Hobbes's head.

"That is not my nose!" he cried, but Frances could only pull him up as quickly as she could and yank the magnet free.

"You still in there?" she said, putting her face close to Hobbes's and tapping his forehead with her finger.

"Of course," he said, flinching. "But I must run a few tests to determine if any data has been corrupted." His eyes went blue as he started his diagnostic subroutines. A moment later, his eyes flicked back to white.

"Well?" Frances said.

"Something seems to be damaged in my language center." He began running through his programmed languages:

"The sly fox sits upon a log.

"Der schlaue Fuchs sitzt auf einem Baumstumpf.

"Le renard sournois s'assoit sur une bûche.

"El zorro astuto se sienta en un tronco.

"Η πονηρή αλεπού κάθεται πάνω σε ένα κούτσουρο.

"La volpe . . . la volpe . . . la volpe . . ."

Hobbes repeated the words as if stuck in a loop until Frances knocked him upside the head.

"Thank you," he said.

"What happened?"

"It appears I no longer speak Italian."

A roar floated up through the Librarian's broken chute and Frances's mood grew dark. "We need to figure out what to do about our big, angry friend."

"Our next step is clear," Hobbes said. "We must summon the proper authorities."

Frances shook her head. "It'll take them forever to get here. And then what? Do you think they'll listen to an eleven-year-old girl and her mechanical head about the man-eating creature loose in their secret underground lab?"

Hobbes considered this. "I suppose it does sound a bit far-fetched."

"No," Frances said, getting to her feet. "We're going to have to do this on our own."

Frances shifted the colander on her head as the elevator descended toward the library, powered by a small generator she dragged in from the carriage house. She'd outfitted herself in a hodgepodge of household items: the colander, safety goggles, oven mitts, and a toilet seat that hung from her neck like a medieval chest plate. For self-defense, she carried a fireplace poker. Hobbes had insisted she don protective clothing before putting herself in harm's way, and this was the best she could do on short notice.

Her great-grandfather's journal lay open on the floor in front of her. She flipped through page after page, searching for some clue that might tell her how to stop the monster she'd helped create. It was no use—the intelligence serum had worn off, taking with it her ability to decipher the journal's code. She slammed it shut in frustration.

"Let's go over the plan again," Hobbes said.

Frances sighed. "Step one: check to see if the coast is clear. Step two: make our way through the lab, staying close to the walls. Step three: pray the creature is in one of the rooms. Step four: lock him inside and hope he can't bust his way out. Step five: come up with the rest of the plan."

The elevator shuddered and lurched to a stop, tossing Frances into the wall. The doors ground in their tracks, jamming only a few centimeters apart. Instead of the pleasant *ding* that usually followed, there was a dull *clink*.

Frances set Hobbes near the back of the compartment and adjusted her porcelain breastplate. She took a deep breath, counted to three, then heaved against the doors. They hardly budged at first, then slammed open all at once, causing the colander to slip over her eyes. She jumped back, waving the poker in front of her like a fencer with a bee in his mask.

"Frances," Hobbes cried. "Frances! He's not there."

She lowered the poker and lifted the colander from her eyes.

Out in the foyer, only a single overhead light was lit, swaying at the end of a frayed wire. In its shifting glow, Frances could see workstations had been ransacked, equipment strewn across the hall. She had to climb over a pile of crumbled plaster and twisted metal just to escape the elevator. When the doors tried to close behind her, she found their metal casing peeled away, as if the monster had tried to pull them apart.

The Librarian was in even worse shape. Several meters of pneumatic chute had been yanked from the ceiling and shattered across the floor. A tangle of wires spilled from what remained of the console.

Even Albrecht Grimme himself had not escaped the incident unharmed. The monster had torn a long gash across his portrait, beginning in the corner and continuing right across his face. Walking farther, Frances found the door to the broom closet, where she hid as a child, splintered on its hinges. Her fairy cave—that's what she told her mother it was. Now it was gone.

Her breath caught in her throat. It was all gone. A bulb flickered above them and popped, showering Frances with glass and sparks.

"Come, Frances," Hobbes said. "We must keep moving." His voice was gentle. Perhaps he was better at reading human emotion than he let on.

Frances sniffed and wiped the tears from her eyes with an oven mitt, then placed Hobbes under her arm. Together, they crept deeper into the lab, staying near the walls as dictated by step two. Every hallway was the same: broken fixtures, crumbled plaster, splintered doors.

They soon reached the Zoo.

"No," Frances cried. The door had been ripped from its frame, and pieces were scattered across the hall.

"Wait," Hobbes called. "It isn't safe—"

But he was already tumbling from her arms, cast to the ground along with the fireplace poker as Frances ran headlong into the darkened room.

"Fritz," Frances called. "Shelley?"

Only silence answered, a deafening absence of scuffling, chirping, and chatter that grew more ominous as she ventured farther into the room. Feed crunched beneath her shoes, filling the room with a thick, musty odor. She covered her nose and continued. Her foot banged against an overturned cage—the rats. When she picked it up to look inside, she discovered the door had been torn away. She found the rabbit pen on its side next to the table, the serpent tank shattered beside it. The animals were gone.

"I'm sorry," Frances said, her shoulders buckling with sobs. "I'm so sorry."

She stumbled to Fritz's empty cage, heartbroken, her stomach filled with dread. "Please be okay," she said, placing her hand on the bars. "Wherever you are, I'll find you. I promise."

When she emerged from the Zoo, her eyes were swollen and red.

Hobbes's head rested on its side in the hallway where he had rolled to a stop after Frances dropped him. "I'm sorry," he said.

Frances nodded. She wondered if he understood what the animals meant to her. If he felt that way about anything. If he even could.

"Here," she said, still sniffling. She set a cage on the floor next to him. Its bars were made of brass wire, with a ring at the top for a handle. It had been home to the yellow-crested cockatoo.

Hobbes looked it over. "What use do we have for a bird-cage?"

Moments later, Frances continued down the hall carrying the birdcage with Hobbes shut inside.

"This is most humiliating," he grumbled.

The trail of destruction zigged and zagged throughout the length of the underground laboratory, eventually leading them to the emergency staircase. The only other way out.

"I guess we know which way it went," Frances said.

The staircase was a dusty relic of a time before electricity, with ornate wooden railings and huge bloodred tapestries that hung from the walls. Frances stared at the tapestries, flight after flight. Each depicted a different medieval scene: plague doctors treating a row of sick children, a ceremony at an open tomb, a hunting party in the woods. In one, a woman knelt before a tribunal while an archer stood off to the side, arrow nocked and ready to fire. As she climbed the endless staircase, Frances felt like she was the one on her way to judgment.

At the next landing, she leaned against the railing to catch her breath. "How many more flights?"

"Only five to go," Hobbes replied.

"Five?" She pulled the toilet seat breastplate over her head and dropped it to the floor. Her shirt was plastered to her skin where she had sweated through the fabric.

"Are you aware that I was designed to carry loads of up to two hundred kilograms?" Hobbes said. "Of course, that was when I had arms. . . ."

"That gives me an idea." Frances dangled the birdcage over the railing. "Maybe I should get rid of some extra weight."

"That is not what I meant!" Hobbes cried.

Frances reached the top with her thighs burning and a worrisome twinge in her knee. She stepped over a chunk of stone and pulled herself to the final landing. The door at the top of the stairs had been wedged between the railings, blocking their path. Frances yanked it free but lost her grip. She watched it slide down the stairs and cartwheel over the railing, wincing as it cracked against the steps somewhere far below.

The doorway led to a storeroom behind the kitchen where the family received deliveries. It looked like a firing squad had come through, splattering raspberry jam and pickled beets across the shelves. Heads of lettuce, cabbages, and a few stray carrots littered the floor.

The delivery bay doors slammed behind her, and she spun around, swinging Hobbes's birdcage like a flail.

"It is just the wind," Hobbes said.

He was right: the doors were creaking in the breeze, the wind slamming them against the doorframe at irregular intervals, only to pull them open again.

Frances dropped the oven mitts and slid the colander from her head, letting it clatter to the floor, wobbling slower and slower until it tapered off in a metallic drone. Through the doorway, she could see the Manor grounds, and beyond that, the rolling hills of the Rosengarten—the famous rose gardens of Bern. At the bottom of those hills flowed the Aare river, and there, just past the water, the city itself. Across the lawn, a line of footprints sunk deep into the mud, marching in a collision course with the population below.

"What have I done?" she said.

"You created a monster," Hobbes replied.

She glared at him through the bars of the birdcage. "It was a rhetorical question."

But he was right. She *had* created a monster.

And now she had to stop him.

Chapter 10

The World Outside

F rances stood at the doorway with her hands on her hips
and the tips of her oxfords squared against the threshold.
She was clad once more in pants, suspenders, and a bow tie.
She'd added a fedora to the outfit, too. It had looked like a hat
made for adventuring—even if the brim sat too low where she
lacked an ear to hold it up.

"You found everything on my list?" Hobbes said.

She hefted a canvas knapsack on her shoulders, feeling the
weight of its contents bearing down on the straps. "Two wedges
of cheese, ten francs, a block of cured ham, a canteen, and a
spindle of thread. And my great-grandfather's journal."

She didn't mention the small wooden case she'd hidden at
the bottom of the bag. It contained something Frances had

whipped up at the chemistry station—what was left of the chemistry station, anyway. Something she could use against the monster. Hobbes would only find a reason to disapprove, so she had decided to keep it to herself.

"Excellent," Hobbes said. "And you are certain there's nothing I can say to talk you out of this madness?"

Frances shook her head.

"Very well. In that case, I suppose we should be off."

"I suppose we should."

Frances breathed in through her nose, holding the evening air in her lungs until it burned, then released it all at once. It was finally happening—she was leaving the Manor, and there was no one here to stop her. Not her parents, not her tutors. Not even Hobbes. It was a strange sensation, being free. Like she'd swallowed a family of crickets and they were bouncing off her stomach lining, trying to escape. Admittedly, the circumstances weren't exactly what she'd imagined, but she wasn't about to—

"Ahem."

Frances looked at Hobbes and frowned. "What?"

"We have been standing here for three minutes and seventeen seconds," he said. "Eighteen seconds now."

"Well, I've been standing." Frances rattled the birdcage. "You've been dangling."

Hobbes sighed. "You truly are an ill-mannered child."

Frances ignored him and, squeezing her bedroom key in her pocket, stepped over the threshold and into the outside world.

The Manor once employed a gardener with a rare talent for topiary. He had covered the grounds with mythical beasts: unicorns and griffins, centaurs and fauns. People traveled from the city just to see them. But that was years ago, and the hedges had long since become hedges again. At least, that's how it had appeared from her bedroom window.

Frances ducked, pushing aside a branch of boxwood, its leaves like thick, waxy clover, and found herself staring into the jaws of a dragon. The branch snapped against the nape of her neck.

"Oh!" she cried, half-startled, half-stung.

The teeth were misshapen, and its horns had fallen to invading honeysuckle, but there was no mistaking it. She found her bedroom window above her and shook her head. All this time, she'd been staring at the back of a dragon.

"I hope that's not an omen," she said, rubbing the welt on her neck.

"Superstition," Hobbes replied, "is the simpleton's answer to fear."

A low-lying wall of smooth, mossy stones bordered the property. Frances felt the grasshoppers in her stomach return as she approached—crossing that wall meant leaving the Manor grounds behind, putting her farther from home than she'd been since the accident. Before she could muster the courage to continue, a dark shape dropped from the branches of a nearby tree.

"Fritz!" she cried as the chimpanzee bounded into her arms for a hug. "We thought you were monster food back there."

Escape, Fritz signed.

"But how did you get out?"

Fritz hopped to the ground and began running in place, jumping up and turning left, then right, then left again.

"You ran through the halls," Frances translated.

He nodded and put a hairy thumb to his chin, then covered it with his hand; the sign for *hide*. Next, he bent his fingers into claws and linked his thumbs to make the sign for *run*.

"You hid and waited for the monster to run by. . . ."

After walking his fingers up an imaginary flight of stairs, he brought his fists together and blew them apart again. Then he made a show of sauntering casually in place.

"He broke through the storeroom doors, and you just walked right through." Frances mussed the fur on the top of his head. "Good boy."

Even Hobbes nodded his approval. "A fine tactical choice. Impressive, for a primate."

"Come on," Frances said. She hefted the birdcage with one hand and, with the other, beckoned Fritz to follow. "We're monster hunting. Race you over the wall!"

Beyond the Manor grounds, everything was vast: the night sky above, the mountain foothills winding into the river, the city spread out like a long, red bruise on the horizon. And the wind! Frances held her fedora in place as it whipped her hair across her face, buffeting her from every side like she was falling from a great height never to reach the bottom. Her head began to swim, so she squeezed her eyes into slits and focused only on her next step.

"You have no reason to fear," Hobbes said, observing her through the bars of his cage. "The probability of injury or death is significantly greater inside the home, particularly under the unique circumstances of the Manor. It is remarkable you haven't met a grisly end long ago, with what goes on in that house."

Frances pursed her lips. "That's not very encouraging."

"I am only stating facts," Hobbes replied. "Would you like me to speak in an encouraging way? Your father programmed me to perform many types of speech, including inspirational."

"Only if it's in Italian."

Hobbes said no more, but Fritz took Frances's hand and gave it a friendly squeeze.

The path twisted down a rocky slope. Once, Frances lost her footing, narrowly avoiding a long tumble to the ground below. Eventually, the path evened out, and the rocks were replaced by grassy knolls and endless rosebushes as they entered the gardens.

Frances had always admired the Rosengarten from afar, but seeing it up close, walking through it, smelling the flowers, was something else entirely. She felt at peace here. Part of her wished it would never end.

But it did end, the tidy rows of flowers replaced by tidy rows of houses that grew bigger and taller every block until they reached a bridge leading across the river into the city.

"I'm afraid the city is not safe for a chimpanzee," Hobbes said. "Those who live here aren't used to beasts running free. You will have to stay off the street."

"He's right." Frances crouched so her eyes were level with Fritz's and stroked the fur between his ears. "We don't know what they'll do if they catch you, so you'll have to keep out of sight. You can act as our scout! If you see anything, come find us. Okay?"

Fritz nodded. He planted a kiss on her cheek and bounded off, hooting and hollering as he crossed the bridge and scaled a building on the other side. Soon, he had disappeared over the rooftops and out of sight.

"I imagine they're not used to girls walking around with severed heads, either," Frances said. She pulled a kerchief from her knapsack and draped it over the birdcage. Now, as far as any passersby were concerned, she was simply transporting a skittish parakeet. As long as no one looked too closely. Or Hobbes didn't open his mouth.

"This is most humiliating," Hobbes grumbled once again. This time, his voice was muffled by the fabric.

Frances leaned over the railing of the bridge and peered into the river below. The oil-black water reflected a shifting, swirling image of her face. Ahead of them, buildings rose from the ground on either side of the street, a tunnel of sandstone walls. With every step, the air thickened, until a smog of coal fires and combustion engines hovered over the cobblestones like a storm cloud.

"Bern looked so much smaller from my window." Frances turned, hoping for a glimpse of the Manor and finding it a mere dot on the hillside. She swallowed.

"Bern, capital of Switzerland," Hobbes recited. "Population 111,783. Founded in AD 1218 by Berthold V. According to legend, he named the city after battling a great bear in the nearby wilderness—"

"Thanks," Frances said. "But this isn't the time for a history lesson."

Hobbes's tone grew serious. "You must keep your wits about you, Frances. You are no longer in the Manor."

"I can handle it," she said, trying to sound sure.

Frances was relieved to find the streets empty. For two blocks, the only sounds were her own leather soles echoing off the cobblestones as she walked in a daze down the center of the street. Then a low rumbling intruded on the quiet.

"What is that?" she said. The noise grew louder and louder until a horn blared, and Frances spun around to find two blinding circles of light expanding before her. She leaped from the path of the truck, close enough to feel the pull of its drag on her clothes. Her toe caught on the curb, and she fell onto her backside, dropping the birdcage.

"Stay out of the road, kid!" the driver yelled, shaking his fist out the window.

Frances's hands shook as she retrieved the birdcage from the gutter. She scooted herself against the wall of a nearby storefront and pulled her knees to her chest, taking quick, shallow breaths.

"We need to turn back," she said, sticking her head between her knees. "I can't do this."

"Turn back?" Hobbes said. "I thought this is what you wanted!"

"It was. It is. I don't know what's wrong with me."

"Your blood pressure is elevated, your face is flushed, and you are shaking. These are signs of anxiety, Frances. You are in a panic."

"I don't panic," she said, the sharpness in her voice muffled by her legs. "I'll be fine. Just let me catch my breath."

"Take all the time you need. This mission was your idea after all."

Frances looked up in disbelief. "You'd rather we let that monster run rampant through the city?"

"I have no responsibility to the people of Bern or any other municipality," Hobbes replied. "Only to you."

"If my parents had just let me come with them instead of leaving me behind with a talking toaster—"

"Panic or no, you will not blame me or your parents for your decisions."

"I wasn't even the one who came up with that . . . that thing," Frances said, momentarily forgetting her fear. "If Great-Grandfather Grimme hadn't created him in the first place, we wouldn't be in this mess."

"At least he had the sense to lock him away. Or was it the late Master Grimme who let him loose on the unsuspecting populace?"

Frances glared. "I knew I should've brought that magnet—"

A sudden clanging echoed through the streets. A crash followed, then a deep, rasping sound like a foraging hog. Frances and Hobbes stopped arguing and listened.

"It's him," Frances whispered. He was close—the noise was coming from an alley nearby.

"Then we stay where we are," Hobbes said.

"No." Frances stood up and brushed off the seat of her pants. "We have to do something."

She grabbed the birdcage and tiptoed to the end of the block, pressing her back against the bricks near the mouth of the alley.

"We shouldn't get too close," she whispered.

"I believe that was exactly the point I was—"

"No, I mean he'll smell us."

"Ah, well," Hobbes said. Then, proudly, "He won't smell me. I am odorless."

Frances clicked her tongue and grinned. "Good thinking. You'll do it."

"Do what? Need I remind you that I could not walk into that alley even if I had any desire to whatsoever? Which I certainly do not."

Frances looked around. The street was empty and the surrounding shopwindows were dark. "People aren't usually in shops at night, right?"

"I do not understand the relevance of your question."

Frances pointed to the closest window. "There's nobody sleeping in there?"

"No," Hobbes replied. "I would think not." He eyed her suspiciously as the corner of her mouth turned up in the faintest smile. "Frances? I do not like the way you're looking at me."

Frances got to her feet and darted to a doorway a few meters from the alley. It was a cobbler shop, with a wooden sign over the door in the shape of a clog. She pulled a hairpin from under her fedora and jimmied the lock like she had in the Zoo. The door clicked open.

Hobbes tried to peer through the dusty windows into the darkened shop, but with no neck to crane, he could see nothing. Frances emerged a few minutes later carrying a broom behind her back.

"I suspect you did not pay for that," Hobbes said.

Frances shrugged. "I'll pay for it later. Mum and Dad can afford it." She unclasped the birdcage and reached inside for Hobbes. "You don't feel pain, do you?"

"Why ask me that?" His whisper became a frantic hiss as she picked him up by his ears. "Frances?"

"You don't, right?"

"No, but I—"

"Good." Frances lifted Hobbes over her head and thrust him onto the end of the broom. He cried out in surprise. She raised the broomstick to test her invention, twisting it around like a periscope.

"I demand that you put me down," Hobbes hissed. "This instant!"

"This should do the trick. Now, hush. He won't be able to smell you, but he doesn't seem to have any trouble hearing."

Frances held the broom in front of her with Hobbes's head suspended at the end. She inched toward the alley until he could peek around the wall.

After a few seconds, he started wiggling, and she pulled him in.

"What did you see?" she said, returning Hobbes to the birdcage.

"The creature sits with his back to us. He appears quite engrossed in a bag of discarded fish. Ugh. I wish I hadn't been outfitted with a simulated sense of smell."

"His back is turned," Frances said. "That's good."

She secured the birdcage and stooped down to gather a few pieces of trash from the curb, rubbing them on her shirt and stuffing them into her pockets.

When she was finished, she spread out her hands. "How do I smell?"

Hobbes grimaced. "Like you tumbled from the back of a garbage cart."

"Perfect. I'll fit right in."

Frances pulled the wooden case from her knapsack, latched like a pencil box.

"We've caught up with him," Hobbes said. "An admirable feat. Now, what do you propose to do? You can't rush into this, Frances—that is exactly the type of behavior that created this mess."

"I'm going to put him to sleep," Frances said. "With this."

She opened the case and extracted a syringe. Holding it up to a streetlamp, she flicked the needle to clear any bubbles that may have formed at the tip. The syringe contained a sedative based on the one her mother used for surgical procedures in the Zoo, modified to account for the body's size. According to Frances's calculations, one dose could knock out a horse.

Hobbes's eyes turned yellow. "This is not a wise plan. Even if you get close enough—which won't be easy—what will you do once you—"

Frances held a finger to her lips. "This is why I didn't tell you."

"Frances—" Hobbes began, but she pulled the kerchief back over the birdcage, muffling his voice.

Frances scooted along the stone wall. When she reached the end, she checked the syringe one last time. The monster was making a racket—digging through bags of trash and cardboard boxes. The rattle of aluminum cans echoed between the stone walls.

She peeked around the corner. In the darkness, she could make out the creature's hulking shape, still bent over the mound of trash. His fingers glistened with grease and saliva, his crushed arm hung limp at his side. Frances crept into the alley, carefully stepping over food containers and fishbones. As she approached him, the smell of formaldehyde and decomposition stung her nose. When she was close enough to reach out and touch his back, she held the syringe over her head, thumb on the plunger, and took a deep breath.

It was at that moment that the alley flooded with light.

"Who's there?" a voice boomed.

Frances spun around and recoiled, blinded by the brightness. She heard a noise behind her and turned again in time to see the monster scramble toward the alley wall, sending an avalanche of crates onto her head, and the syringe flying from her hand.

Chapter 11
Constable Willermus Montavon

F rances pushed the crates aside and found the monster standing over her, his hulking mass blotting out the moon. She tried to crawl backward, one hand lifted like a shield against the light that still shone in her eyes while the other frantically traced the veins between cobblestones, searching for the dropped syringe.

"My, my," the monster said. His voice was gruff, but warm. "Aren't you a jumpy little tadpole."

At last, the tips of her fingers brushed against a cool glass surface on the ground beside her. Her fist closed around the syringe just as the light switched off with a *click* and the dark mass stepped into the moonlight. Frances squinted. It wasn't the monster after all, though he was nearly as large. It was a constable. He had wide shoulders and a round belly, and a bushy white mustache that began at each ear and joined under his nose. He clipped the flashlight to his belt, then stretched out his hand to help her up. Frances shook her head, wincing as pain throbbed from the lump where the crates had struck her.

"I'll stay right here, I think," she said.

"There on the cobblestones?"

"Is there a rule against remaining on the ground after I've fallen down?"

The constable let out a hearty laugh. While he was distracted, Frances slipped the syringe into the pocket of her trousers.

"My dear boy," the constable said. "If one tries hard enough, one can find a rule against just about anything."

"I'm not a boy," Frances corrected him.

"No? My apologies, lass. Now, let's take a look at you."

The constable held out his hand again, but this time he didn't wait for Frances to take it. Instead, he wrapped his meaty fingers around her wrist and hauled her effortlessly to her feet.

"Good heavens," he cried once he got a whiff of her. He pulled out a handkerchief to cover his nose. "I'll be off fish for a week!"

Frances pulled her hand away and attempted to sprint out of the alley, but the constable stepped in front of her. She bounced off his belly and fell back onto the ground.

"Now, now," he said. "There's no need to be frightened. My name is Constable Willermus Montavon. I am here to help."

Constable Montavon bowed with a flourish and paused, eyebrows raised. Frances realized he was waiting for her to speak.

"Um, thank you. I'm Frances."

"Frances! Francis Drake, Francis de Sales, Saint Francis of Assisi. A lovely name, steeped in history. I must say, you gave me a fright, rustling about in the shadows. I thought I'd seen a proper ghost."

He prodded her shoulder with a large, gloved finger. "You appear more or less solid, though I'd wager a healthy meal wouldn't be lost on those bones of yours." The constable straightened up and gestured with his hands like a preacher. "We've all known hunger, haven't we? One can't blame a child for resorting to less . . . noble means of supplying their needs. Come, now. The weather is mild enough tonight, but they say we're headed for a nasty cold snap in three days' time. I would hate for you to be caught out in the elements."

Three days? Frances scoffed. *I'll be back in the Manor long before then.*

The constable's words sounded grand, but she couldn't make much sense of them. Ghosts and hunger and "less noble means"? It wasn't until she caught a glimpse of herself in a broken window that she understood.

"You think I'm a street urchin," she said. "No, no, no—I'm not looking for something to eat." She stood and shook the constable's hand. "Thanks for your concern, though. Glad we got that figured out. Good night!"

She tried to walk away, but the constable did not release her hand.

"If you're not scavenging for food," he said, raising an eyebrow, "what are you doing out at this time of night?"

"I'm just . . . I was—" Frances fidgeted while her mind searched for a suitable lie. She could tell him she was lost, but he'd only insist on taking her home. What if he saw the damage the creature had done to the Manor? Maybe her dog had run away, and she was looking for it. That might work, but what if he offered to help? No, she had to get rid of him.

Or did she? She looked him over. He was big—almost as big as the monster. That could be useful. And he did say he wanted to help. . . .

Frances took a deep breath and exhaled. *Best to breach the subject cautiously*, she thought. "I'm looking for a body."

"A body? Has someone died?"

"No. Well, yes . . . a long time ago. But then I—I . . ."

The constable was looking at her sideways. She could tell she wasn't making any sense, so she shook her head and started again.

"I'm looking for a—for a monster."

"A monster . . ."

She nodded, wincing. "You didn't see him?" She pointed to the back of the alley. "He was right there."

"Did I see a monster that lives in alleys and roots through good Bernians' trash?"

"He doesn't live in this alley." Frances rubbed the bridge of her nose. She wasn't used to dealing with non-brilliant people. "I tracked him here, and I was about to catch him. I would have, too, if you hadn't scared him away."

The constable narrowed his eyes.

"It was an accident, I'm sure," she said. "I'm not saying it's your fault or anything."

He studied her for a moment, then broke into a grin. "A monster!" He put his hands on his belly and laughed. When he finished, he brushed away a tear and sighed. "Isn't it remarkable, how even the youngest among us find ways to cope with the challenges we're dealt? Jest is a powerful elixir, able to soothe the downtrodden soul. Still"—he became serious—"as a man of the law, I can't abide pranks."

"It's not a prank. And, I told you, I'm not downtrodden."

When he spoke again, any trace of laughter that had lingered in his voice was gone. "Where are your parents, girl?"

Frances realized she'd made a mistake in telling the constable about the monster. Of course he didn't believe her—that's why she didn't call the police in the first place. Now she had no idea what to tell him about her parents. If he found out they had left her alone—because if he didn't believe her about the creature, he certainly wouldn't believe her about Hobbes—he might try to take her away and stick her in an orphanage, or arrest her parents when they returned.

The constable frowned. "Either I take you to your parents or I take you to the station. So, where do you live, little girl?"

Frances saw no way out, so she sighed and told the truth. "The Manor. Up on the hill."

The constable raised his eyebrows. "Grimme-Stenzel Manor?" Frances nodded. He stroked the tips of his mustache and examined her. "My, my. This is an unexpected twist!"

"Yes, well, it's true," she said. "I am Frances Stenzel, daughter of Victor and Mary Stenzel of Grimme-Stenzel Manor. Now please let me be on my way—my parents would not appreciate their daughter being harassed by a local constable."

"Let you be on your way?" The constable laughed good and hard at that. "And I thought you were a ghost! Why, you're not the spirit of poverty but the specter of privilege! Perhaps you've come down from the hill to haunt us common folk with your games."

Frances's heart dropped. Somehow, she'd only made things worse. *I liked him better when he assumed I was poor.*

The constable pointed to the overturned trash cans. "So, what is the reason for this vandalism? What need do you have that your Manor doesn't provide?" He took her by the hand. "I'll return you to your parents, and you'll explain to them what you've been doing here. You need to face consequences for your actions like all good folk."

Frances tried to protest, but Constable Montavon pulled her along by her wrist. When they reached the end of the alley, her pulse began to race. There, on the street, was the constable's paddy wagon.

The squeal of tires, the crunch of metal, the twinkling glass . . .

"I—I can't," Frances stammered. "I can't go in there. I can't get into that truck."

"It is discipline that shapes us into citizens worthy of this fine city," Montavon replied, ignoring her pleas.

Frances dug her heels into the cobblestones and squirmed, trying to yank her arm free, but the constable hardly seemed to notice. He dragged her around to the back of the wagon and pulled open the rear door. Frances gaped at it like she was staring into the mouth of a tiger.

"Please," she cried. "I can't."

In the darkness, a scream pierced the air, ricocheting off the walls of the alley. The constable stood at attention, still gripping Frances's wrist.

"It's the monster," Frances said.

"Quiet," the constable barked. Another scream, this one even louder. It sounded close, only a few feet away.

Frances stopped resisting. "Someone needs your help," she said. She slipped her hand into her pocket. "I'll stay here and wait for you, I promise."

"I said be quiet! If someone is in need, I will not allow you to . . ."

The constable's words trailed off as he reached his free hand to his neck, where he felt a sharp prick. His fingers closed on a smooth, cylindrical object sticking out of his flesh. He pulled the half-empty syringe free and turned it over in his hand, his eyes wide with surprise.

"What . . . what have you done?" he said.

Frances felt his grip loosen on her wrist. "I'm sorry," she said. "But I was telling the truth. There's a monster loose in this city, and I have to stop it before it hurts someone."

"I won't stand for this," the constable mumbled, and fell face-first into the gutter.

Frances laid his head on a rolled-up rag she found in the alley and covered him up to his shoulders with a tarp so he wouldn't freeze in the cool Swiss night. Back at the mouth of the alley, she found Hobbes's birdcage right where she left it. She lifted the cloth.

"Not bad," she said.

"Not bad?" Hobbes echoed. "It was humiliating! I think I ruptured one of my vocal processors."

"Well, next time don't scream so high."

Hobbes turned up his nose in a huff. "It worked. That is enough for me."

"It did. But I had to use one of the sedatives. We'll only get one more chance."

"I don't suppose simply going home is an option."

"No. We have to find the monster."

"In that case," Hobbes said. "We'd best get out of here before the constable comes to."

"Him?" Frances gave the man's foot a light kick and watched it flop back into place. "He won't be bothering us any time soon."

Hobbes sighed. "You are always solving the problem in front of you, never considering the consequences down the line. I'm afraid we have made a formidable enemy tonight."

Frances scowled, unable to disagree. "Then we'll just have to catch the monster before the constable catches us."

She replaced the cloth covering and picked up the birdcage, setting off on the trail of the monster.

As she made her way through the city, the signs were everywhere: broken windows on Post Street, overturned trash containers on Junkerngasse, the grisly remains of a rats' nest near Nydegg Church. The problem was finding any pattern to the destruction. The monster seemed to be everywhere at once, always just beyond their grasp.

The birdcage grew heavy as the night dragged on. Soon,

Frances could go no farther.

But where would she sleep? She couldn't head back to the Manor, not with a monster still loose in the city. Besides, she wasn't sure she could make it all the way back without collapsing. It had never occurred to her that they might not find the creature right away.

Frances walked on until she found an alley behind a bakery. It was hidden from the street and had only one entrance, so nothing could sneak up on them while they slept. It would have to do.

She gathered an armful of loose newspapers and laid them down as a bed. BRITAIN DECLARES WAR ON GERMANY, one headline announced. She pulled her great-grandfather's journal from her knapsack and placed it under her head. The leather was coarse, and the raised lettering would leave marks, but it was better than nothing. She lay on her back, looking up at the night sky. The three stars of Orion's belt, the pinched square of the raven Corvus. She wondered if her parents were looking up at those same stars, or if they could see them, wherever they were.

After a few minutes, she grew restless.

"I have to pee," she announced, turning to Hobbes. "What do I do?"

"Do I look like an expert in human bodily functions? Find somewhere out of sight and get to it."

Frances walked a few paces and squatted behind a trash bin. "Turn off your ears," she called.

When she was finished, Frances lay back down on the newspapers and turned the journal over. The other side was just as uncomfortable.

"I will wake you in four hours," Hobbes said.

"Why only four?"

"Because that is how long I estimate we have before the constable's sedative wears off."

"Fine." Frances rolled onto her side so her back was to the birdcage. "Four hours."

"Good night, Frances," Hobbes said.

But Frances didn't hear him because, for the first time in as long as she could remember, she was fast asleep.

Chapter 12

A Helping Hand

Frances awoke gasping and clutching her side.

"Get up," said the man who had just kicked her in the ribs. He was tall and thin, with a large flat nose like the butt of a pistol. The baker, Frances assumed. She scrambled to her feet, holding her knapsack to her chest and grabbing the birdcage. "Go on, filthy beggar. You'll get no scraps from me."

"Beggar?" she said, dodging another kick. "Why does everybody keep— OW!"

Frances ran until the bakery was out of sight and leaned against a streetlamp to catch her breath. "Why would he kick me?" she said.

"We are not in the Manor any longer," Hobbes answered matter-of-factly. "You have been raised by loving parents with the means to provide everything you need and more. Few are fortunate enough to share in such privileges."

Frances examined the fresh bruise on her side and winced. "So, they go around kicking each other over stale bread, or because they need a place to sleep?"

"The pursuit of money and property have justified countless atrocities throughout human history. The correlation is quite clear."

Frances imagined the francs clinking together at the bottom her knapsack with their notched edges and smooth silver faces. She wouldn't even have thought to bring them if Hobbes hadn't included them on his list of supplies.

"You mustn't dwell on it," Hobbes said. "We have work to do. The creature is out here somewhere, and that constable could be lurking behind any corner."

The city was still dark outside the pools of orange lamplight. Frances's legs and back ached. She slept so rarely that four hours had left her groggy and slow. Still, she soldiered on, following a line of torn-up butcher paper between a grocer and a store with colorful hats in the window, and examining uprooted hedges on Kramgasse. If either were the monster's doing, they offered little clue as to where he went next.

Morning came on gradually through the mist—Frances hardly noticed until she turned a corner and was blinded by the sun. As her eyes adjusted, the city came into focus. Empty streets and darkened alleys gave way to early morning strolls and bleary-eyed pedestrians beginning their commutes. A new day had arrived, and the trail had gone cold.

"How could a giant, destructive monster just . . . vanish?" Frances said, kicking an empty can down the road. She stayed close to the shopfronts as she walked, avoiding the open spaces of the streets and sidewalks.

"He likely found a concealed place to sleep until nightfall, when he can move without being seen," Hobbes said. "Perhaps he's not entirely without wits."

He convinced her to turn back to the last place they found evidence of the monster, the hedges on Kramgasse. From there, they searched every alley and trash pile, until they reached a crowded market. People milled about in a disjointed mass, this way and that, making it hard to see.

"I can't go in there," Frances said, her breath catching in her throat at the sight of so many people.

"I'm afraid we must, if we hope to pick up the creature's trail."

She huddled against the wall of a china shop with her eyes squeezed shut. Why did she feel this way? They were just people. But she'd never seen so many together in one place before. She took a deep breath, then another.

"Frances—" Hobbes began.

"Give me a minute," she snapped.

Hobbes's voice remained calm. "We can always go home. The creature will be apprehended eventually—perhaps by our zealous Constable Montavon. There is no shame in defeat."

"Of course there's shame in defeat," Frances said, shaking her head. "That's where shame comes from."

She grit her teeth and squeezed the key in her pocket. The Manor was just over those hills, she reminded herself. If only she could see it, even just a glimpse. She took a breath and held it until she could hold it no longer, then exhaled and waded into the crowd. People jostled her on every side, like storm-chopped waves.

"Remember, we're looking for signs of the creature's presence," Hobbes whispered inside the cage.

Frances stood on the tips of her toes to look around the shoppers and merchants. She searched for anomalies, anything suspicious at all. But the crowd was too thick. A short woman with a large purse pushed past her, and Frances stepped into the path of a man with impossibly long limbs. She turned to move out of his way and lost her balance, swinging the birdcage in an arc over a nearby vegetable cart and nearly clobbering an old man squeezing tomatoes.

"Are you bleeding, sir?" the merchant said, but the startled old man had only squeezed too hard and splattered tomato juice down the front of his shirt.

I have to get out of here. The city was closing in, wringing the air from her lungs. Her vision was beginning to swim when a hand gripped hers. She turned to see a boy about her age, with round cheeks and a curl of blond hair on his forehead.

"Follow me," the boy said.

He weaved through the crowds like he had done it a thousand times. Frances tried to keep up. The birdcage was cumbersome, but she held it close, terrified someone would glimpse what was inside.

When they broke through the edge of the crowd, the boy led her to a quiet spot beneath a stone arcade. A bike was tied there, bent nearly in half, with two flat tires.

"You okay?" the boy said.

"I'll be fine," Frances replied, leaning against the arcade.

"I'm Luca, by the way. Luca Frick."

"Frances Stenzel. And you can let go of me now."

The boy looked down at his hand as if he had just remembered it was attached to his arm, then pulled it away, red splotches blooming on his cheeks.

When she no longer needed the wall to steady herself, Frances adjusted her knapsack and started down the street. "Thanks for your help," she said without looking back.

Luca hurried to untie his bike, fumbling with the knot in his haste. "That your first time in the market?"

Frances ignored him and kept walking. Behind her, Luca chewed his lip and tugged at the tangled mess he'd made of the string. When it finally slipped free, he balled it up and stuffed it in his pocket.

"Mum sends me out for supplies almost every day. Even when we don't need anything." He wheeled his bike after her, both tires spinning off-kilter and squeaking like frightened piglets. "Frances?" he called. "Frances, wait up!"

"I'm in a hurry," she said.

"I'm not, so I'll come with you."

The boy had been sweet to help her, but he would only slow her down. That, and his sincerity was already getting on her nerves. Frances's mind ran through possible evasion scenarios. Then she noticed his bike.

"What happened?" she said, pointing to the mangled tires.

"Not sure. It was like this when I woke up. I left it next to our trash bins, and the bins were busted, too. There was trash everywhere." He wrinkled his nose. "My bike still kind of stinks."

It certainly did, but Frances didn't care. Luca's busted bicycle might be her first new lead all morning. Stopping to investigate would be risky with the constable no doubt on her trail, but she had to try.

"Can you take me there?" she asked.

Luca's eyes went wide. "You want to come to my house?"

"I want to see your trash bins."

"They're just regular bins. About this high." He held his

hand up to his shoulder. "Same as anybody's."

Frances stopped walking and turned to Luca. "Are you going to take me or not?"

He opened his mouth like he wanted to say something, then closed it and exhaled through his nose. "If you really want to go," he said at last.

They set off at once. Luca led the way. Or tried to. He struggled to keep up with Frances's pace. Several times she got so far ahead he had to call out because she'd missed a turn. In her eyes, every street looked the same, all sandstone arcades and fountains and so very many people.

Before long, Luca was wiping sweat from his forehead. "We sure are going awful fast," he said.

"I'm being pursued," Frances replied.

"Ooh, a chase. Who's chasing you?"

"A constable. A particularly determined one."

Luca eyed her sideways. "What'd you do?"

Frances tugged at her sleeve, pulling it over the bruise left by the constable's fingers when he dragged her by her wrist. Her face darkened. "It's just a misunderstanding."

Luca watched her for a moment, then nodded, apparently satisfied. He pointed to the birdcage. "What do you have there?"

"None of your business," she said, smoothing the cloth that concealed Hobbes's disembodied head.

"If it's a bird, it's real quiet. Quietest bird I ever heard."

"I like quiet."

"It's not a parrot," Luca went on, undeterred. "'Cause if it was a parrot, it would repeat everything I say." He leaned his face close to the birdcage and said, "Polly want a cracker. Polly want a cracker."

Frances scowled and pulled the birdcage away. The sudden movement jostled Hobbes, and he said, "Ow!"

"What?" said Luca.

"Ow," Frances said. She affected a limp. "I stubbed my toe. Or something."

Frances and Luca (and, beneath his cover, Hobbes) walked on in silence after that. The farther they went, the more Luca's pace seemed to slow. He looked both ways two, even three times before crossing a street. He stopped to peer inside a storefront selling aprons until Frances pulled him away. Once, he ducked behind a postbox because he swore he saw the constable.

"Never mind. Just a guy wearing a blue shirt," he said.

By the time they reached their destination, the sun hovered almost directly overhead.

"Here we are," Luca said, setting his bike on the ground. "Number 1401 and a half."

"And a half?" Frances repeated, looking around.

Luca's face reddened as he cleared his throat and pointed. The house was crammed between two others as if it had been added after the rest of the neighborhood to use up leftover materials. If Luca hadn't been there to guide her, Frances wasn't sure she'd have found it. No wonder he hadn't been in any hurry to arrive.

Frances knelt to examine the trash bins. Scraps of food, bits of paper, and mounds of day-old porridge littered the street. It was the monster's handiwork all right, but there was no way to tell which direction he had gone. Until she noticed a pattern. The mounds of porridge were staggered in two straight lines, side by side. When she looked closer, she found that each was hollow at the center, with a row of five smaller indentations across the top. These weren't random splatters—they were footprints.

"Still fresh," she said, turning to the birdcage. This earned an odd look from Luca, whom she had already forgotten was there. "The mess, I mean," she added quickly. "When did you say you first discovered it?"

"Oh. Um . . ." Luca put a finger to his chin. "I guess it was right when I left for the market. Maybe an hour ago?"

Frances followed the trail of porridge with her eyes until it disappeared behind the houses. It wasn't much, but it was something.

"You should stay here," she said, wiping her hands on her trousers. "Your mother will expect you for lunch."

"Oh, no," Luca said. "She told me to stay out as long as I please because she had a migraine headache. A real bad one, she said. Been getting a lot of those lately. She packed me a snack."

Luca reached into his back pocket and pulled out a peanut-butter-and-jelly sandwich wrapped in wax paper. The sandwich had been flattened on one side, the other molded in the concave shape of his left buttock. He examined the sandwich suspiciously before sliding it back into his pocket.

"Well, anyway," he said. "I'm not hungry."

"You have to go home," Frances insisted.

"I told you, I can stay out as long as I need to."

"Luca," Frances said. "Go home."

Luca's smile faltered, and he tilted his head to one side like one of the rabbits in the zoo. This made her think of the monster, and the terrible fate the animals met at his hands. This boy would suffer the same if she didn't get rid of him.

"Leave me alone!" she shouted, stomping her foot.

Luca's face fell further, his bottom lip quivering. Frances worried he might cry.

But he never got the chance. At the other end of the street, a voice bellowed above the automobiles and pedestrian chatter.

"Stop right there, girl!"

It was Constable Montavon, no more than thirty meters

ahead of them, shoving his way through the crowd at the end of the block, his face red as a beet behind his mustache. From the look of his uniform, which was still stained with soot and grease from his nap in the gutter, he must have been searching all morning.

Frances cursed herself for raising her voice. "Come on," she said, and reluctantly grabbed Luca's hand.

This seemed to brighten him up. Soon, he was running so fast he had to pull Frances along behind him. They ducked between houses and across the street, then darted through the arched gate of a small park. They ran along a winding path, weaving in and out of sight, looking for the perfect place to hide.

"There," Frances said, pointing to a marble fountain.

Just then, the constable thundered around a bend in the path behind them. A passing line of schoolchildren blocked his way, but it wouldn't hold him off for long.

Frances dived out of sight, landing hard on the stones behind the fountain, the birdcage skittering out her hands and crashing into a park bench. When she looked up, she found Luca frozen in place, his mouth agape.

"Move, Luca," she cried. "He'll see you!"

But Luca didn't move. Instead, he slowly raised his hand and pointed over Frances's shoulder. Behind her, the birdcage lay on its side with its door hanging open and Hobbes's head tipped onto his ear, looking annoyed.

She heard a muted thump and turned back around. Luca had fainted.

Oh no . . . Her only choice was to drag him out of sight.

"Over there," Hobbes called.

She followed Hobbes's eyes to a row of evergreen hedges a few meters away. "It's too far. The constable will see us when we cross!"

"We have no choice," he said, his voice calm. "You must try."

Frances stuffed Hobbes's head back into the birdcage and put it under her arm, holding it tight, even though the wires dug into her skin. She grabbed Luca by his ankles and took a few steps backward, dragging him facedown on the stones.

"He's too heavy," she grunted.

"You're almost there."

She took a deep breath and pulled. Sweat dripped into her eyes. Just as she felt the prick of pine needles on her back, the constable appeared across the fountain. Frances stifled a cry and gave one final heave, using all her strength to yank Luca through the hedge.

The ground gave way under her feet, and she tumbled down a hill, landing with a slap on the muddy bank of a small stream. Hobbes came tumbling down after, and she only just grabbed the birdcage before it splashed into the water.

Frances held her breath as the constable's heavy boots clomped on the stone path above them. She glared at Hobbes, who was rattling his cage, moving his eyebrows wildly and clearing his throat. She put her finger to her lips to shush him.

"The boy!" he whispered.

Somehow, Luca had not followed them down the hill. He remained at the top, lying on his stomach, with his arms splayed out in front of him, one of his hands poking right through to the other side of the hedge.

Frances turned to Hobbes, but there was nothing the disembodied head could do.

Above them, the constable's footsteps continued, growing fainter as he circled the fountain. Frances scrambled up the hill and grabbed Luca's ankles. Needles rustled loudly as his hand slipped free of the hedge. Frances lost her balance and slid back down the hill, landing again in the mud. This time, Luca landed right on top of her. She gasped as the air was forced from her lungs all at once. The constable's footsteps grew louder again. He was right on the other side of the hedge. Luca began to stir. Of course he would choose that moment to come to. Frances clamped her free hand over his mouth to keep him from crying out.

"I will find you, Frances Stenzel," Montavon bellowed. "You

may think yourself above consequences, but I will not stop until I show you how wrong you are!"

The constable's footsteps grew quieter again until they disappeared. Frances took her hand off Luca's mouth. It was hot and clammy from his breath.

Luca rolled off her and sat up, rubbing his head. He breathed in sharply, remembering.

"That's a head!" he cried, pointing at Hobbes.

"Calm down," Frances said.

"A head!" His eyes went wide. He turned toward Frances. "You killed him. You killed somebody, and that's why the police are after you."

"Luca—"

"You killed somebody and chopped off his head, and now you're walking around town with the dead guy's head in a cage!"

"Luca, please," Frances said, looking anxiously toward the top of the hill. "You need to quiet down. He'll hear us."

"Are you going to kill me, too?" Luca touched his neck and dropped his voice to a whisper. "Are you going to chop off my head?"

Hobbes, who had been rolling his eyes and sighing and making all sorts of frustrated noises, suddenly spoke.

"Boy," he said. "Boy!" Luca's mouth snapped shut. "Stop

blabbering. You are acting the fool."

Luca looked from Hobbes to Frances, who shrugged. He opened his mouth as if to say something, then fainted again into the mud.

Chapter 13

1401 and a Half

Frances stuck her head between the hedges and peeked down either side of the path. A bicyclist zipped by. A woman pushed a carriage while her baby grasped at a butterfly and cried when it fluttered out of reach. Two men argued about the war; one, walking with a cane, became so angry he spat onto the sidewalk. No sign of the constable—or the monster.

"If you continue to do that every minute," Hobbes said. "It rather defeats the purpose of hiding, does it not?"

Frances scowled. "Nobody's out there. Nobody important, anyway."

She crawled back behind the hedge and pulled her knees to her chest. The noise of the city was getting to her again. She could feel her lungs tightening and her throat constricting.

Beside her, Luca remained unconscious on the dirt. She watched his stomach rise and fall like a buoy on the river. Almost peaceful.

She kicked him.

Luca snorted awake, squinting in the sunlight. He sat up with a groan.

"I had the strangest dream," he said, scratching the small of his back. He pointed at Frances and smiled. "You were there, and there was this—" He noticed Hobbes propped up next to Frances and his face fell. "Oh."

"Sorry, Luca," Frances said. "I'm real. Hobbes is real, too. Well, real-ish."

It was Hobbes's turn to scowl. "The creature we hunt is quite real as well, and we are no closer to finding him than we were last night."

"Creature?" Luca said, his eyes growing wide. "Like, a monster?"

"Yes, a monster. A terrible monster who is very much on the loose." Hobbes tilted his head toward Frances. "We have her to thank for it."

"It was an accident," she said, glaring back at him. "At least, I didn't mean for all this to happen. And anyway, we're going to stop him."

"What about that constable?" Luca's eyes had taken on a kind of glazed look as he attempted to process everything he was hearing. "He seemed pretty unhappy with you, Francie."

"Frances," she corrected. "He's going to be a problem. We need a place to lie low until dark. Someplace out of the way. Hidden, where nobody could find us, even if they knew where to look."

An idea dawned on her. She turned to Luca and grinned. "What if we stayed at your house? Just until nightfall."

Luca climbed to his feet and put up his hands. "Wait, my house? We were just there!"

"You may be onto something," Hobbes said. "It's remote, nondescript—"

"It's perfect." Frances stood and brushed off the seat of her pants. "I almost walked right past the front door, and you were pointing at it!"

"But my mum is there," Luca said. He began to pace, running his fingers through his hair, leaving thick blond tufts sticking up in every direction. "If she caught me with a girl in my room . . ."

Frances snorted. "What difference does it make that I'm a girl?"

"You know . . . 'cause I'm a boy?"

Frances stared blankly.

"Never mind," Luca said.

"Just tell your mother you've made a new acquaintance," Hobbes offered. "You invited her over to play age-appropriate games and forgot to inform her."

"It doesn't work that way. Not for me."

"Why not?" Frances was growing impatient. Luca's house was the perfect choice; why couldn't he see it?

"Because I don't have any friends," Luca said. Then he sat in the dirt with his face in his hands.

Frances fell silent. Even Hobbes knew enough about human emotions not to speak.

"I'm sorry, Luca," Frances said finally. She sat down next to him and took a deep breath. "To tell you the truth, I don't have any friends, either."

Luca looked up. His eyes were wet as if he had almost cried but fought it off. "Really?"

"Really. You're actually the first real kid I've seen in seven years."

Luca nodded, which struck Frances as strange.

"You don't look surprised," she said.

Luca shrugged. "You *are* kind of spooky."

Am I? She didn't think she was, but she hadn't been around other children enough to know.

"I am not," she said, and decided she didn't care if it was true.

The trip to Luca's house was a quiet one. Rather than doubling back on the same route, Luca led them in a roundabout manner that took them several blocks out of the way but minimized their chances of running into Constable Montavon. It annoyed Frances at first, having to let Luca lead, but his knowledge of the city did make the web of streets easier to navigate.

"Your monster's not a dragon, is it?" Luca said, thrusting an invisible sword at a sandwich board sign touting *Festival Specials—Limited Time Only!* "I'm pretty sure I could slay a dragon."

"*Our* monster, as you say," Hobbes said, "is not a dragon. Nor should you be in any hurry to meet him. You might fancy yourself a knight, but he will more likely take you for a meal."

Luca gulped and let the invisible sword fall to his side.

When they finally reached number 1401 and a half, it was late afternoon.

"Stay quiet, okay?" Luca whispered. "It's best if Mum doesn't know you're here."

He pulled a key from the front pocket of his trousers and inserted it into the lock, turning it slowly until he heard a soft click. The door opened without a sound, and they tiptoed inside. Luca had clearly done this before and knew every loose floorboard. Frances did her best to match his footsteps.

Inside, the house was no bigger than a hallway—smaller, in fact, than the hallways of Grimme-Stenzel Manor. It was furnished with three mismatched wooden chairs and a table that folded out from the wall on a hinge. A potbelly stove took up the far corner, along with a small pantry. The walls were papered with a pattern of violets and aster that peeled at the seams. A threadbare carpet ran the length of the room. It was purple, as were the curtains on the windows at either end. Frances felt like she'd stepped into a hollowed-out eggplant.

"Luca?" a voice called from upstairs. "Is that you?"

Luca froze. His eyes darted across the room, looking for a place to hide as his mother descended the stairs. She appeared on the landing wrapped in a bathrobe, a sleeping mask over her eyes.

"I told you to stay outside," she said. "Oh, great God in heaven, why'd you curse me with a son who can't follow simple instructions? I swear, Luca, when the midwife dropped you on that thick head of yours, you—" She pulled the mask from her eyes. When she noticed Frances, her demeanor transformed. She clasped her hands together, and her face lit up with a wide smile that didn't quite reach her eyes. "You . . . wonderful boy, you! I'm just so glad to see you home early. And who might this young man be?"

"Hullo, Mum," Luca said, his voice sullen. "This is Francie. Er, Frances. She's a girl."

Luca's mother rushed forward to take Frances's hand in hers. She squeezed so hard that Frances had to grit her teeth to keep from crying out.

"A girl! Are you from the neighborhood?"

"No, Mum," Luca said before Frances could reply. "She's Frances. Frances Stenzel?"

"A Stenzel! From up on the hill?" Luca's mother turned and began tidying up as she spoke. "My stars!"

Frances sighed. She wished people would stop making a big deal out of where she lived.

"What in heaven's name are you doing in a house like this, with a boy like Luca?"

"Luca is . . ." Frances tried to think of what to say. "We're friends. He said I could come over and play age-appropriate games."

"Did he, now?" The woman turned to her son, her smile growing even wider than before, though the fire in her eyes was unmistakable. "He didn't bother to say a thing about it to his poor mother. Isn't that right, Luca?"

"Sorry, Mum," Luca mumbled.

She noticed the birdcage in Frances's hands and took a step back. "That's not a bird, is it? I don't allow animals in my house."

"Oh, no," Frances said. "It's, uh . . . it's—"

"It's a thing all the kids are doing," Luca said. "All the kids Frances knows."

"Ah, yes." His mother did her best to hide her confusion.

"I recall now, quite the fad! I've been keeping my eye out for a birdcage for Luca, but I'm waiting for just the right one. You understand."

An uncomfortable silence followed, and Frances felt the need to fill it. "I don't mean to be a bother, Mrs.—"

"*Ms.* Frick, if you please. Luca's father, *Mr.* Frick, may he rest in peace"—she made the shape of a cross over her chest—"passed away eleven months ago. Caught a dreadful pneumonia delivering the mail."

Frances turned to Luca. "The postman was your dad?"

He nodded.

"Seventeen years trudging through this godforsaken city in all manner of weather," Ms. Frick continued. "I begged him to find more respectable work, but he was a bullheaded man."

The postman. Frances pictured a round red nose and a double chin. A smile that spread all the way across his face and up to his eyes, like he meant it.

"I remember him," Frances said. "We didn't get many visitors, and he would always tip his cap and smile. He was sometimes the only friendly face I saw for weeks when my parents were away."

"Mm-hm," Ms. Frick said. "He probably caught his pneumonia up on that hill, come to think of it. Now it's just me, all alone in this world. And Luca, of course."

"There's a new postman now," Frances said, then winced.

"But he's not as good," she added quickly. "We miss Mr. Frick terribly."

"That's so kind of you to say," Ms. Frick said, her voice flat.

"Can we just go up to my room?" Luca asked. "To play?"

"Not dressed in those clothes, you can't!" Ms. Frick looked at Frances and shook her head. "You poor thing. You look like you tumbled from a barge."

Frances looked down. Sure enough, streaks of mud and grease covered her pants, and her white shirt had been dyed the color of oatmeal by the dew that morning.

"Stay right here," Ms. Frick said. "I'm sure I have something that will fit."

"That's okay, Mrs.—Ms. Frick. You don't have to trouble yourself—"

"Trouble? I think I am more than capable of scrounging up a few spare articles of clothing, thank you very much."

"What?" Frances said. "No, I didn't mean to—"

But Ms. Frick had already disappeared up the stairs.

"Your mother is quite a woman," Hobbes said.

Frances punched Luca on the shoulder. "Those better be pants she's bringing down for me."

"I tried to warn you," he said, rubbing his arm.

Frances was about to give him a warning of her own when Ms. Frick returned with a bundle of fabric draped over her arm.

"Here we are," she said, handing the clothes to Frances.

"Not what you're used to at the Manor, I'm sure, but see if they won't keep you warm, nonetheless."

Frances pulled a blouse from the bundle and held it up. It was bright yellow, with a ruffle of lace at the neck. She grimaced and folded it back in with the others.

"I really don't need—"

Ms. Frick leaned forward, eyes narrowed and lips pursed. "I insist."

The choice was clear: do as the woman said or take her chances in the street. Frances bowed her head and allowed Ms. Frick to lead her to the bathroom.

"I'd like to have a word with your mother," she said through the door. "Letting you out of the house in trousers."

"On that subject you two would probably get along," Frances grumbled under her breath.

A moment later, Frances emerged wearing the yellow blouse and a purple skirt with a bold print of green flowers. She had to cinch the skirt and tie it into a knot in the back to keep it from sliding down to her ankles. Luca's eyes went wide when he saw her, until she caught him staring and sent him retreating into his shoulders with a scowl.

Ms. Frick looked her over. "They're too big, of course, but then, you *are* small. Leave your old clothes on the floor—I'll burn them in the furnace tomorrow evening. Supposed to be a cold snap on the way."

"But I—"

"Now go," she said, waving them away. Luca wasted no time scrambling up the stairs. "But you leave that door wide open, young man! Surprise inspections. You hear me?"

Frances hurried after him, tripping over the skirt and wondering if all families were so bewildering.

Chapter 14
An Unexpected Visitor

"Who does she think she is, dressing me up like this?" Frances tugged at the skirt, wishing herself back in the privacy of her own room so she could rip it off and throw it out the window. "I might as well be wearing the drapes!"

For years, she'd fought her mother over skirts and blouses and flowers and bows and purple. "I am only trying to help you," Mary would say. Help her what? Frances wondered. Become more like her, spending hours applying makeup and curling her hair so she could act like she didn't handle rabbit pellets and hydrochloric acid and brain specimens all day? Her father didn't have to do any of that.

All those arguments, all those fights, and Frances had always held her ground. Now look at her. She had endured some terrible things since coming to the city, but this skirt was almost more than she could bear. At least her mother wasn't there to see it.

"I think you look nice," Luca said. "And you don't smell nearly as bad as you did before."

Frances's lip twitched on its way to a snarl.

"Here," Luca said quickly. He reached under his bed and pulled out a shirt and a pair of trousers. "These are mine. You can change into them as soon as we leave."

Frances unfolded the trousers and held them up in front of her. "Thank you," she said. She stuffed the borrowed clothes into her knapsack along with her fedora, bow tie, and the odds and ends she'd salvaged from the pockets of her soiled clothes. She paused over the Manor key before hiding it at the bottom of the bag. "But I'm still mad."

"Of course," Luca said, holding up his hands.

Luca's bedroom, like the rest of the house, was impossibly narrow. It couldn't have been more than four paces across, with olive walls and a wick-stained ceiling that began just above Frances's shoulder and rose to a peak at the center of the room. A cot was shoved into the far corner beneath the room's lone window, which was so slender it was only a single pane across. Beside the bed stood an ancient radiator that produced a disconcerting *CLANG* at regular intervals.

Luca's sheets were straight and smooth, tucked beneath

his mattress and topped with a throw pillow that matched his quilt. Clothes were folded and stacked on a stool in the corner. She could tell he worked hard to keep the cramped space tidy. The only adornment was a single shelf affixed to the wall across from the cot displaying two rows of wooden figures—a battalion of soldiers.

Curious, Frances picked one up. "These dolls are nice."

"They're not dolls," Luca said, politely lifting the figure from her hands. He gave it a brief inspection and returned it to its spot on the shelf. "And I'm still learning."

"You made those?"

Luca nodded, a flush of pink blossoming on his cheeks. "My dad taught me. Even gave me his carving knife before he died." He pulled a pocketknife with a wooden handle from his front pocket and opened it. He turned the blade so the light from the window glinted off its edge; then he folded it back into its handle with great care. "I also made this."

He knelt down and pulled a large wooden mask from beneath his bed. It had a bulbous nose, a wide grin, and pointed teeth.

Frances scrunched up her face. "What is that?"

"It's for the Tschäggättä festival," Luca said.

"Tasha-gotta?"

"You know, the big parade where people put on scary masks and chase kids through the streets, throwing candy? The whole city's getting ready for it. My dad used to make the scariest masks. He even won an award a few years ago."

Frances couldn't picture such strange behavior. Instead, she tried to conjure her memories of Luca's father. Sometimes the friendly postman would have little presents for her when he caught her at the door, peeking out from behind her father's legs: a red bottle cap, or a piece of string tied in a bow. She wished she'd thought to pay more attention.

"Excuse me," Hobbes said from his birdcage, "but I believe we still have a reanimated body to recover."

Frances winced. She had nearly forgotten he was there. She set the cage on the bed and removed the cloth covering. "Try to be quiet, okay? Ms. Frick might get a little suspicious if she hears a third voice up here. Especially if that voice sounds like yours."

Hobbes looked her over. "You are more presentable than usual."

Frances held a finger up to his cage. "Say another word about it, and the next flock of pigeons we find, you're getting a roommate."

Frances kicked at the hem of her skirt and began pacing the length of the room. She pictured the porridge tracks behind the house, following them in her mind. She turned to Luca. "What's near here?"

"Well, there's a bookshop, a general store—"

Frances shook her head. "Someplace out of the way, where a person could hide all day without being seen."

Luca thought for a moment. "There's an empty lot between two houses up the street. Used to be a playground until some older kids busted it up."

Same direction as the footprints. Frances stopped pacing. "We need to check out that lot. That could be where the monster is hiding."

"*After* we wait for the cover of darkness," Hobbes reminded her. "You will be of no use to anyone in the back of the constable's paddy wagon."

Frances groaned and flopped onto the bed. "I finally have a lead, and we're stuck in this tiny room all day!"

Luca looked around self-consciously but said nothing.

Frances pulled Grimme's journal from her knapsack and thumbed to the page where she'd left off. She could remember reading the coded text, what it *felt* like. But without the intelligence serum, its meaning remained just out of reach. Like a shadow that fades as soon as it's exposed to light.

She did find one spark of recognition in the text. It was scrawled above a sketch of the body attached to the tentacled machine. "*Prometheus*," she said. "Where have I heard that word?"

"Name," Hobbes replied. "Not word. Prometheus was one of the Titans of Greek mythology, said to be the creator of man."

Frances considered this for a moment, then turned the page.

"Is that Latin?" Luca said, peeking over her shoulder.

"I wish."

Luca stared at her. "You know Latin?"

"Don't you?"

"Er . . . yeah," Luca said. "I mean, pretty well. Not, like, all of it, I guess."

Frances closed the book in frustration. "The answers are in here," she said.

If only I could read them.

A moment later, they were startled by a knock at the front door. The walls were so thin the sound could have been coming from inside the room.

Frances set down the journal and crawled to the window to investigate. "Was your mother expecting visitors?"

"Don't think so," Luca said. "She doesn't usually invite people to the house. She's embarrassed, I think."

Frances craned her neck to see who'd come calling, but the window was too narrow and an awning obscured the front stoop. A series of locks and latches rattled below her, followed by the creak of the door.

"Why, hello," she heard Ms. Frick say. "What a pleasant surprise."

"Who is it?" Hobbes asked.

"I can't see." Frances got to her knees for a better angle. "It sounds like she knows whoever it is."

Luca shook his head. "That's just how she talks. Usually to men, or"—he glanced at Frances—"rich people."

Outside, a man was speaking. Frances couldn't make out his words, but something he said sent Ms. Frick into an unlikely fit of laughter.

It can't be. . . .

"Here, help me get this open," Frances said, wedging her fingers under the window. She had to be sure.

Luca hesitated. "Mum wouldn't like us spying on her."

"Do as she says, boy," ordered Hobbes.

Luca sighed and crawled across the bed to join Frances at the window. It wouldn't budge, at first. Even with both of them straining. Then, all at once, it popped open with a squeal and slammed into the top of the frame. Frances and Luca ducked their heads, but the adults below didn't appear to notice the noise.

Frances instructed Luca to hold her feet and began threading herself through the window frame. She had to angle her body sideways in order to fit, making it difficult to balance. Partway out, her hips caught. She was suddenly very aware of her skirt and reached back to smooth it over her legs. Luca chose that same moment to heave forward, nearly causing her to fall. She held her breath as loose chunks of wood skittered off the awning, then glared up at Luca.

Sorry! he mouthed, and tightened his grip on her feet.

"I apologize for the intrusion," the visitor was saying. Frances could hear him more clearly now, though he was still hidden beneath the awning. His voice was kind but gruff. It was a voice she knew. "I am here in search of a fugitive and her possible accomplice. A young boy. I believe he lives here with you."

Constable Montavon. He had found them.

Frances motioned frantically for Luca to bring her in. He bit his lip and pulled.

"Luca? An accomplice?" They could hear Ms. Frick laughing. "Beg your pardon, sir, but you seem to have the wrong house. My Luca doesn't have the constitution for *accomplicing*."

Frances wriggled until her hips were back through the window and she could get her knees on the other side of the wall. Luca's hands tugged at her waist.

"The fugitive I seek is a crafty one," Montavon replied. "He may be helpless against her charms."

"*Her*, did you say?"

"Yes. Have you seen your son today? With a young girl, perhaps? Short, dark hair, eyes brimming with guile?"

"I knew it," Ms. Frick exclaimed. "I knew there was something odd about that girl! What would a Stenzel be doing traipsing about these parts? There's some wicked motive here, I said. Truly, I did."

"A woman's intuition is a mighty force." The constable's patronizing tone made Frances's blood boil, but Ms. Frick either didn't notice or didn't care—Frances could hear her giggling. "Do you know where the children are now?"

Come on, Luca, Frances shouted in her mind. *Pull!* As she struggled to turn her body, Ms. Frick and the constable stepped out from beneath the awning.

"They're right upstairs," Ms. Frick said, pointing up at the window.

The last thing Frances saw before tumbling backward into Luca's room was the constable's steel-blue eyes, and the corner of his mouth turning up in a smirk.

"Hello again," he said.

Chapter 15

Any Way Out but
Through That Door

F rances tumbled into the room and collided with Luca, the
two of them rolling off the bed and landing in a heap on
the floor. Above them, Hobbes shifted helplessly as his birdcage teetered on the edge of the mattress before gravity had its
way and he tumbled to the floor, too.

"She sold us out," Frances cried, scrambling to her feet.

Luca held his belly where she had rammed into him. "What
are you talking about?" he wheezed. "Sold us out to who?"

"The constable—he's here." Frances pulled Luca to his feet
and grabbed Hobbes's birdcage. "Your mother is bringing him
right through the front door."

"He spotted us earlier just outside this house," Hobbes said.

"He must have known we'd come back."

Frances paused at the doorway. Voices echoed up the stairway and into the hall. The constable was already inside, blocking their only escape. "We're trapped."

Luca, still breathless, closed his eyes and knuckled the small of his back. "We're only sort of trapped," he said.

"What do you mean? We're either trapped or we're not."

"There's another way out, but it's—"

Frances swung her knapsack over her shoulders and ushered Luca into the hall. "Lead the way," she said, dropping her voice to a harried whisper.

"Okay . . ." Luca paused to reach back into the room to grab his jacket before Frances shoved him forward. "But it really is—"

"Just go!" she cried.

They ran single file through the narrow hallway between Luca's bedroom and his mother's. In his rush, Luca failed to turn the knob all the way on the first try, and Frances nearly crushed him against the bedroom door. He fumbled with the knob until they burst into his mother's bedroom.

"Luca?" Ms. Frick called from the end of the hall. "What kind of trouble have you brought on this house?"

The constable reached the top of the stairs, forcing his way past Ms. Frick. His movements were powerful and deliberate.

"Where are you running off to, children?" he said. His voice was calm. He had them, and he knew it. "You see now that the long arm of justice reaches into every corner of this city. There is nowhere to hide."

"Don't you have anything better to do than chase an eleven-year-old girl?" Frances said. "Like try to catch actual criminals?"

The constable counted on his fingers. "Petty vandalism, destruction of property, resisting arrest," he listed. "I'd say you've left quite a trail of criminal acts."

"I haven't vandalized anything. It was the monster."

"Monster?" Ms. Frick gasped. She gripped the constable's arm, but he shook it free and took a step closer, leaving only a couple of meters between him and Frances. She could hear Luca's breathing quicken beside her in the doorway, but she didn't dare take her eyes off Montavon.

"Ah, yes—this monster you mentioned. I have a theory." He waved his hand in front of him. "There is a girl who lives in a grand house perched high above the city. With no work for her hands, she grows idle. She looks out her window at the common wretches toiling in the city below, and thinks, 'There's the cure for my boredom! I'll descend from this hill and prey upon the ignorance and superstition of the common folk. What fun it will be!'"

"You don't know anything about me," Frances said. Despite herself, tears welled in her eyes.

"I wonder, what could have brought you to a house as miserable as this?" the constable continued.

"It's nothing special," Ms. Frick said, "but I'd hardly call it—"

"And this boy—what does he have to do with your game?"

"Leave him alone," said Frances.

The constable turned his eyes on Luca. "Tell me, boy, have you seen this monster?"

Luca thought for a moment. "No, but I—"

"You haven't!" The constable laughed. "Yet, you believe her?"

"Sure," Luca replied.

"In the time you have known her, has she shown herself to be a truth-teller?"

Lucas scratched the back of his head and looked over at Frances. "Well, we only met today."

"Today! Is that so? Quite the coincidence, isn't it? A young woman of means takes an interest in you, the son of a peasant woman, on the very day a monster appears on the scene? A boogeyman no one else has witnessed."

Luca opened his mouth to speak and, after a moment, let it snap closed again. Even Ms. Frick was silent.

"Don't listen to him, Luca," Frances said, but he didn't seem to hear. He was staring into the empty space between Frances and the constable, a frown pulling at the corners of his mouth. She imagined him replaying their interactions that day in his mind. Had she given him any reason to distrust her? She hadn't lied to him. Had she been kind? She tried to pull him farther into the bedroom, but his feet remained planted, one hand still gripping the door.

"Son," the constable said, his voice softening. "I am an officer of the law, sworn to protect the citizens of this municipality." He inched closer. Another step and he'd be able to reach out and grab them. Still, Luca didn't budge. "Put this nonsense behind you. Don't allow this mischief-maker to bring you down with her."

"Do as he says, Luca," Ms. Frick pleaded.

Frances bit her lip as Luca looked first at his mother and the constable, then at Frances. After a moment, his back straightened.

"No, thank you," he said, and slammed the door in the constable's face.

Frances stood in shock for a split second before springing to aide Luca, who was already pushing his mother's dresser against the doorway.

"This won't hold them long," she grunted as the constable's

heavy fists rattled the door in its frame.

"Surely you have a plan," Hobbes said from his birdcage.

"I told you," Luca replied. "There's a way out. But it's not safe."

Frances winced as a candlestick rolled off the dresser and smashed against the floor. "I'll take any way out but through that door."

Luca sighed. "Over here." He led them into a tiny closet next to his mother's bed.

"You want us to hide?" Frances scoffed.

Luca ran his hands along the wall of the closet. "It's around here somewhere. . . ."

"Allow me." There was a small *flick*, and Hobbes eyes became illuminated, casting light in two thin shafts across the closet.

"Here it is." Luca reached for a rickety ladder that led up to a trapdoor in the ceiling and began to climb. "It goes to the roof," he said over his shoulder.

Frances could hear the squeal of wood scraping against wood as the constable shoved the dresser partway across the floor. "You open this at once," he shouted through the door, "or I will be forced to break it down!"

"Oh, please don't," whimpered Ms. Frick behind him.

Frances hiked up her skirt and followed Luca up the ladder.

After struggling for a moment with the latch, he lifted the trapdoor and the closet flooded with sunlight.

"Luca, you're a genius," Frances said as she felt the open air on her face.

"I would not be too quick with commendations," said Hobbes, switching off his eye lights. "I'm afraid we may be stuck yet again."

Hobbes appeared to be right. The roof of 1401 and a half was flat and narrow, covered in aging brown shingles. The houses next to the Fricks' were at least a half story higher.

"Over here," Luca called.

Frances turned to find him on the far end of the roof, climbing a thin brick chimney, putting him within reach of the neighboring house. Frances hurried to join him, gingerly avoiding several weathered patches. The last thing she wanted was to come crashing through the ceiling, right on top of the constable.

Luca dropped to his belly on the roof above her and reached out his hands. "Toss Hobbes up to me!"

"Hold on tight," Frances told Hobbes with a smirk. Then she heaved her bodiless tutor into the air.

"You truly are an ill-mannered child!" he cried, tumbling within his cage like clothes in a wash bin.

Luca fumbled the birdcage from hand to hand, and for

a moment, it looked like he might catch it. Instead, Hobbes crashed back down to the roof of 1401 and a half and began to roll, nearly toppling over the edge before Frances grabbed him. She cursed as the cloth covering flitted away in the wind.

"Fritz, where are you?" she said, scanning the rooftops. If ever she needed her beloved chimpanzee, it was now.

"I'll get it this time," Luca said. "I promise."

"My confidence abounds," muttered Hobbes.

Frances gave them both an exasperated look and tossed the birdcage once more to Luca's outstretched arms. He caught it, and Frances scrambled up the chimney to join him.

The neighbor's roof was larger, covered in orange tiles like the scales of a dragon. She looked up and found the city spanned out before her, its rooftops curved around the bank of the river in waves of orange, peach, and brown, dipping downhill and spiraling inward like the ridges of a seashell. Crooked chimneys sighed curls of smoke, perfuming the riverfront air with the smell of countless family dinners. Gulls cawed. In the distance, the water was aflame in the setting sun.

A glint of metal caught Frances's eye. Below her, she spied a small dome made of steel bars crisscrossed like netting, tucked into the corner of a courtyard two doors down. The playground Luca had told her about! Several bars were missing, and rust had claimed much of what was left. But even in its dilapidated state, Frances could imagine children running and climbing, or dangling by their knees from the bars.

Luca must have played here, too. The thought was followed by an empty feeling, like a small hole had opened in her chest.

If the monster hadn't moved, she might have missed him. He was crouched at the center of the dome with his shoulders curled forward, all but filling the space. The coarse gray skin on his back could have been cut from the same weathered steel as the playground bars.

He was focused on something in front of him. At first, Frances thought he was eating. But when she stepped to the edge of the roof for a closer look, she noticed a thin red wire gripped between his fingers. It appeared to be attached to the arm that was crushed during his escape from the laboratory. She watched him pull the wire until it snapped, then cast it aside.

Frances blinked in disbelief. *Did he just remove a piece of his own arm?*

Behind her, the trapdoor slapped against the roof and the constable's hand emerged, grasping at the shingles. "That is far enough," he bellowed as he struggled to squeeze through the narrow opening. "I am warning you."

The monster must have heard the commotion, too, because, when Frances turned her attention back to the playground, she found him staring up at her through the bars. For a moment, their eyes locked.

"Frances," Luca called. "We have to go."

She broke her stare, briefly, to risk another glance at the trapdoor. The constable now had one leg free and his knee braced against the roof. In a few seconds, he'd be on his feet.

Not again. Not when I'm so close.

But when she looked back, the dome was empty.

The monster was gone.

Chapter 16
Every Calculation Ends
in Your Deaths

F rances scanned the playground, searching for the monster.
How could he just disappear? But he hadn't disappeared—
at least, not yet. She spotted him at the far end of the courtyard,
just in time to watch him pull himself over the wall and drop to
the ground on the other side.

"No!" she cried. "I will not lose him again."

"Him who?" Luca said behind her. "Hey—wait for me!"

Frances took off in pursuit, sprinting along the rooftops
and vaulting a series of dormers before scrambling over the
eave onto the next building. The tiles were slick and the pitch
steep, making footing difficult to find. Frances cursed when
her toes caught in the hem of her skirt.

Eleven years and this is the day I have to dress like a girl!

On the ground, the monster lumbered across courtyards, swatting at clotheslines and reducing wooden gates to splinters with his powerful shoulders. When the row of houses Frances was following split into two, with one row curving left along the river and the other veering right toward the Old City, Frances turned right after the monster without hesitation.

"Wait," Luca cried as he scrambled over the rooftop behind her, Hobbes's birdcage cradled awkwardly under one arm. "You're going the wrong way!"

Frances ignored him, pumping her legs to match the monster's speed.

The buildings on this side were taller. Soon, Frances reached a rooftop so steep she was forced to climb on her hands and knees. When she reached the top, she swung her legs over the ridge and slid down the other side, scattering a flight of pigeons.

She skidded to a halt at the edge of the roof. The next house over was at least a meter and a half away, with a three-story fall in the gap between. In the alley below, the monster paused to look up at her again before ducking beneath an awning and out of sight.

Luca appeared beside her a moment later, panting for air after running to catch up. "I told you, we can't go this way," he said. He set the birdcage down to shake a cramp from his hand.

"We can make it," she insisted.

"That's not what I mean—"

"We can make it. I'll go first."

Frances backtracked, putting as much distance as she could between her and the edge of the roof. Then, breathing sharply in through her nose, she gathered her skirt and took off at a sprint, pushing off with both feet and soaring through the air. She hit the next roof with a slap, grabbing hold of a chimney to keep from sliding down the slope.

"Toss me the cage," she called. Luca sent Hobbes over the gap and she caught him, letting go of the chimney for just a moment.

"The boy will have to hurry," Hobbes said. "The constable was not far behind us."

"He'll hurry," Frances called out across the gap. "Your turn, Luca. You can do this."

"Let us hope," Hobbes added solemnly.

Luca walked back toward the center of the roof, just as Frances had done. He started to run but stopped at the edge, spinning his arms like a windmill. After regaining his balance, he retreated to his original position.

Frances glanced at the street below her. Still no sign of the monster. He could be two blocks ahead by now, and the constable was closing in. *Come on, Luca. . . .*

"You just have to go for it," she called. "Like adding titanium tetrachloride to water."

"I don't know what that means," Luca said. He leaned forward like an Olympic sprinter and stuck out his tongue. Behind him, Frances watched a large hand reach over the edge of the roof as Constable Montavon hoisted himself up.

Luca noticed her eyes and looked over his shoulder. He let out a yelp and ran, still looking back.

"Jump, Luca—jump!"

He turned just in time to see the end of the roof approaching and leaped, flailing like a child learning to swim. He hit the second roof hard on his stomach, his fingertips sliding along the tiles until his feet dangled over the three-story chasm between the houses. Frances stretched to her full length—unfortunately not very long—and managed to grab two of his fingers.

"Ow, ow, ow," he said as Frances strained to pull him up.

They scrambled over the gable as Montavon landed with a thump behind them. He swiped at Frances's knapsack, but she ducked and slid feetfirst down the tiles. On the street, the constable's size and strength gave him an advantage. Up here, Frances and Luca were lighter and quicker. Each rooftop they crossed put more distance between them.

"We're losing him again," Frances said.

"Not for long." Luca pointed up ahead, where one building rose higher than the others, topped with a white spire. "That's the Zytglogge," he said. "An old clock tower."

"So?"

"It's on the other side of Grocers Alley. We're running out of rooftops."

Frances craned her neck to peer over the buildings ahead of her. Luca was right. The rooftops had been narrowing as the streets on either side converged at the plaza. The buildings dropped off altogether before they reached the clock tower. They were headed straight toward a dead end.

Luca shook his head. "I tried to tell you."

A dog barked below them, and Frances looked down to see a German shepherd pulling on its chain. Then she saw what the dog was barking at: the monster had broken through the gate and was cutting across its yard.

"There he is," she said.

"The monster? Where?" Luca whirled around, his face lit up with excitement and terror at the prospect of finally laying eyes on the monster. But Frances was already charging ahead. She forgot all about the approaching clocktower as she climbed, her eyes fixed on the fleeing monster. She wasn't going to lose track of him again.

"Frances, wait!" Luca cried. He followed her over one house, then another, lunging forward and grabbing her shirt, yanking her back just as her feet reached the edge of the final rooftop.

When she looked down, the street appeared to rise up to meet her, spinning as it expanded, until her feet were once more planted firmly on the rooftop. She blinked, shaking the vertigo away. By the time her vision steadied, the monster was nowhere to be seen.

"No," she growled, and kicked one of the orange tiles, sending it cartwheeling over the edge.

Luca watched it shatter against the cobblestones below and gulped. "What now?"

"I am afraid I see no escape," Hobbes said. "Every calculation ends in your deaths."

"We're going to die?" said Luca, his voice cracking.

Frances reluctantly pushed the monster from her mind and surveyed the landscape. "No one's going to die. Look!"

A radio antenna was mounted above a dormer window two meters to her right, with a thick black wire that ran across Grocers Alley to the clock tower on the other side. A guard station stood at the base of the tower, just below the junction box where the wire terminated. No more than a meter and half drop, Frances estimated. *We can survive that.*

Luca reached up and tugged on the wire. It sprang back with a *twang*. "I don't know," he said.

"Even if you both possess the necessary upper body strength," Hobbes said, "and I doubt very much that you do, it will take far too long to cross that cable hand over hand."

Frances smiled. "Who said anything about hand over hand?"

The roof shook under the constable's weight as he slid down the side and landed against a gable a few meters away. "This is as far as you go," he said. He was clutching his side and panting, his face bright red behind his mustache.

"No," Frances said. "This is as far as *you* go."

She grabbed the birdcage from Luca and hooked the ring over the wire. "Hold on," she said.

Luca, wide-eyed and ghostly pale, stuck his fingers through the wires, and together, they pushed off from the edge. Frances felt the roof drop away as her body tilted forward.

Almost at once, the birdcage jerked to a stop, sending her feet kicking wildly out in front her as she dangled dozens of meters over the street. Below her, someone gasped. People began to point. Frances blushed and cursed her skirt once again.

"Frances!" Luca squeaked. He was stretched and straining as he struggled to keep his toes on the edge of the roof. Constable Montavon loomed behind him, his fingers wrapped around Luca's belt. Frances kicked her legs, but the constable was too strong.

"I'm going to let go," Luca said. "Get yourself to the other side."

"No." She glared at the constable. "Let go of him!"

Montavon laughed. "Why do you care what happens to this

boy? There are many more playthings to choose from. Why not leave him and save yourself?"

"I'm afraid I must agree with the constable on this one," Hobbes said, as discreetly as he could within the birdcage. "Our mission is more important than the fate of one boy. If he is willing to surrender, we must leave him."

"He helped us," Frances said.

Luca hung his head. "You can go, Frances. I don't mind. I don't even care if you made the monster up. I had a lot of fun today."

"I'm not going anywhere without you," she said, gritting her teeth. "You're my friend."

Luca looked up at her. "You mean it?"

"I said it earlier, didn't I?"

"That was just for my mum."

"Well, I mean it now," she said. And she did.

Luca's eyes narrowed and his jaw set, transforming his face into something fierce. "Let me *go*!" He kicked out with one of his legs and hit the constable's kneecap with a crack like a stalk of celery snapping in two.

Montavon howled in pain. At the same time, a black blur sped past Frances, leaping from somewhere she couldn't see. Fritz! He landed on the constable's chest and scrambled onto his shoulders, pounding him on the head like a conga drum.

The constable swung his billy club and reached up to cover his face, letting go of Luca.

Escape, Fritz signed as they fell away from the rooftop.

"Good boy," Frances said, though she wasn't sure he heard her over Luca's screaming. The birdcage had begun to slide, and they were left holding on for their lives.

Chapter 17

A Clock Strikes Midnight
at 7:15 in the Evening

Whven her father described the accident—usually to visiting colleagues late at night while Frances spied from the landing—he always said the same thing: it happened in a moment. Or it was over in a flash. This always struck Frances as strange, for it was nothing like what she remembered.

She remembered the world slowing to a halt, as if the car was filled with invisible gelatin. Broken glass hung in the air all around her, held in place except for a barely perceptible motion, the way stars appear fixed against the night sky. She could have reached out and plucked them if she hadn't also been at the mercy of that frozen moment: flung into the air like a rag doll, her body limp, unable to scream. She didn't even feel the cut that severed her ear—she learned of it later, when she woke with her head bandaged like a fisherman's cap.

It had happened in a moment, maybe, but it was the longest moment of her life.

Now, dangling from a birdcage, speeding high above the cobblestones, everything was happening too fast. The rooftop fell away; the wind whipped her hair. And the clock tower—it was approaching much too quickly.

Even in those few seconds, she could see that the Zytglogge was beautiful. Its face was black and gold, with a gilded sun and moon mounted on either end of the hour hand, each orbiting a starburst in the center. Below it hung an astronomical clock inlaid with the signs of the zodiac. Rotating dials told the month and year, with a series of rings showing the position of the planets in the solar system. Beside that was the bellworks, an elaborate mechanical display featuring the city's founder, Duke Berthold V, and several well-dressed bears on a track below him. Atop the tower, just below the spire, hung a massive bell, with the bell ringer's golden hammer ready to strike on the hour.

The birdcage jumped the cable on impact, slipping through Frances's fingers. As she began to fall, she grabbed on to the only thing she could reach: the gilded moon at the end of the hour hand.

Luca grabbed onto the only thing *he* could reach: Frances. With his weight on her ankle, it took all her strength to cling to the moon.

Hobbes swung helplessly inside his birdcage, Luca's fingers still threaded through the wires.

The hour hand creaked into motion under the unexpected load, its gears grinding within the tower. It began slowly, but as Frances ticked passed the three, then the four, they picked up speed. When the moon reached six, the bottom of the clock, it stopped. Luca kept swinging, taking Frances's ankle with him, until he swung back in the other direction.

All at once, the hour hand's sudden change of position triggered the bellworks and the clock tower sprung to life.

GONG. GONG. GONG.

The bell tolled, and the mechanical bears began to spin along their track, circling the Duke's throne.

GONG. GONG. GONG.

Frances's felt the moon slip from her fingers. She fell, arms and legs flailing, landing on her back on the guard station at the base of the tower. Something soft broke her fall, saying "Ow!" when she landed on it. Luca. She rolled down the sloped roof and tumbled over the side.

GONG. GONG. GONG.

Frances's stomach dropped as her skirt caught on the edge of the roof and her body spun in midair. The skirt gave way with a terrible rip, and the cobblestones rushed up to meet her. The impact sent a shock wave of pain through her leg and hips as she landed hard on her ankle. She tried to stand, but her leg couldn't bear her weight and she crumpled to the ground with a gasp.

GONG. GONG. GONG.

Then, quiet. Every man, woman, and child in the plaza stood in stunned silence, struggling to accept that the great clock had just rung twelve at seven fifteen in the evening. Someone broke the silence, and soon the plaza erupted in shouting and laughter and cheers.

"Frances," Luca called. He hopped down from the guard station, Hobbes's birdcage swinging at his side. "We thought you'd gone splat"—he clapped his hands together—"but you're okay!"

The color drained from his face when he noticed her foot, which twisted at a strange angle. "Oh no, your leg . . ."

Through her pain, Frances heard Constable Montavon somewhere above them, shouting her name. "Fritz," she said through gritted teeth.

"The chimp has proven he can take care of himself," Hobbes said. "We must hurry."

Luca gathered the courage to look once more at her leg, his face white as an onion. He turned away again. "You sure you can walk?"

At that moment, a man dressed in the yellow-and-blue-banded uniform of the Swiss Guard rushed out of the station to investigate the sudden commotion, brandishing an ornamental spear. "You there," he said, noticing the children, but his head whipped about so quickly that his pointed helm slipped over his eyes.

"We don't have a choice," Frances said. She pulled her good leg under her and used the guard station wall to stand. Even still, the pain made her feel dizzy and sick.

"I'll help you." Luca hurried to her side and offered his free hand. Frances took it and put her arm over his shoulders.

"You're so small," Luca said, grunting. "I thought you'd be lighter."

"Gee, thanks," Frances replied.

Together, they limped under the archway beneath the tower and let the city swallow them up.

Several blocks later, Frances rested against the back door of an Italian restaurant, leaning on her elbows while Luca did his best to tie a dish towel around her leg. She bit down on a stale breadstick to keep from crying out. It was the third time they'd had to stop since Frances's fall.

"'Would it kill you to put on a skirt every now and again?'" Frances said in a mocking voice. She turned her face to the sky. "Yes, Mother. Almost!"

Luca pressed a finger to his lips. "Not so loud. We shouldn't even be stopping."

"Look at her, boy!" Hobbes said. "At best, she loses consciousness from the pain. At worst, the ankle is broken, fails to heal properly, and she is one limb closer to looking like me."

"I'm not going to lose my leg!" Frances cried. "Look, no one hates it more than I do when Hobbes is right, but I really can't go much farther."

"Of course I'm right," Hobbes said. "Now then, where is the nearest doctor?"

Frances shook her head. "No doctors. Constable Montavon saw me fall. He'll know I'm injured. For all we know, he's got officers canvassing all the physicians in town right now."

"Perhaps a veterinarian?" Hobbes offered. "Human and animal physiology are quite similar, all things considered."

"And perhaps," Frances replied, "instead of reattaching your head myself, I'll phone the vacuum cleaner repair man."

"Well," Hobbes huffed. "I see the fall has not damaged your impertinence. Tell me, then—if you refuse to see a doctor, where do you expect to find medical care?"

"I might know somebody who can help," Luca said, raising his hand. "And she is definitely not a doctor."

With Luca's help, Frances limped down a winding street to a row of shops in the heart of the Old City. They grunted to a halt, sweating despite the evening chill. Frances looked around.

"So, where is this place?"

Luca pointed at the ground. "Right there." At his feet was a door mounted at a forty-five-degree angle from the sidewalk. Its purple paint was dingy and faded, with the shape of a willow tree carved into the wood and a sign that read *Madame Melina's Medicinal Herbs.* "It's underground. A lot of the shops in the Old City are."

"Not many of the reputable ones, I would imagine," Hobbes said.

Frances eyed the door. "What's down there?"

"It's where my mum comes for her migraines. It's owned by some kind of healer."

"An apothecary," Hobbes spat. "You brought us to an apothecary?"

"I . . . guess so?"

"This is not a medical facility. It is a sorcerer's den. A witch's hovel. A place where rational science is tossed out with the chamber pot by petty charlatans looking to separate the simpleminded from their money."

Luca shrugged. "My mom says they make her migraines go away." He put a finger to his chin and thought for a moment. "She also smiles a lot more when she comes home and says she feels like she's flying."

"Witch or not," Frances said. "We have to try."

Luca bent over to lift the knocker and banged three times. No one came to the door. He tried the knob and found with some surprise that it turned freely. The door swung open with an ominous creak. "Does that mean we can go in?" Luca asked nervously.

Frances rolled her eyes and threw her arm over his shoulder. Luca grabbed Hobbes's birdcage with his free hand, and the three of them squeezed through the doorway and limped down the stairs.

Even in the oncoming dusk, the shop was dimly lit. Strange plants hung drying from the rafters, spilling over shelves filled with all manner of strange vials, colored liquids, and pickling jars with contents that could have belonged in the lab. There didn't seem to be any order to the way the items were arranged: blue vials next to red, pickled roots next to dried pig's ear. Frances smelled lavender, ginger, rose hip, and something ancient and vinegary.

Luca helped her to the floor, where she rested against a case displaying suede pouches filled with mysterious powders, then set out to find something they could use to dress her wound. He held Hobbes aloft to scan the shelves.

"What about this one?" Luca said, picking up a jar of purple gloop.

Hobbes read the label. "Not unless she wishes to grow hair over her entire body."

Luca grimaced and set the jar back onto the shelf.

"This one?" He picked up a small spray bottle that could have held women's perfume.

Hobbes sighed. "I was not aware that Frances had flesh-eating nasal parasites."

"Golly, I hope not."

"I thought you said all these treatments were a sham," Frances called from the floor.

"If we're going to treat you with a sham tincture," Hobbes replied, "we might as well use the right one."

"How about this one?" Luca held another bottle in front of Hobbes's face.

"An excellent choice," came a voice from behind them, followed by the sound of the bottle slipping from Luca's fingers and shattering on the floor.

Chapter 18
Madame Melina's Medicinal Herbs

The oldest woman Frances had ever seen emerged from a door on the far side of the shop. Her back was stooped at the shoulders, curling her over a gnarled wooden cane. An orange tabby perched at the summit of the hump, his eyes stoic and alert. Wiry gray hair stuck out of the woman's head in every direction and a leather patch covered one eye. Madame Melina, Frances presumed.

Frances and her companions watched in silence as she shuffled from behind the counter to join Luca in front of the display. Luca had enough sense to drop the birdcage and hide it with his legs.

"This particular tonic," Madame Melina continued, plucking a bottle from the shelf to replace the one Luca dropped, "is a special blend of herbs stacked in the saliva of an Egyptian fruit bat. It has been known to allow the patient to see beyond the mortal plane and experience great insight into the realm of spirits." The woman twisted the cap and spritzed a few drops into her mouth, smacking her lips. "It also does wonders for bad breath."

"We weren't sure you were open," Frances said.

"Open, closed . . ." The woman shrugged. Her voice was thin and raspy, and she spoke German with a heavy Bernese accent. "I am here and you are here; that is what matters. Now"—she turned her one eye to Luca—"what brings you to my apothecary?"

Luca gulped down the lump that had formed in his throat and pointed to Frances. "She's hurt. Pretty badly."

Melina squinted across the room. "Let me look at you."

She set the bottle of third-eye breath freshener back on the shelf and shuffled to where Frances was laid out on the floor. Gripping her cane until her knuckles turned white, the woman lowered herself to a crouch, her bones creaking and joints popping in a symphony of age. She placed a hand on Frances's foot, just above her ankle. Frances hissed and pulled away.

"My, my," Melina said. She nodded and began the arduous task of standing up. When she got stuck about halfway, Luca rushed in to lift her by her elbow. She waved him away.

"Well," she said, her back finally straight (or as straight as it seemed to get). "Now that that's finished. I'm afraid you have a rather nasty sprain, dear. If I did not know any better, I might think you had fallen from a great height and took a tumble on your way down."

She is *a witch*, Luca mouthed.

"Will you help me?" Frances said.

"Of course I'll help you. But in return, you children will tell me what sort of trouble you've gotten yourselves into."

Neither of them spoke. It occurred to Frances that they hadn't discussed what to say in a situation like this. As the silence grew longer, a tense awkwardness set in. Luca bit his lip and scrunched up his face.

"Well, you see—" Frances began.

"We're hunting a monster," Luca blurted. "And a nasty constable is hunting us."

"A monster, you say?"

"Sorry," Frances said, glaring at Luca over Melina's shoulder. "Sometimes Luca speaks without thinking. What he means to say is . . . What he meant was . . ."

As Frances struggled for a plausible explanation, the old woman looked toward the back of the shop and stroked the purring cat on her shoulder.

"A monster," she said. "That would explain the missing rats."

Frances blinked. "You—you believe us?"

"Why shouldn't I?"

"People usually don't, is all."

Melina cackled. "People are fools." Shuffling behind the counter, she lowered herself onto a stool and produced a small dish of milk as if by magic. The orange tabby purred as Melina set the dish on the counter. "That's why I choose more discerning company."

A second cat appeared, hopping noiselessly onto the counter and joining the tabby at the dish. He was smaller, with cloudy-gray fur, like old pewter. Soon, the counter was crawling with cats, each with different colors and markings, all jostling for a spot around the dish. When the milk ran out, she shooed the cats away and placed the dish back under the counter. Only the orange tabby remained. He climbed back to his perch on her hump, curled up, and went to sleep.

Melina closed her eye, and for a moment, it looked like she might fall asleep, too. Luca looked at Frances, but she could only shrug. Finally, the old woman's eye flicked open.

"What did I come over here for?" She turned and began rooting through a cabinet, pushing aside jars and containers until she found a small, green pouch. She held it out in front of her, squinting to read the label. Satisfied, she poured the contents of the pouch onto the counter and mashed them with a wooden tamper. It appeared to be some kind of dried plant, dark green like the needles of a fir tree.

"My kitties spend all day in the streets," Melina said, "feeding on the rats. They come home full and sleepy, wanting only to lie about in the crates I keep in back. They're terribly lazy, the lot of them, but they make for good company. Today, they weren't gone a full hour before they returned, mewing and mawing, begging for a bite to eat. I went out to the alley and watched for a bit. Didn't see a single rodent or hear so much as a squeak. The rats were gone. I couldn't explain it, but if there's a monster roaming these streets . . . well, mystery solved."

Melina squinted at the birdcage still tucked behind Luca's legs.

"That him?" she said, pointing with the wooden tamper.

Frances's eyes went wide as she realized what the old woman was implying. "Oh, no, this isn't the monster; he's still out there somewhere. This is just my tutor, Hobbes."

Luca held the birdcage aloft to give Melina a better look.

"That melon there is your tutor?" She raised her eyebrows. "My, my. I'll do my best to stay on your good side."

"It's not what it looks like," Frances assured her.

"It is exactly what it looks like," Hobbes said.

"The melon speaks!" Melina's laugh was throaty and coarse, like stones rubbing together.

She turned back to her pile of dried herbs, which were now

a fine powder. She added a few drops of water from the faucet before continuing to mash. Soon, she'd created a thick green paste.

As Melina continued her preparations, Frances did her best to explain what had happened, how she discovered the body in a secret laboratory under the Manor, how she'd used Hobbes's hardware to complete the body and awaken him, and how nothing after that point had gone as planned.

Hobbes snorted. "That would suggest you had a plan at all."

Frances wasn't sure why she was telling Melina all of this—she was a stranger, and an odd one at that—but it felt wonderful to tell somebody, even better to be believed. When she finished, the old woman was smiling.

"So, you're the Stenzel girl."

Frances nodded.

"I had my suspicions the moment you entered my shop—those eyes, my God! The soul of Albrecht Grimme peers out across the void. Your story only confirms it."

Frances looked up in surprise. "You knew my great-grandfather?"

Melina nodded, gathering the paste in a cheesecloth. "I was the cook up at the Manor. For a time."

"An unlikely coincidence," Hobbes said.

"You don't believe me, Melon?"

"A young girl finds herself in a shop full of tricks with an elderly woman who claims a connection to her wealthy family? Highly improbable."

Melina waved him off. "The Manor employed a great many people. You never saw the old house in its heyday. I fixed his meals, stocked the pantries. Ran a tight ship, too, until the help started to leave. First the maid ran off with the footman and took all the good silver. Then the gardener, talented chap, accepted a position at the museum. And the butler . . ." She furrowed her brow. "I don't exactly know what happened to poor Mr. Glauser. No one does. Disappeared one day without a trace. Left all his effects in his quarters, even. Very strange. That was just a few months before young Victor came to live with his grandfather."

"My dad," Frances said. She tried to picture the Manor as it was then, bustling with staff and activity. Such a different place than the one she knew and loved. "Why didn't you leave like all the rest?"

"I should've; I know that. Everybody begged me to, my mum, my sister . . . but I couldn't bring myself to leave the poor fool alone in that old house." A wistful smile appeared in the corner of her mouth. "I loved him, you see. I suppose he loved me, too, in his way."

Luca's mouth dropped open. Frances stifled a laugh.

"The manners on these two," Melina said, addressing Hobbes.

"If only you knew," he muttered from his cage.

"I'm sorry," Frances said. "I was just surprised."

"I was once young and beautiful, you know. Now I'm only beautiful." She struck a pose and winked at Luca, who blushed and looked at the ceiling. "I can see you don't believe," she said as she hunched back over her cane.

Frances tried to protest, but Melina waved a hand to shush her.

"Let me show you." She opened a drawer under the counter, pulling out a golden pocket watch, a dusty ledger, and a glass eye. "Aha!" she exclaimed as she produced a tattered photograph, yellow and faded with age. She held it out for Frances and Luca. "You see?"

Frances squinted her eyes. Melina was right; it was difficult to make out much detail, but the girl in the photo was lovely, with shining dark hair, round cheeks, and pouting, rosebud lips. Her eyes—still two of them—were sharp and coy, framed by long, curved lashes. A name was scrawled at the bottom: Melina Moon.

Studying the woman standing over her, under the wild, coarse hair and wrinkled skin, Frances could see her younger form take shape. It required some imagination, but it was her. Frances wondered about the years in between and decided that, if she survived this, she would come back one day to ask Melina about her life. She had the feeling it would be quite a story.

Luca peered over Frances's shoulder and glanced at the old woman. "You used to be real pretty," he said.

Melina yanked the photograph away and cackled. "Here is a boy who could not tell a lie if he wanted to." She turned to Frances and winked. "There are worse qualities."

"He has some of those, too," Frances muttered. "What was my grandfather like?"

"Oh, he was a wretched man, at the end. At the beginning, too. Does that surprise you?"

"It might have a few days ago," she said.

"His first priority was always his work. I never knew where we stood while he was alive, but when he passed, he left me enough to open this shop. So, I suppose that's something."

"I wonder what he would think of this place," Hobbes said. His voice was thick with disdain.

"You think none of this is science?" She gestured toward her powders and herbs.

"Not proper science," Hobbes replied, turning up his nose (an act that loses much of its impact when the head isn't attached to a neck).

Melina shrugged. "I suppose he would have hated it. Though, I don't believe he was quite so rigid as you seem to think, Melon. He was always pushing boundaries. By the time he died, his peers had rejected him. He was a laughingstock, my Albrecht. But there never lived anyone so determined to change the world. You there," she said, nodding to Luca. "Set that melon down and make yourself useful."

Melina handed him the cheesecloth and a roll of bandages and explained how to apply the paste and dress Frances's ankle.

When she was finished, Luca stared at the bandages, rubbing the nape of his neck. "You sure I should be the one to do this?"

"If I get back down on the floor," Melina said, "I may never make it up again."

Luca's hands shook as he scooped out a dollop of the paste and, under Melina's guidance, packed it onto Frances's leg. She hissed in pain.

"Sorry," Luca said, wincing.

Melina nodded for him to continue. "You're doing fine, boy."

Almost at once, the pain in Frances's ankle began to subside, replaced by a cooling sensation from the paste. Soon, every muscle in her body had loosened. She exhaled in relief.

As she rested, the old woman leaned over her, squinting her good eye. "Interesting," she said, rubbing her chin.

"What is it?" The old woman was looking at her scars, but Frances was too relaxed to be self-conscious.

"Nothing, I'm sure. It's just . . ." Melina paused, retreating into her thoughts. "Tell me, child. You've been injured before?"

The squeal of tires, the crunch of metal, the twinkling glass . . .

"I was in an automobile accident when I was little," Frances replied.

"I see. What do you remember?"

"I remember the crash . . . the car rolling. Waking up in the Manor with a bandage over my ear." She pulled back her hair to show the coarse skin where the doctor had sewn her up.

"What about before the accident?"

Her mother and father. She's cooking; he's reading a newspaper. They're in the kitchen, except it's too small. The sun is coming in through the window behind them, and she can't quite see their faces . . .

"It's all a bit foggy. My dad says it was the bump on my head."

"Hm," Melina said. "A reasonable explanation, I'm sure."

Hobbes was looking at Melina with a strange expression. "What are you getting at, woman?"

Melina snapped free of her thoughts and smiled. "Nothing of any consequence. After all, I am but a batty old witch!"

When Luca finished wrapping Frances's leg, Melina gave it a quick inspection and seemed satisfied. Frances stood with a great deal of help from Luca and tested her leg with a little weight. It still hurt, but the pain was much more tolerable. Melina dragged a stool over and Frances sat, already grateful for a rest.

"So, my great-grandfather—he wasn't . . . evil?"

"Albrecht Grimme? Oh, he was mean as a toothache. Not even dear young Victor could soften him up." Melina's eye misted over, and she fell silent for a moment. She shook her head. "No, he wasn't evil. His burden was simply too heavy, if you ask me. All he did, he did for science."

The old woman's words comforted Frances, though they did little for the guilt that had nagged her since the monster escaped. She hadn't been acting for the good of mankind when she brought the monster back to life; she just wanted to prove she could do it. And look what happened. Who knew what harm the creature was doing even now?

"We should probably be going," Frances said, suddenly anxious to resume their search. She slid to the edge of the stool and set her injured foot on the floor before pulling it back again with a hiss.

Melina wagged a bony finger. "If you think I intend to send you off without a hot meal, you've got another think coming. Eat something. Gather your strength. When you've finished, the swelling in that ankle will have gone down enough for you to put some weight on it."

Luca sat up at the mention of food. Catching Frances's eye, he clasped his hands together and stuck out his bottom lip, pleading silently. She had to admit, a hot meal did sound nice.

"Okay," she said. "We'll stay for dinner."

"Yes!" Luca cheered, earning a good-natured cackle from Melina.

The meal was delicious—baked chicken with red peppers and leeks, washed down with hot cider. It was the first food Frances had eaten all day, and she was grateful for the full belly. Luca wolfed his portion down and asked for seconds.

"A healthy appetite, too," Melina said, giving Frances a sly grin.

Once they were finished eating, Melina showed Frances a back room where she could change out of her now-tattered skirt and blouse and into the clothes she'd borrowed from Luca. Frances had to poke an extra hole in the belt to keep the trousers up, but she already felt more like herself. With her bow tie in place and the fedora on her head, she surveyed her reflection in the mirror and smiled. *Much better.*

"Thank you," Frances said as they were leaving. "For fixing my leg and feeding us. For the stories, too."

"It was my pleasure, dear," Melina said, pulling Frances to her bosom for a tight embrace. When she released her, she cupped her thin fingers around Frances's cheek and looked her in the eye. "You may find yourself in your great-grandfather's shadow now, but you'll make your own way. I did." She released Frances and ushered her and her companions to the door. "The docks are due east. If I had a nose for vermin, that's where I'd be. Now, go catch that monster of yours. My kittens need to eat!"

For a moment, Melina's joyful cackling filled the streets. Then the old purple door swung shut and Frances and her companions once again looked out into the city, braced for the task at hand.

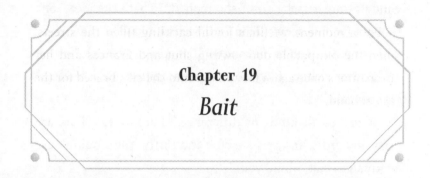

Chapter 19

Bait

"That's not a rat."

Frances looked at the gray tabby in her arms, then back at Luca. She shrugged. "It's all I could find."

They stood in an alley near the docks of the Matte district, an isolated section of the city just off the river that became a ghost town when the stevedores packed up their lunch tins and headed home for the night. Frances had been away for over an hour, hunting rats beneath the piers. She had gotten the idea from Melina: if the monster was feeding on rats, she could use one to lure it into a trap. The few she found proved more difficult to catch than expected.

Cats, it turned out, were much less suspicious.

"So, the monster's going to . . . eat her?"

"Her?" Frances shook her head. The last thing she needed was Luca getting attached to the bait. She was having a hard enough time herself. "Yes," she replied. "That's the idea." She thought for a moment. "Don't tell Melina, okay?"

Luca put a hand to his mouth. "I'm going to be sick."

"Rodent, feline; I do not see what difference it makes," Hobbes said.

"It makes all kinds of difference," Luca cried. "Rats are dirty and gross, and cats are cute and fluffy. You wouldn't use a human as bait, would you?"

"I suppose not," Hobbes said, after considering the question far longer than even Frances was comfortable with. "But feline will have to do. Night has fallen, and we have no time to waste."

"Look, I don't like this any more than you do," Frances began. She pictured the empty cages in the Zoo on the night the monster escaped and felt a pit form in her stomach. The rabbits, the cockatoo . . . She shoved the mewling cat into Luca's arms. "Just help me tie her down."

Luca stroked the mangy cat behind her ears as Frances tied a string around each of her paws. "I'm so sorry, little Bernadette."

"Now you've named her?" Frances cried.

"I couldn't help myself." He nuzzled her whiskers with his nose.

Getting Bernadette into place took some effort—cats were

not well suited for leashing, and Luca insisted she be as comfortable as possible—but they managed. With their bait finally secure, Frances laid the trip wire and pulled it taught.

She examined her work. The trip wire ran up the alley walls and through a series of pulleys salvaged from a warehouse near the docks. At the other end hung a counterbalance comprising loose cobblestones, the rim of an automobile tire, and an iron beam.

"Like a chandelier," Luca had said, "made of junk."

The trigger was the final piece.

Luca gave the reluctant Bernadette one last scratch behind the ears, then fetched the wood he'd been carving. The entire trap relied on a hook and base—two pieces that linked together until the trip wire snapped, pulling them apart and triggering the snare. These weren't pieces that could be scavenged, so Luca volunteered to make them himself, according to Frances's specifications. He'd been working on them since Frances left for the docks.

"The secret to good whittling is to keep your knife sharp," Luca said. "I keep a whetstone in my pocket next to my dad's knife. And always cut with the grain. That way, the wood curls off in neat little—"

"Almost done?" Frances interrupted.

Luca blinked in surprise. "I, er, just need to smooth out some rough spots."

Frances could tell she'd come across harsher than she'd intended. "It looks great," she added, forcing a smile.

When he finished, Frances tied the trip wire to the hook and secured it to the base. She strummed the wire with her finger. *Perfect.*

"All we need now is the monster."

Frances shifted her weight between her sprained ankle and her uninjured leg, which had fallen asleep and now tingled like it was full of bees. The final step had been to leave a trail of old fish from the docks to the alley to draw the monster. Now she and Luca were crouched shoulder to shoulder behind a row of trash bins, with Hobbes stowed at their feet.

The waiting might have been bearable if Hobbes hadn't insisted on announcing the time every quarter hour.

"Will you stop doing that?" Frances snapped after forty-five minutes.

"I'm sorry," Hobbes replied. "Perhaps you are unaware that the city's clock tower was recently closed for repairs."

"I hope the monster gets here soon," Luca whispered. His face was so close to Frances's she could smell the leeks from dinner on his breath. "You've been talking about him all day, but I don't even know what he looks like. Does he have claws? Sharp teeth?" He pushed up his lip with his finger and pointed to one of his incisors. "Ike this, vut allavay across?"

Frances sighed. "They're just teeth."

Luca's shoulders drooped but quickly perked back up again. "Still. I know I shouldn't be, but I'm kind of excited. It's not every day you get to see a real live monster."

"You're right." Hobbes's voice was grim. "You shouldn't be excited. Terrified, perhaps. But not excited."

"If he's so dangerous, why'd Dr. Grimme make him in the first place?"

Frances had been wondering this herself and had come up with a theory. "I think my great-grandfather was dying."

". . . So he made a monster?"

Frances shook her head. "It wasn't supposed to be a monster. Grimme was brilliant, like Melina said. But he was old, and even great men die."

Luca thumbed his father's knife as Frances went on.

"He must have figured, he had the knowledge, the resources—why not cure death?"

Luca considered this. "So, why wake it up now?"

"I only found his workshop because I was looking for a way to get rid of Hobbes."

"I knew it!" Hobbes cried.

"But once I found him, I knew I had to do something," she continued. "War is coming, and my parents needed help. Mr. Byron said we might even lose the Manor. And . . ." She paused. When she spoke again, her voice was quiet. "I guess I thought if

I did something even my father couldn't do, they wouldn't have to leave me behind anymore."

Even as she spoke, Frances felt a check in her mind. She suspected there was more to the story than she wanted to admit. When she had discovered the body, and the equipment used in the experiment, it felt so strange. So familiar.

But she didn't have long to ponder it.

"Quiet, both of you," Hobbes said. "My sensors are picking up movement at the mouth of the alley."

Frances turned her ear to the street. She couldn't hear anything at first. Then, a scratching sound against the cobblestones.

Bernadette hissed and mewed, pulling at her leashes.

"It's him," Luca said. "It's him, isn't it?"

Frances peered between the bins. Bernadette was knotted in the rope, trying to wriggle free but only tangling herself further. The alley appeared empty, until Frances looked down.

"It's only a rat," she said, sinking back to the ground. "Where was he hours ago?"

"Odd," Hobbes muttered. "My sensors should have easily identified the auditory signature of a rat. Perhaps they were damaged in the fall."

"Bernadette," Luca cried. He slid out from behind the trash bins and shooed the rat away, then dropped to his knees and untangled the cat, knot by knot. "Poor kitty. You just wanted a snack."

"Careful, Luca," Frances said. "You'll set off the trap."

"We can't leave her tangled up like this." He pulled the final knots from around Bernadette's legs and yanked her free, cradling her to his chest even as she pushed against him with her paws. "And we can't let her get eaten, either—I don't care how important that monster is."

Frances was about to remind him that cats were likely next on the monster's menu either way, when something caught her eye. Bernadette no longer struggled. Instead, she was staring over Luca's shoulder, hackles raised. A guttural sound issued from her throat, like the winding of an air-raid siren.

What's gotten into her? She followed Bernadette's gaze to the mouth of the alley, searching the shadows.

"My diagnostic subroutine is complete," Hobbes announced. "My sensors are functioning at a reliable eighty-seven-point-six percent capacity. The sound I observed could not have been the rat. I believe it may have been—"

"The monster," Frances whispered.

At first, she could see only the faint glow of his chest panel blinking in the darkness, before his malformed silhouette took shape against the lamplight spilling in from the street; muscled shoulders hunched forward, dead arm listing at his side. The shadows pulled back from his face as he advanced, gathering in the hollows of his cheekbones and the wells of his deep-set eyes. Something wriggled in his fist. The rat.

"I suppose that is one possibility," Hobbes said, his voice skeptical.

He can't see him, Frances realized. The trash bins keeping Hobbes hidden were also blocking his view. Luca was just as oblivious, still busy doting on the cat, his back to the street.

The monster had come at last, and they weren't ready.

"Luca," Frances whispered, keeping one eye on the creature. He approached slowly, deliberately. He had them cornered—why rush? When Luca didn't respond, she called again, louder. *Is he ignoring me?*

"Luca," she hissed. "You have to listen to me!"

"I've been listening to you all day," he said without looking up. "I've been chased by a constable, embarrassed my mum, fallen from a clock tower, and I helped tie up poor Bernadette even though I didn't want to." When he lifted his face, tears glistened in his eyes. "I don't think I really want to listen to you anymore."

His words stung, but the pain was quickly smothered by the urge to sting him back. *I didn't ask you to follow me around*, she wanted to yell. Instead, she set her jaw and tried to keep the hurt and indignation out of her voice.

"We don't have time for this," she said. "The monster is here."

Luca wiped the tears from his cheek with his shoulder and looked at Frances like he wasn't sure he'd heard her.

"He's . . . here?"

She nodded. Luca froze as the color drained from his face.

"The creature is here?" Hobbes repeated at her feet. "Will somebody please move these blasted bins!"

In that moment, several things happened at once. Bernadette, sensing Luca was distracted, seized the opportunity to escape. She scrambled from his arms, knocking him off balance. He stepped back to catch himself, and Frances watched helplessly as his right foot landed on the trip wire, straining it against the trigger. The fleeing cat then bolted down the alley and disappeared over the far wall but not before ricocheting off the trash bins and sending them clattering the ground, leaving Frances and Hobbes exposed.

"That is not exactly what I had in mind," Hobbes said as the bins rolled to a stop against one of the buildings.

The creature recoiled from the sudden pandemonium but quickly recovered. He paused to sniff the air while his eyes darted from Luca to Frances before finally settling on Hobbes. A look of recognition passed over his face, and he dropped the rat, which ran squealing into the night.

"What do I do? What do I do?" Luca cried, sucking air in quick, shallow gulps.

Frances held up her hands and took a cautious step forward. "You need to stay calm."

It would take another three steps, at least, to reach the trigger and disable it so Luca could escape without springing the trap. At the other end of the alley, the monster snarled a warning.

Luca squeezed his eyes shut. "Shouldn't we be running? Why aren't we running?"

"No!" Frances cried. She took a breath and calmed her voice. "We can't do that right now."

"Why not?"

"Because," she said, edging forward, "you're standing on the trip wire."

Luca opened his eyes. He stared at Frances, his brow furrowed, wearing a mix of emotions she couldn't decipher. "I'm . . . the bait?"

Then he leaned to one side and lifted his foot to see.

The hook snapped off its base with a terrible *CRACK* as the snare cinched around Luca's ankle.

The chandelier of junk crashed to the ground, flipping him into the air.

The monster roared and lurched backward, stumbling from the alley.

Frances limped after him, ignoring Hobbes's demands that

she stay where she was.

When she rounded the corner, she skidded to a stop, scanning left and right. But she was too late.

The street was empty. The monster had escaped.

Chapter 20

A Brief Respite

Purple shadows dripped from windows and rooftops, coating the pale stone buildings like oil. A trio of bats cartwheeled around a chimney before darting beneath an eave.

Frances resisted the urge to peek over her shoulder where Luca followed half a block behind her. He hadn't spoken since they abandoned the trap. None of them had.

Frances had to cut the rope to release him, and a pulley had broken off the wall. The rusted metal shattered on the cobblestones in a cloud of orange dust, the entire night's work evaporating before her eyes.

"Don't be too hard on the boy," Hobbes said. Frances had taken the birdcage before Luca could grab it. He had carried it most of the day, but Hobbes was her responsibility and she no longer felt like sharing it.

"I didn't want the cat to get hurt, either," she replied. "Especially not after what happened in the Zoo. But that trap was our best chance at catching the monster. We had him, and Luca ruined it." She shook her head. "I told him not to name her."

Hobbes looked up at her through the wires of his cage. "I am no expert in human emotion, but even I can see he is experiencing embarrassment. Perhaps even shame."

Frances glanced over her shoulder. She watched Luca shamble forward, his eyes fixed on the stones beneath his feet, and felt a prick of guilt.

"Tell me what to do," she said. "I've never been in this situation."

Hobbes's eyes turned from white to blue. "Humans are animals, are they not?"

Frances raised an eyebrow. "I suppose. . . ."

"What would you do if you noticed Fritz looking down and out?"

"I'd give him a banana. But I don't have any bananas."

"Forget about bananas. You must give Luca a gift, a gesture of care and support."

What kind of gift would show Luca I care? She reviewed her limited catalog of human interactions for an example. "I've seen my dad give Mum flowers."

"Flowers, yes!" Hobbes replied. "Bright colors, pleasant aroma—both known mood stabilizers."

Frances spotted a planter outside the window of a nearby shop. She pulled out a handful of edelweiss by their stems and waited for Luca to catch up. She cleared her throat.

Luca looked up in surprise.

"Um, here." Frances shoved the impromptu bouquet into his hands. Clumps of dirt fell from the exposed roots onto his shoes.

He examined the flowers, frowning.

"They're flowers," she said, shooting Hobbes a worried glance. "It's a gesture of care and support."

Luca raised them to his nose and sniffed. "Thanks," he said at last. "Apology accepted."

"Apology?" Frances sputtered. "You think I'm— Why should I apologize to you?"

"You were going to let your monster eat that innocent kitten," Luca said, jabbing the flowers into her shoulder. "You didn't care that I didn't want you to. Now she's gone!"

"It was a cat. What about all the people in this city? Would you rather the monster eat them?"

"He almost ate *me!*"

"Children!" Hobbes bellowed. "It has been a difficult day. Each of us have made mistakes."

"But he—" Frances began.

"You have not slept in twenty-four hours," Hobbes went on. "You've crossed rooftops, zipped over the city on radio wire, and fallen from a clock tower. It is the nature of human physiology that exhaustion produces—"

"We get it; we're tired," Frances said, cutting him off. "Hobbes is right. We shouldn't be fighting. I'm sorry about the cat."

"Bernadette," Luca corrected her.

"I'm sorry about *Bernadette*. And that you almost got eaten."

"And I'm sorry I ruined your trap. It was a good trap."

Frances nodded.

Luca held up the flowers, shaking off the last bits of dirt. "These are nice. Although, girls don't really give flowers to boys."

"Why not?"

Luca shrugged. "It's usually the other way around. I don't know why. Just the rules, I guess."

"The rules are irrational," Frances said.

"Yeah," said Luca. "They are."

Day broke as they shuffled down the street, dragging their feet on the cobblestones.

"Maybe we should have slept," Luca said, stifling a yawn.

"We would have awoken in the back of the constable's paddy

wagon if we had." Hobbes's voice was muffled beneath the new cloth Melina had given them. It was stitched with an ornate pattern of flowers and cantaloupe. He had not been amused. "Frances, talk some sense into the boy. Frances?"

Frances was a few paces back, having slowed to a stop in the middle of the sidewalk. A group of soldiers that had been talking and laughing behind them nearly tripped over her. One turned back to glare and, finding only a child, made a joke of it and moved along. More soldiers appeared on the streets each day. Whenever Frances saw them, the specter of war ignited a fresh pang of worry for her parents. This time, she was too preoccupied to notice.

"We failed," she said, hanging her head.

"We didn't fail," Luca said. "We just haven't succeeded yet."

Frances leaned against a building and sank to the ground, wincing at the pain in her ankle. "Another night with nothing to show for ourselves. Now the sun's out and the monster will hide. Tonight, we'll be right back where we started. We've accomplished nothing."

"Nonsense," Hobbes said. "We know the creature hibernates during daylight hours. We know he has limited himself to small, easy prey like rats and discarded fish. He hasn't revealed himself to anyone, which means he knows he's vulnerable. This is valuable data. Tonight, we will put it to use."

"Tonight?" Luca said, rubbing his eyes. "That's hours away.

And I can't exactly go home after what happened with the constable." Suddenly his face brightened. "Does that mean we have the day off?"

"Of course not," Hobbes said. "We have supplies to gather, details to clarify."

Luca gave Frances a pleading look.

She shrugged. "There's a lot to do."

"You're in the big city for the first time in your life—well, almost, anyway—and all you've done is hunt a monster and read an old book. You've got to do something fun before you hide away again in that creepy old house." Luca held out his hand. "Come on. We're going swimming."

Frances hesitated. "I don't know how to swim."

"You don't need to—the river does all the work."

"This is not a prudent use of our time," Hobbes said. "We must prepare for this evening."

"We'll have plenty of time to do that after we swim. Besides, my mum said a cold snap is coming. It might even snow—in September! This may be our last chance all year." Lifting the collar of his shirt to his nose, Luca added, "Also, we smell really bad."

Frances felt her resolve fading. The look on his face was so earnest, and a break did sound nice. She'd always wanted to try swimming. . . .

"Fine," she said. "We'll take the day off."

Luca pumped his fist in celebration. "Follow me."

Boys and girls of every age were already gathered at the water's edge, stripping to their undergarments and placing their clothes into blue lockers opened with francs, or retrieving their clothes and dressing, river water still dripping from their hair.

"We can't wear our clothes?" Frances asked, a look of horror on her face.

"No," Luca said. "I mean, they'd get all wet." He nodded toward the lockers and smiled. "At least we won't have to pay."

He led her to a stand of trees twenty paces from the riverfront. A thick carpet of broad-leafed ivy covered the ground.

"My dad showed me this spot." He shrugged sheepishly. "We never had much money for things like lockers."

"I've got money," Frances said, pulling a franc from her knapsack. Luca stared at the silver coin. When he didn't say anything, she slid it into the pocket of her trousers. "We can use your spot, though."

"I must reassert my opposition to this plan," Hobbes said from beneath his melon-trimmed cover. "The Aare river current runs at five hundred and fifty-nine cubic meters per second—dangerous conditions for even a strong swimmer. Besides, I've run the calculations and I am fairly certain that, without my body, I will not have enough buoyancy to stay afloat."

"That's why you're staying right here," Frances said, setting the birdcage on its side between the trees.

"I beg your pardon?"

"Relax." She gathered an arm full of ivy and draped it over the cage with a sly smile. "It's a really nice spot."

"You cannot leave me here. Frances!"

Moments later, Frances and Luca stood opposite one another in silence, scuffing their feet in the ivy, their cheeks flushing a darker shade of red with every breath. Finally, Luca turned so his back was to Frances. Frances did the same.

"Promise you won't stare," she said over her shoulder.

"Promise," Luca replied. After a pause, "You promise, too?"

"I promise."

Frances untied her shoes and kicked them aside. She pulled apart her bow tie and unbuttoned her shirt, rolling it tightly before setting it down in the ivy. The ankle bandage would have to go, too, she supposed. She sucked air through her teeth as she pulled it away from her skin and set it atop her clothes so it wouldn't get dirty.

She stood in her undergarments, shoulders curled inward against the breeze, and looked at the pile of clothes. Trousers, oxfords, bow tie; Luca's clothes weren't so different from hers. It had always given her a sense of protection, dressing that way. Like putting on a hard shell. She had never really thought about why.

Maybe it had to do with the way she saw people act toward her mother. Victor and Mary were both brilliant scientists, and for all his eccentricities, that was all Victor had to be. With Mary it was different. She had to be more than just brilliant. She had to be witty, poised, fashionable, beautiful. She wore the reddest dresses, the tallest heels, the brightest lipstick.

Even then, when colleagues or investors came to the house, they asked Mary about the food, the Manor, and Frances, but as soon as talk turned to work, they deferred to Victor. Frances never understood why her mother tolerated it. All she knew was that *she* wouldn't.

Without her shell, she felt small and fragile. Like a little girl.

Behind her, Luca coughed. She wrapped her arms around herself and turned to face him.

Luca stood in his undershorts, mouth agape.

Frances hugged herself tighter, trying to cover the scars with her arms. The largest ran from her collarbone down the center of her ribs. Another ran the length of her left shoulder, just below the one on her face. The final wrapped around her right leg like the cut of a carrot peeler, next to the fresh bruise that ringed her ankle.

Luca blinked and looked away. "You ready?" he said, unable to meet her eyes. Frances nodded, and Luca waved for her to follow. "This way."

They walked down the hill to the riverfront path, but when

they reached the water, Luca turned and headed west. "We have to get upstream," he explained.

The path was wide and dotted with people, mostly children. Frances had been counting on getting into the water right away. On land, she was exposed. Several times she caught children looking at her scars. One boy made a gagging sound, and his friends laughed. The crowd grew thicker, and the familiar sensation of the world closing in returned; only this time, she didn't have the Manor key to anchor her. Her breathing quickened, and stars dotted her vision. Every sound was a firecracker, every image a blinding light.

"This should be a good place to jump in," Luca said. Frances didn't wait to hear more. She pushed her way through the other children, planted her feet on the edge of the water, and jumped.

Frances hit the water hard, stinging her injured leg and sending shock waves of cold through her body. The water parted, then rushed in to envelop her, closing over her head and shutting out the noise and commotion and stares of the city above. All was quiet. She was alone in a world separate from everyone else. She thought she heard the muffled sound of Luca's voice shouting her name, but she didn't care. For the moment, she was all there was.

Then the water was coursing too quickly, pulling her deeper, drawing her downriver. She kicked her legs, looking up at the sunlight filtering through the surface of the water and splintering into rays of light. She pumped her arms as hard as she could, but she was small and the river was large. Her chest tightened and her lungs burned. *If I die down here*, she thought, *it'll prove Hobbes right.*

She kicked harder.

Just when she thought she'd be lost to the current, an arm closed around her waist. Luca was beside her, his cheeks puffed out like a blowfish, swimming toward the sunlight with Frances in tow. When they broke the surface, she coughed and gasped, gulping air.

"Easy," Luca said. Frances realized she was still thrashing for her life. "I told you, you've got to let the river do the work."

This time, Luca showed her how to float on her back, and they drifted, arm in arm, letting the current carry them instead of fighting it.

The water comforted Frances, the sensation of floating so different from the normal way of life. She dipped her head so that only her face was above the surface, her ear underwater, every sound muffled and quiet and calm.

Above them, maids beat rugs draped over clothes lines, young men in fatigues smoked cigarettes on balconies. Shop owners hung banners to prepare for the Tschäggättä festival. Many were covered in strange horned faces, like the mask she had seen in Luca's room. No one paid any attention to the children floating by.

"That's our stop up there," Luca said as they rounded the inlet. They paddled to the water's edge and caught a rocky ledge as the river continued rushing on its way. They climbed onto the grass and collapsed on their backs, laughing and catching their breath.

"I can't believe you'd never done that before," Luca said.

Frances couldn't believe she'd done it now. The sun was right overhead, its rays warm against her skin. For a moment, the world was peaceful and safe.

"Why do you dress like a boy?" Luca said abruptly.

Frances's smile faded. "I dress like me."

"Well, 'you' dresses like a boy."

"You'd rather I put on a skirt, like the one your mum made me wear?"

"No, no!" Luca said, putting up his hands. "I don't care what you wear."

A group of young children swam by, giggling and splashing. Their mother walked along the shore, waving and telling them to stop roughhousing.

"It's just that . . . whenever somebody calls you a boy, you correct them."

Frances sighed. "So?"

"So, if you don't want people to think you're a boy, why dress like one?"

One of the kids was crying now. The mother reached over

the water as far as she could without falling in, as the child swam teary-eyed to the shore. Frances could hear her scolding as they hurried along the path.

"Just because I think pants are more practical and long hair is bothersome doesn't mean I don't want to be a girl."

Luca mumbled something Frances couldn't hear.

"What?"

"I knew you were a girl," he said, louder. "I could tell."

Frances frowned. "What is *that* supposed to mean?"

Luca's eyes went wide. "Nothing! I was just saying— What I mean is—"

He continued stumbling over his words until he was drowned out by an approaching siren. The noise started faint and rose in volume and pitch until a police car whizzed by on the street overhead. Frances and Luca watched, propped on their elbows in the grass.

Luca's shoulders relaxed as the siren faded. "I never really noticed the police before. Now they're everywhere."

Frances knew the feeling. The constable had been dogging her every step since the moment she set foot in this city. She shouldn't need to be out here in the first place! If he were to apply even a fraction of the time and resources he spent chasing her toward finding the monster . . .

She rolled onto her back and sat up. "Of course."

"Of course what?" Luca turned but found only a damp

depression in the grass next to him. "Oh, are we leaving now?" He scrambled to his feet and hurried to catch up with Frances, who was already limping back up the riverbank. "Frances?"

When they reached Luca's hiding spot, the sun had begun to set, and a chill had crept into the air. Hobbes greeted them with an irritated huff.

"The mer-children return," he said. "I'm sure you didn't once consider that I might worry. I was only trapped in a cage under a pile of weeds with the worms, calculating the probabilities of various gruesome fates that might be the cause of your delay. Perhaps now we may begin planning for tonight's search?"

"No need," Frances said, rewrapping her ankle, "I know how to find the monster."

Chapter 21

Impersonating an Officer of the Law

The bell over the entrance to the Confiserie Münsterplatz jingled as a uniformed officer backed through the door, holding a horseshoe-shaped pastry in each hand. A patrol car was parked out front. The officer passed one pastry through the window, then opened the door and climbed inside. Moments later, a balled-up wax-paper wrapper was tossed out onto the street.

Frances and Luca hid behind a low sandstone wall a half block from the car where they could spy on the officers without being seen. They set Hobbes's birdcage on the wall with the covering pulled aside so he could peek.

"Hey," Luca said, starting to rise. "Isn't littering a crime?"

Frances grabbed his arm and pulled him back down.

"I do not know what you have planned," Hobbes said from his perch. "But I am confident I will not approve."

"I'm with the melon," Luca said. "Shouldn't we be staying *away* from the police?"

Frances pointed to a long, thin antenna at the back of the car. "See that? *That* is how the constable stays a step ahead of us. When someone reports a crime, a dispatcher radios the officers, telling them were to go. The technology is only a few years old—I read about it in one of my father's magazines. Calls were probably coming in all night. But since no one actually saw the monster, the constable assumed it was me."

"I imagine he's been quite busy, between the monster and the two of you," Hobbes said.

Luca's mouth fell open. "Me?" He looked like he was about to protest further, then changed his mind and crossed his arms in a huff. "You know, I never broke a single law before I met her."

"The sun is setting," Frances continued. "The monster will come out of hiding soon. Someone's bound to see something. When they do, we're going to make sure *we* get the call before the constable."

"And how do you propose we do that?" Hobbes said.

Frances smiled. "First, Luca will need to break a few more laws."

● ● ●

A short time later, as the sun dipped behind the rooftops and streetlamps flickered to life throughout the city, Frances crept up behind the patrol car. She pretended to browse a shopwindow while surveilling the street behind her in the glass. The birdcage hung at her side.

"We'll wait here for Luca's signal," she whispered.

"Do you believe he has it in him?"

Frances shrugged. "As long as he doesn't meet a cat."

Hobbes was unconvinced. "You are putting a great deal of faith in that boy doing the right thing. Which happens, in this instance, to be entirely the *wrong* thing."

She eyed the car's reflection. *It's not Luca I'm worried about,* she wanted to say.

As if on cue, the window of the confiserie shattered with a loud crash, raining bits of glass onto the sidewalk. A crowd was already gathering as the officers jumped out of the car and waded into the commotion. "It was a kid," someone shouted. "A boy wearing dirty trousers. He ran that way!"

Frances sighed. "I suppose I'll get blamed for that, too."

"As well you should," replied Hobbes.

Frances watched the officers take off in pursuit, then knelt beside the car and tugged on the latch. The heavy door swung open, sending her sprawling onto the curb. The sharp scent of old leather and petroleum filled her nose. At once, she felt as if she was being dragged under, plunged into a different time.

Her father. Lifting her into the back seat.

The door, slamming; a snowflake drawn inside. It flits about the cab, lingering in the air above her head as streetlamps pulse in the darkness outside her window like heartbeats, quickening.

Her mother pressing her hand to the windshield as headlights split the night like a curtain ahead of them. Her mother's mittens coarse wool instead of leather, her coat a muted brown. This is what she notices as the world turns sideways.

Then: snow. Rushing in through the window—above her now—the lone snowflake lost in the flurry. Soon, snow will cover everything, mingling with the broken glass until she can no longer tell the difference.

"I can't do it," Frances gasped. She tossed Hobbes into the driver's seat and slammed the door, her heart pounding in her chest.

"What if a call comes in?" Hobbes shouted from inside. "I can't operate the radio without arms!"

Frances collapsed against the door and slid to the ground. Why didn't she appoint herself the decoy? Luca didn't want to smash a window! But no—she had to be in control. She certainly didn't feel in control now.

Inside the car, Hobbes dutifully relayed each transmission through the window. The first few were uneventful: an elderly woman dropping her house key through a sewer grate; a fight breaking out at a pub on Postgasse Street.

"A small boy has broken a window at a local—" Hobbes paused. "Ah, yes. I believe we are already familiar with that one. . . ."

Frances pressed her palms against her eyes until stars popped across the backs of her eyelids. After everything she had been through, all she'd accomplished since discovering her great-grandfather's journal, she was still the same fragile, helpless girl who climbed into that automobile all those years ago. Sometimes it felt like she had never really climbed out again.

"Here's another one," Hobbes called. "It seems there has been a break-in." He fell quiet as the transmission continued. From outside, Frances heard little more than a static hum. "Reports describe the perpetrator as a 'hideous ogre.' Not a very charitable description, I must say, criminal or otherwise . . ."

Frances pulled herself to her feet. "That's the monster. It has to be."

"An ogre?" Hobbes said. "Of course! An apt analogy, I'm sure. Quickly now, we must respond before another officer beats us to it."

The radio was mounted to the dashboard next to the steering wheel. Frances leaned through the window, stretching to her full length. Her fingertips hardly grazed the handset.

"I'm afraid you must get inside the vehicle," Hobbes said.

Frances shook her head. "I'm not sure I can."

"In that case, allow me to be sure on your behalf."

"Hobbes—"

"Listen to me. These past two days, I have witnessed you facing challenge upon challenge with vigor and determination. And while many of your decisions have been questionable, no one could deny the bravery you've shown. You are Frances Victoria Stenzel. What man or monster can stand against you?"

Frances turned away, pulling the cuff of her sleeve over her wrist to wipe the tears from her eyes. She wasn't about to let a tutor see her cry. *He's just a machine*, she reminded herself. In truth, his kind words meant more to her than he could know. She decided it would be best to keep it that way, since knowing would only make him that much more insufferable.

Before she could talk herself out of it, Frances threw open the door and hoisted herself into the car. The cab was unexpectedly spacious, with a high, curved ceiling and wide leather seats. Though none of this made her want to remain inside any longer than she had to.

Hobbes seemed to share her impatience. "Quickly now," he said.

"I can't."

"How many times must I say it? Your bravery—"

"No, I mean, *I* can't. If an eleven-year-old girl answers the radio, it'll raise suspicion. You have to do it."

"Me?" Hobbes scoffed. "I will not impersonate an officer of the law!"

Frances didn't give him the choice. She shoved the handset against the bars of his cage and clicked it on.

"Er, uh . . ." Hobbes stammered, at a loss for words for perhaps the first time since his creation. When he spoke again, he had modulated his voice an octave lower. "What I mean to say is, we—'we' being the officers assigned to this vehicle, of course"—Frances rolled her eyes—"are near the scene of the crime and will investigate further. Over. Uh, over and out."

Frances clipped the handset to the dashboard and let her head fall against the seat. Her plan had worked—even if it was in spite of her. She turned to Hobbes, a playful smile on her face. "That was the least convincing police officer I have ever heard."

Hobbes wasn't smiling. When he spoke, the warmth had all but disappeared from his voice. "Let us hope it convinced whoever was on the other end of that radio," he replied. "Or we may be headed straight into the constable's grasp."

Chapter 22

A Propane Lamp, a Coil of Wire, a Roll of Tape

When Frances and her companions arrived at the scene of the break-in, they found a general store in disarray: windows blown out, shelves overturned, merchandise strewn across the sidewalk.

"It *was* the monster," Luca said, leaning his hands on his knees. He had run three city blocks before losing the officers, plus two more to reach the café Frances picked for their rendezvous point, and he had yet to catch his breath.

Hobbes nodded. "We seem to have just missed him."

They scouted from a quiet corner at the far end of the block, keeping to the shadows until they could be certain no actual police officers were on their way.

Even in the waning light, amid a gathering crowd, the shop

owner was impossible to miss. Helga Portsmouth stood over six feet tall, her formidable girth wrapped in a tight orange dress that made little pretense to contain her bosoms. She was pacing back and forth, wringing her hands and shouting.

"I'll kill him," she cried, lunging forward so that two men had to hold her back. "Don't think I won't!"

The object of her wrath appeared to be the handsome man in a leather apron sulking on the opposite side of the street, flanked by another, smaller crowd of people—his friends, judging by the way they glared at Helga.

"You measly excuse for a man," she shouted, shaking her fist. "Leaving me alone with that vicious ogre. Might as well have served me up on a silver platter! You worthless, beautiful, good-for-nothing lout . . ."

"We have to get inside that shop," Frances said, ducking back behind the corner. "The monster might have left some clue as to where he's going next."

"We'll be exposed the moment we set foot out there," Hobbes said. "And the constable could appear at any moment."

"We have to risk it."

"I strongly advise you—"

Frances huffed and stepped onto the street before Hobbes could finish, her eyes trained on Helga. Hobbes sputtered and looked to Luca, who shrugged and jogged after her.

"Excuse me," Frances called out. She walked the long way

around—the crowd was nothing like the throng in the market the morning before, but she still felt her palms begin to sweat. "What happened here?"

Helga looked around for the source of the question and made no effort to disguise her annoyance when she discovered it came from a child. "Where are your parents, young man? The grown-ups are talking."

Frances scowled but didn't bother to correct her. "Who did this?" she said.

"Some kind of giant," said a woman in the street. She wore a simple blue dress and clutched an infant to her breast. "Must've been seven feet tall!"

"Aye," an elderly man added. "With hands the size of wagon wheels."

"And he glowed with a green flame," declared a man in a top hat.

"That isn't the half of it," Helga said, her face growing serious. Everyone fell silent, leaning into her words. "None of you were close enough to see its teeth—they were razor-sharp." The crowd erupted in hushed murmurs.

Luca turned to Frances, his eyes saucers. "I knew it," he whispered.

Helga continued, emboldened. "Rows and rows of teeth, he had. Each more terrible than the last." The crowd's murmurs grew louder and more excited. "And . . . he had six fingers on each hand. And his hair was snakes!"

Luca gasped, putting a hand over his mouth. "Snakes?"

"Of course not," Frances said. "That woman is a twit."

Helga continued to describe the monster in increasingly unbelievable terms while Frances and Luca turned their attentions to the crime scene. The front door was dangling off its hinges, so they let themselves in. Glass crunched beneath their shoes as they wandered the aisles, making a sweep of the shop until an overturned shelf blocked them from going farther. Frances picked up a shard of something porcelain and examined the thick black goo congealed on its edge.

"There's no blood except the creature's." Frances turned to Hobbes, her eyebrows scrunched together. "No one was hurt."

"That's good, right?" Luca asked.

"Certainly," Hobbes said, peering out from beneath his cover. "But why?"

"Exactly," Frances said. "If he attacked the shop before dark, he must have been desperate. So why didn't he hurt anybody?"

"That lady would've made quite a meal, too." Luca turned back toward Helga, who was busy describing the monster's six-centimeter claws.

"Why didn't he feed?" Frances bit the inside of her cheek and scanned the shop. *We'll never find anything useful in this mess.*

Then she had an idea.

"Excuse me," she called, stepping gingerly across the shop floor and making her way back toward Helga. "Excuse me!"

". . . so he could throw me over those hideous, muscular shoulders and carry me back to his lair," Helga was saying as she approached. "But I looked at that foul—"

"Excuse me!"

Helga threw up her hands. "What is it now, child?"

"I was just wondering," Frances said. "How did you escape?"

"Ah, my escape!" Helga turned back to the crowd. "I thought I was done for. No—I *knew* I was done for! The ogre was coming at me, snarling and growling. I did the only thing I could think to do: I gathered my wits and screamed with all my might. I screamed so terribly that the beast whimpered and jumped right through those windows there."

"You do have quite a pair of lungs," a man said with a wink.

"Oh, Peter," Helga cooed.

"But if he wasn't going to eat you," Frances said, "what was he doing in the shop? Is anything missing?"

"Do I look like I've had time to take inventory? I just had a near-death experience—my life is still flashing before my eyes." Helga pointed vaguely toward the sky. "There's me as a young girl. . . ."

Frances sighed and motioned to Luca. "Come on," she said, nodding back the way they came. "We won't get anywhere with this woman."

But as they began to walk away, Helga held up a finger. "Come to think of it, he *was* holding something under his arm. I remember now—I thought he was a common shoplifter until I got a good gander at him. I asked that spineless Philippe to deal with him"—she glared at the handsome man across the street—"but of course *he* fled like a frightened rabbit."

"Do you remember what it was?" Frances asked, leaning forward.

"It was odd, really. A propane lamp, a coil of copper wire. A roll of tape, I think. Maybe a few other items. It all happened so fast."

"I think this poor thing has had enough," the man called Peter said, putting his jacket over Helga's shoulders. "Haven't you, dear?"

"Such a gentleman." Helga batted her eyelashes. "Unlike another so-called man I know!" Philippe scowled and slunk off down the street while his friends patted his back in solidarity.

In the distance, a siren began to wail.

"The jig is up," Hobbes said. "I believe it is time for us to leave."

Frances and Luca crept away while Helga kept the crowd's attention on herself. When Frances reached the edge of the block, she stopped. Along the curb, there was a metal grate just wide enough for a man. She crouched down to examine it. The grate was in place, but along its edges Frances could make out a row of deep scratches, each about three centimeters apart.

"Frances," Luca called as the sirens grew louder. "We have to go!"

"Right behind you," she said. She lingered a moment longer, then got to her feet and ran.

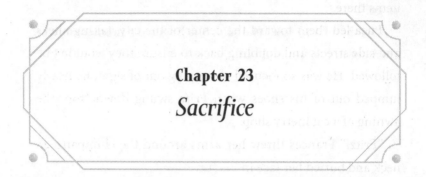

Chapter 23
Sacrifice

N ews of the attack on Helga's shop spread quickly, along with rumors of a rampaging monster on the loose. Shops were closed and barred; curtains were drawn. A young housemaid peeked her head out a window and withdrew again, pulling the shutters closed behind her.

"At least now we can move around without being seen," offered Luca.

"On the contrary," Hobbes said. "If anyone happens to look outside tonight, we are all they will see."

A propane lamp, a coil of wire, a roll of tape . . . Frances ran the items through her mind again, searching for a logical explanation. No food, no shelter. Other than perhaps the lamp, the monster hadn't taken anything at all that might be useful to a hungry creature stalking the city by night. She consulted the journal, but of course there was no mention of any of the items there.

Luca led them toward the center of the city, taking alleys and side streets and doubling back to ensure they wouldn't be followed. He was so focused on staying out of sight, he nearly jumped out of his shoes when Fritz swung down from the awning of a cabinetry shop.

"Fritz!" Frances threw her arms around the chimpanzee's neck and buried her face in his fur.

Fritz planted a sloppy kiss on the top of her head and held aloft two loaves of bread gripped in his feet. Luca accepted his portion eagerly, tearing into the crust with his teeth. Frances wrinkled her nose at his lack of manners, but Luca only shrugged.

"Monster hunting makes me hungry," he said, half-chewed bits tumbling from his mouth.

Frances thanked Fritz for the bread, but she was much more interested in what news he had brought. "Did you see the monster?" she asked.

He began to sign, though much of it was hard to follow. The intelligence serum was wearing off, Frances realized. He was reverting to his normal chimpanzee self. She felt a pang of guilt—the last vial could have boosted his mind back to peak functionality if she hadn't used it on herself. He still retained enough of his training that, with a bit of back-and-forth, Frances was able to decipher most of what he was saying.

"You were scouting for the monster."

Fritz nodded. He curled his hairy fingers around his eyes like binoculars and pointed them north.

"You found him outside the city. . . ."

Fritz nodded again, hooting with excitement. He raised his hands as if he wanted to sign something else, but the words wouldn't come. He banged the heel of his palm against his head in frustration.

"It's okay, boy. You can do this."

Fritz thought for a moment, then drew a circle on the ground. Standing inside the circle, he puffed himself up as big as he could and made swiping motions with his arms.

"What is he doing?" Hobbes said.

Frances shook her head. "I have no idea. Sorry, Fritz. I don't understand."

Luca's eyes lit up. "That's a bear. He's talking about the bear pits!"

"The bear pits?"

"Yeah, it's a park just north of here with real bears and everything. People come from all over to see them."

Fritz grabbed Luca's hands and danced him around in a circle. When he was sufficiently dizzy, Fritz let him go and motioned for them to follow.

"The creature could not have made it across town so quickly without drawing attention to himself," Hobbes said. He turned to Frances. "Are you sure it's wise to put our fates in the hands of a primate?"

She smiled, watching Fritz scamper down the street. "Fritz would never let us down. You'll see."

Two blocks later, the tunnellike maze of city streets opened up as they climbed a steep hill toward the bank of the Aare.

Luca pointed to a narrow bridge that spanned the width of the river a few meters upstream. "We'll have to cross there."

Frances stepped up beside him as Fritz scampered off to scavenge. The wind was stronger here with no buildings to impede it, and the temperature was dropping fast. Thin gray clouds approached from the west, like a dark sheet being pulled across the sky over the Old City. She peered over the wall at the water below and remembered the way it had rushed around her, surrounding her, so clear and cold. She hugged herself, suddenly aware of the chill.

Luca noticed her shivering and set the birdcage down in the grass. "Do you want my jacket?" he said, already tugging at one of his sleeves.

"I—" Frances stopped, unsure of the correct response. "That would be nice. Thank you."

She placed her great-grandfather's journal on the ground next to Hobbes so she could slip the jacket over her arms. She was still fastening the top button when Fritz hissed and leaped onto her back, nearly knocking her over.

"Easy, boy," she said. "What's gotten into you?"

The chimp's hands were a blur, signing the same word over and over: *hide.*

"Quickly," Frances whispered. "Behind those bushes."

Luca grabbed Hobbes's birdcage and followed her behind a row of low-lying junipers. When they were flat on their bellies, Frances pushed aside a swath of branches and peeked through. It was Constable Montavon, marching down the street where they had just emerged. Two officers followed on either side. One was thin with dark, sunken eyes; the other shorter, with a potbelly and a scraggly beard. She noticed with some satisfaction that Montavon favored his right leg—Luca's rooftop kick must have been a good one.

"He never gives up," Luca moaned.

Montavon and his deputies continued until they reached the bridge, then stopped to look around. Frances could see the constable's mouth moving, the white of his mustache doing a sinister dance in the moonlight as he barked his orders. One of the deputies turned and began marching farther up the river. The other headed straight toward Frances and her companions.

"These bushes will not conceal us at close range," Hobbes said, turning his volume down low. But with the empty street in front of them and the river at their backs, they would be spotted the moment they tried to run. They were trapped.

The deputy continued to advance, his lantern casting a circle of light that inched closer and closer. Frances held her breath. *One more step and he's got us.* But as he lifted his foot, his toe caught on something, and he fell, dropping the lantern and snuffing out the light.

When he stood up, he held something over his head and called to the constable. Montavon summoned him back to the bridge.

"What is it?" Luca whispered once the deputy was out of earshot.

Frances strained her eyes but couldn't see anything until the deputy stepped into the light of Montavon's lamp, and she felt her heart sink into the mud. "The journal," she answered. "Constable Montavon has my great-grandfather's journal."

"But how?" Hobbes said. "You've had it with you since we left the Manor."

"I set it down when Luca gave me his jacket," she replied, fighting back tears.

Luca's face fell. "I'm sorry."

"It's not your fault. The constable came, and we had to hide and I . . . I forgot it."

"What's done is done," Hobbes said. "The constable will soon have us all if we cannot keep quiet."

His tone was sharp, but Frances could hear the worry in his voice. He knew the journal held knowledge of the monster and the procedure that created him that couldn't be found anywhere else. Answers they might need to stop him. *How could I be so careless?*

On the bridge, the constable and his men stood huddled together, flipping through the journal's pages, blocking the only way across the river for two kilometers. Frances could hear Luca's teeth chattering next to her as the temperature continued to drop. She felt guilty wearing his jacket, but she couldn't risk moving to give it back.

Finally, the constable spoke.

"Frances!" His voice boomed against the stone buildings. "It seems you've dropped something. Looks rather expensive, though I suppose that shouldn't surprise me. And should it have surprised me to find my city the victim of yet another act of wanton vandalism? Or that witnesses reported a child matching your description fleeing the scene?"

"It's over," Luca whimpered. "We're goners."

Frances was afraid he was right. Now that the constable knew she was close, he would never leave until he had her. It would only be a matter of time before she was discovered, along with Luca and Hobbes and—

"Wait." She reached for the empty patch of grass next to her. "Where's Fritz? He was right here."

"I see him." Luca pointed through the bushes to the far end of the street. There was Fritz, knuckle-walking down the center of the road, chattering away in chimp.

No, Fritz—come back! I'll think of something, I promise.

But it was too late. One of the men pointed, and Montavon looked up from the journal, snapping it shut when he saw the chimpanzee. He barked an order, and the deputies began to advance. One approached Fritz from the right, the other his left, while the constable strolled casually down the middle of the street.

Reaching into his pocket, Montavon produced an apple. "If it isn't my friend from the rooftop," he called. He took a bite so the crunch echoed across the cobblestones. "All that climbing and swinging . . . perhaps you've worked up an appetite?"

Fritz hooted and scratched under his arms, dancing a silly little jig and doing his best to act like a simple beast. The deputies snickered, but an icy look from the constable shut them up.

"What is he doing?" Luca whispered. "He's walking right into their trap!"

"Have you ever played chess, young man?" Hobbes said.

"Once or twice. My dad and I played. Before he died."

"Then surely you can see what the chimpanzee has in mind."

"He's sacrificing himself." Luca turned to Frances, a look of sadness on his face. "That's his plan, isn't it?"

Frances was silent. She watched as Montavon held out the apple. Fritz walked right up to it and plucked it from his hand, dropping it into his mouth whole.

"Now," cried Montavon.

The deputies sprung at Fritz, wrapping their arms around him and pinning him between them. Fritz let out a howl, spitting out the apple and kicking his legs, but the constable was ready. He snapped a pair of handcuffs around his ankles and, taking another pair from the belt of the potbellied deputy, snapped those around his wrists.

"No . . ." Frances whispered. She wanted to cover her eyes as the three men dragged her first and closest friend down the street, but she couldn't bear to look away until they disappeared behind a row of buildings, and the sound of his howling faded into the night.

Chapter 24

The Bear Pits of Bern

I t was only a short walk across the bridge, but it felt like kilo-meters. With each step, Frances's feet grew heavier, as if the stones were grasping at the soles of her shoes, shouting, "No, your friend is the other way!" Luca turned off the road ahead of her, taking a narrow path through a park. He stopped after only a few paces.

"Are we turning back?" Frances asked, looking around. They stood before a stone wall, about as high as her shoulder, broken by a four-foot section of wrought-iron fencing.

"No," Luca said. "We're here."

It felt like a slap; they had been so close. Fritz had sacrificed himself for less than one hundred meters.

Sensing her grief, Luca reached out as if to put his hand on her shoulder, then reconsidered and ran his fingers through his hair instead. "Are you . . . okay?"

"I'm fine," she lied.

"Perhaps it's for the best that the constable found the journal," Hobbes said. "Consider this: Why is he so determined to catch us?"

Frances sighed. "Because I stabbed him in the neck with a hypodermic needle and sedated him against his will?"

"You did what?" Luca cried, his eyes wide. "Oh, God. We really are going to jail."

"Yes, yes—that was all very unfortunate," Hobbes continued. "But you would not have needed to sedate him if he had believed your report about the monster. Albrecht Grimme's journal is full of information about the creature—not proof per se, but it corroborates your story."

"It's my great-grandfather's life's work. Everything he lived for, maybe even died for. We have to get it back."

"We will," Luca said. "I promise."

Frances could tell Luca still felt responsible for what happened. She wanted to reassure him but couldn't settle on the right words. It was more difficult than she had anticipated, having friends. In less than two days, she had lost Fritz and upended Luca's entire life. And when she thought about what she had done to Hobbes . . .

No. She couldn't dwell on that now, not until the monster

was stopped. Fritz sent them here for a reason, and she wasn't about to let him down again.

She leaned over the fence and peered through the iron bars. Below her was a circular enclosure about twenty feet deep. In the center stood a large, cliff-like structure built using rectangular blocks of cement arranged at different heights and depths to create a kind of expressionist interpretation of natural rock.

"There are real bears down there," she said, turning to Luca in amazement.

"I told you." He grinned. "Why'd you think they call it the Bear Pits?"

There were six of them, full grown with shaggy black fur and wet snouts, huddled against the eastern wall, asleep. The air above them was dotted with flies.

"You don't think the monster . . . ate any, do you?" Luca said.

Frances shrugged. "The bears look fine to me."

I just hope they didn't hurt him. The thought surprised her. Only a few hours ago, she would have been relieved to find the bears had stopped the monster and saved her the trouble. Wouldn't she?

They walked farther around the perimeter of the pit, searching for any signs of the monster.

"Well, looks like he wasn't here after all," Luca said, rubbing his hands together. "I guess we won't have to meet the bears. Shame, really."

"Wait," Frances said, grabbing Luca by the shoulder as he tried to leave. "Look." She pointed to a dark spot on the floor of the pit, a few feet from the stones at the center. It was a sewer grate, with one corner ajar. "That's where the monster went."

"Show me," Hobbes said. Luca held him over the side. "A reasonable hypothesis. But we cannot know for sure."

"Back at Helga's shop," Frances said, "nobody saw the monster leave. He just . . . disappeared. As we were running away, I noticed a sewer grate just like that one. The bars were all scratched up. It makes sense; that's why no one has spotted the monster during the day, and how he's been able to get from place to place so quickly—he's been hiding in the sewer."

"There's got to be another way down there," Luca said.

"Do you see any other openings?"

His shoulders slumped. "No."

Frances scanned the pit. They would have to go over the railing, rappel to the bottom of the enclosure, open the sewer grate, climb inside, and replace the grate—all without waking the six rather large, rather intimidating bears.

"Bears don't eat people, do they?" Luca peered over the railing at the six furry bodies rising and falling with the rhythmic breathing of sleep.

"Humans are not a traditional staple of the black bear's diet, no," Hobbes replied. "Mauling is a different story, however, with an estimated two hundred and fifty bear attacks reported each year and ten times that many injuries."

Luca gulped.

Frances leaned over, calculating the distance to the bottom. She gripped the railing and shook. *It should hold.*

Frances checked her estimates with Hobbes, who had a few minor adjustments. They would need rope, and a distraction for the bears. After some scavenging, Luca returned with a garden hose. Frances cradled a dead pigeon that appeared to have flown into the window of the groundskeeper's office and broken its neck.

"You really are spooky," Luca said, watching her lay the lifeless bird on the ground.

"Everything dies," she replied, using Luca's pocketknife to make an incision down the bird's belly.

"See?" Luca said, jumping back. "That's the kind of thing I'm talking about."

Frances shrugged. "We need the bears to smell it."

Luca looked like he might gag. He turned to Hobbes for support, but all he said was "Please remember to wash your hands at the next available opportunity."

Frances set the bird aside and secured the end of the hose to one of the wrought-iron bars. She worked quietly so as not to rouse the slumbering bears.

Luca puffed up his chest and insisted on going first, though Frances couldn't figure out why—he was clearly terrified.

"Maybe this wasn't such a good idea," he said once he was climbing over the railing. He took his first hesitant step, sliding his foot off the edge and dragging the toe of his shoe down the smooth concrete wall, searching for his next foothold. He found nothing—no crack or fissure wide enough to catch the edge of his leather sole.

"Lean back more," Frances coached him. "Put your feet flat against the wall and walk down backward."

"I'm too heavy," Luca whispered back. His knuckles were already starting to tighten under the strain of holding himself up.

"It's simple physics!"

Luca leaned back the way Frances instructed, careful not to lose his grip on the hose. He reached the bottom sweaty and sore, misjudging the final few feet and dropping to the ground in a panting heap. Above him, Frances stifled a gasp. The bear nearest Luca growled in its sleep.

When she was sure the bears hadn't awoken, Frances exhaled and pulled the hose back to the top of the pit. She looped her belt through the ring of Hobbes's birdcage and climbed over the railing, careful not to let the cage rattle against the bars.

"You're not afraid of heights, are you, Hobbes?" she said, looking back over her shoulder to her bodiless tutor, dangling over the pit in his cage.

"I am composed of a lightweight alloy with a tensile strength of over eighty thousand kilograms per square centimeter. It's your brittle frame I worry about."

"I was joking," Frances muttered. Rappelling came easily to her. She understood the physics, and her small body put little strain on her arms or legs.

Below her, Luca was trying to get her attention.

"What is it?" she hissed.

Luca pointed. "It's slipping."

Frances peered up at the railing where she had knotted the hose. "It's fine. I'm almost down."

"Not the hose," Luca whispered. "Hobbes!"

Frances dropped her eyes to her belt and found the leather stretched against its buckle, ready to snap. She pushed off the wall with both feet, rappelling faster, but halfway to the ground, her foot slipped. She spun and slammed shoulder first into the wall. The birdcage hit next, and her belt snapped.

Luca squeezed his eyes shut and held up his arms to catch the cage but missed. It crashed to the ground, popping open and sending Hobbes rolling across the concrete—right into the arms of a six-foot black bear. Frances and Luca stared in horror as the sleeping bear rolled over, her massive arm coming to rest over Hobbes's face and pulling him in toward her body as if cradling a cub. Hobbes's eyes blinked madly, his mouth covered by the bear's arm. It was a miracle none of the others stirred beyond a few snorts and stretches—the cage crashing against the stones sounded like a cymbal being struck.

Frances and Luca backed away from the bears and ducked behind the rocks.

"What are we going to do?" Luca asked. "We can't leave him there. Can we? Can your dad just . . . make a new one?"

Frances pondered this. If Hobbes's head was lost, could Hobbes himself be restored? Could his memories, or his essence, or whatever made him *him*, be saved?

"We have to get him back," she decided. She looked around for something to help retrieve Hobbes from the arms of the sleeping bear. Vines, straw, a few sticks and stones. The hose. The dead bird folded in the handkerchief. A plan formed in her mind.

She set the blade of Luca's pocketknife between her teeth and shimmied up the hose. About two meters up—the highest distance she could fall without injury, she estimated—she took the knife in one hand and began to saw. The rubber was tough, and the sawing motion was difficult to perform while the hose swung side to side. When it snapped, Frances dropped so suddenly that she almost forgot to toss the knife to keep from landing on it.

She tied the bird to the end of the hose and dangled it over the bear holding Hobbes. It sniffed, still asleep. When she drew it away, the bear followed the scent with its nose, lifting its arm off of Hobbes and rolling onto its side. Then came the hard part. If they tossed something for Hobbes to grab with his teeth, they'd risk hitting the bear. Someone had to creep up and grab him.

"It should be me," Frances said. "It's my fault we're in this mess." Luca looked conflicted but didn't argue.

At Frances's instruction, Luca held the bird aloft while Frances tiptoed around the bears. A fly buzzed near his face, making a few passes before landing on the bridge of his nose. He flared his nostrils, but the fly didn't move.

"Keep it steady," Frances hissed. The bear was much larger up close—even its smell was terrifying. She held her breath and plucked Hobbes from the ground.

Meanwhile, Luca watched the fly cross-eyed as it crawled to the tip of his nose. He stuck out his bottom lip and blew a puff of air. The fly flew off—and Luca sneezed.

Frances watched, helpless, as the bird slipped from Luca's hands and landed on the bear's chest. The bear's eyes snapped open, and Frances found herself face-to-face with a very large, very unhappy animal.

Soon, all six were on their feet.

"Luca," Frances cried. "The bird!"

Luca grabbed the hose and tossed the bird as far as he could. The bears watched it arc through the air and hit the ground with a lifeless *thunk*.

Frances took advantage of the momentary distraction.

Cradling Hobbes in the crook of her arm, she grabbed the broken birdcage and sprinted out of reach of the bears' powerful arms. Luca remained frozen in place.

"Run, Luca!" she shouted, but still he didn't move. The bears lumbered toward him, hungrily sniffing the air. The largest tilted its head back and roared, a string of saliva trailing from its mouth. "Luca!"

At last, he managed a small step back, then another, until he was pressed against the rocks at the center of the pit. Soon the bears were only centimeters from him, huge paws raised like boxers. Frances turned away, unable to watch. When she looked again, Luca was gone.

The bears reeled back, bewildered. They pawed at the wall where Luca had stood moments before, growling and snapping.

"Luca," Frances called. One of the bears turned and growled. It stomped toward her, swatting the air. The others soon followed. They weren't about to let another meal get away.

Frances ran to the sewer grate and pulled with all her strength, but it only moved a few centimeters.

"I'm sorry, Frances," Hobbes said. "I have failed in my primary directive."

Frances found a stick the bears had been gnawing on and wedged it under the bars. She could hear them snarling just around the corner.

"You kept the Manor tidy," she said, leaning her weight on

the stick. "You made lunch and taught my lessons. You did what you were supposed to do."

"None of those were my primary directives. I was created to protect you."

She heard the scrape of metal against stone as something started to budge. "Protect me from what?"

Hobbes looked up at her, eyes glowing blue, his expression approximating sadness. "Everything," he said.

Then the grate popped open, and they tumbled into darkness.

Chapter 25

Lights-Out

No sooner had the grate fallen back into place than six wet snouts and two dozen paws appeared, snuffling and clawing at the bars. Frances rubbed her head and pulled Hobbes out of something slimy and green.

"I never thought I would say this," he grimaced, "but I would like to get back into my birdcage as soon as possible, please."

The cage was mangled, but Frances was able to bend a few wires back and put the pieces together. Misshapen but sound. As she finished, she heard her name whispered from somewhere down the tunnel.

"We're over here," she called.

Luca splashed toward them, slipping and sliding across the muck. He still clutched the hose, which dragged behind him.

"Frances! Hobbes! I'm so glad you didn't get eaten." He leaned against the curved wall and rested his hands on his knees. "I'm so glad *I* didn't get eaten."

"How did you escape?"

"There was another grate over there. I fell down here by accident."

"That sounds in character," Hobbes said.

"Come on." Frances coiled the hose around her shoulder. She wasn't sure what good it would do against the monster, but it was all they had. "We may have a long way to go."

They followed the tunnel until it ended at a stone staircase. A few steps down, darkness fell across them like a curtain. It was impossible to know how far down it went, but they had no choice, unless they wanted to turn back and face the bears. They descended in silence.

At the bottom, Hobbes switched on his lights. Luca held him aloft, and they surveyed the tunnel. It was narrow enough for Frances to touch both sides at once. A trickle of water ran down the center of the floor, but a distant sound like rainfall suggested the current would grow stronger as they descended.

"The tunnels beneath this city are ancient," Hobbes said. "Some dating as far back as the medieval era. If my calculations are correct, we should be underneath the river by now."

Luca swallowed hard and eyed the arched ceiling. "Is it safe?"

"Don't worry," Frances said. "If it collapsed, we'd be crushed instantly. We wouldn't feel a thing."

"I suppose that's . . . something," he mumbled.

It was a strange feeling, walking deeper and deeper underground. Luca looked over his shoulder every few feet. But there was nothing to see; the entrance had been swallowed up by the darkness.

"Hold him still," Frances said.

Luca faced forward and raised Hobbes a few centimeters higher. "Sorry."

At the first fork in the tunnel, Frances chose the path leading to their right. The echoes were more spread out in that direction, suggesting larger tunnels. "The monster is seven feet tall," she reminded them.

After traveling this way for nearly a quarter hour, Luca spoke. "If the monster's dead, how does he . . . know things? Like, where to go, what to eat, or how to hide in the sewer?"

"He's not dead," Frances replied. "Not anymore. That's what the procedure does; it takes something dead and makes it alive again."

"Whether you can call that creature 'alive' is debatable," Hobbes said.

"He's breathing, isn't he? Walking around? He's alive enough."

"So, what happens if he dies a second time?" Luca asked.

"He goes back to being dead, I'd imagine."

"And then you'd bring him back?"

"I don't know," Frances said. "No one's ever gotten this far before."

They walked in silence after that. Every tunnel led to other tunnels, sometimes splitting in three directions at once. Hobbes offered some guidance, but he only had a partial blueprint in his memory banks. Before long, Frances was choosing at random.

"Are we almost there?" Luca said. "I don't want to be down here with the rats any longer than I have to be."

"We'll stay down here as long as it takes."

"There are kilometers of tunnels, Frances," Hobbes said. "We won't find him by wandering about."

"If you have a better plan, I'm listening."

Hobbes didn't reply, but Frances could hear him grumbling to himself in his cage.

"I was thinking," Luca said. "Why'd the monster take that stuff from the shop? A propane lamp, a coil of copper wire, a roll of tape . . . ?"

"I have a theory," replied Frances. "Hobbes, do you remember back at the Manor when—"

Frances stopped; Luca was following so close behind he ran right into her, nearly knocking her over.

"What's wrong?" he said, anxiously scanning the shadows.

"A minute ago, you said 'down here with the rats.' That's what you said, right?"

"So?"

Frances gestured at the floor. "Look around."

Luca swept the twin beams of Hobbes's eye lights across the tunnel in front of them. Frances blinked. *Did the light just flicker?*

"I don't see anything," Luca said.

"Exactly. Where are all the rats?"

He waved Hobbes around, illuminating every inch of the tunnel in both directions. There were no rats. The lights flickered again, this time winking out entirely until Luca gave the birdcage a shake.

"Easy, boy," Hobbes said. "I won't be rattled about like a common lantern."

Frances squatted down to peer into the birdcage. The lights were steady again, but they were dimmer; there was no mistaking it. She could hear it in his voice, too; his words had slowed, their pitch lower.

"We need to turn back," she said, rising.

"What? Why?" asked Luca.

"We have come too far to turn back now." As Hobbes spoke, his eyes dimmed further. The circle of light that surrounded them began to collapse. "It would be wiser to continue. Up ahead there is a . . . there is . . . there . . .”

"Hobbes," Frances said. "Stop talking. I need you to save your—"

"There . . . th . . . th—" His eyes faltered once more, then went out altogether.

Frances had never been afraid of the dark. She liked it, in fact. It had a certain leveling effect she appreciated. No one was bigger or smaller or better dressed. There were no scars in the dark.

This was different. This darkness was complete. It was a wall that had fallen on them, and if they didn't get out from under it, it would crush them. Frances closed her eyes and opened them, but it made no difference. All was darkness.

"Frances." It was Luca's voice, somewhere to her left.

"I'm here," she answered. She held out her hand until he found it. "Hobbes?" Silence. She'd expected as much but had to be sure.

"What happened to him?" Luca asked.

"It's his battery." She heard Luca shake the birdcage again and squeezed his hand. "Don't bother. It's dead."

"He's dead?"

"No, just his battery. He'll be fine once we charge him back up. At least, I hope so."

"You have a plan, right?" His voice was fraught with panic.

Frances took a deep breath. "Before he shut down, Hobbes was telling us to keep going. It sounded like he was about to say there's another exit up ahead."

"We're not turning back?"

"It's too late for that now. We'll never find our way back to the bear pits without Hobbes. We have to keep going."

Frances ran her fingertips along the stone walls as she inched forward. Luca kept a hand on her shoulder so they wouldn't get separated. She kept expecting her eyes to adjust to the darkness, but they never did. Progress was slow.

After a while, Luca spoke. "What was that you were saying? Before Hobbes . . . shut down."

"You said something about rats," Frances said. "But there aren't any. The whole time we've been down here, I haven't seen or heard a single rat."

"Just like at Madame Melina's apothecary. You think it's the monster?"

"I don't know."

"It has to be him. What else could it be?"

Before Frances could answer, she heard a yelp behind her as Luca's hand slipped from her shoulder and the birdcage clattered to the floor.

"Luca?" Frances whispered. But he was gone.

Chapter 26

Nobody of Any Consequence

"**L**uca," Frances called. She whirled around, searching for him, but found only darkness. Then someone spoke.

"He can't hear you," the voice said. It was the voice of a man, hoarse and broken like a motor turning over after years of disuse.

Frances stumbled back. "Who's there?"

"Nobody important," answered the voice. "Nobody of any consequence at all."

"What have you done with Luca?"

"I'm afraid I don't know any Lucas. Don't get many visitors. Now"—the man struck a match against the stone wall and lit a lantern—"let's have a look at you."

There was a hiss of propane as the tunnel flooded with an

orange glow. Frances raised a hand to shield her eyes from the shock of brightness. The man was small and stooped, with a curtain of greasy, white hair over his brow and teeth Frances could count on one hand. His eyes were bulging and blood-shot, with pupils so large they seemed poised to overtake the thin halo of white that remained and flip them inside out like a pair of used socks.

"You a boy or a girl?" he said, squinting his eyes.

Frances sighed. "Does it matter?"

"Suppose not." He held his lantern aloft and nodded at a spot behind her. "That your friend?"

Luca dangled upside down by his ankle, still swaying, his fingertips dragging in the muck. His face was red and swollen. He appeared to be unconscious.

"What did you do to him?" Frances ran to Luca's side, but her arms couldn't reach to untie him. She glared at the strange man, who only shrugged.

"Wouldn't say I did anything, really," he said, shuffling over to Luca. "Hold him steady, now." He set the lantern on the floor and began to untie Luca's feet. "Got traps all over these sewers. Not usually for"—the ropes pulled loose and Luca collapsed onto the floor—"not usually for children. Just rats."

Frances dropped to her knees and flipped Luca onto his back. His eyelids fluttered open, and his eyes rolled forward until they found Frances's face. "Francie?"

"Luca, you had me worried. And don't call me Francie."

"Okay. You know, I've never been upside down before in my life and then, *BAM*, twice in two days." He rubbed his head and looked around. When he noticed the old man, he scrambled back against the wall. "Who's that?"

"You don't know?" the man said. Frances and Luca looked at each other and shook their heads. "Why, I'm the sewerman, of course. Either that or I'm frightfully lost." He chuckled. "Been waiting for a chance to say that. Little joke I thought up."

The old man gave a long, phlegmy cough and spit before speaking again. "I repair what needs repairing down here, unclog what needs unclogging. Nothing but my wits and my bare hands." He held up his hands and examined them; then he looked up and offered one to Frances. "You can call me Gangie. Mr. Gangie."

Frances recoiled from the handshake and offered a half-hearted curtsy instead.

"So, what brings you down below?" Mr. Gangie continued. "You running from the law?"

They were, Frances supposed. But she wasn't sure she wanted the sewerman to know it. "We were looking for someone. But we didn't find him."

Mr. Gangie nodded sagely. "Big fella, bum arm, flickering light in his chest?"

Luca's eyes widened. "How did you know?"

"Said I don't get too many new faces down here. Besides, I heard you talking about him to your lantern over there."

Luca scrambled over to the birdcage and held it to his chest. "We weren't talking to our lantern. I mean, he's not a lantern—"

"Won't get no judgment from me," Mr. Gangie said. "Gets lonely down here. I been known to do some deep conversing with an old boot." He drew a smile in the air with his finger. "Had a rip in the toe like this. Jolly old thing, he was."

"Do you know where he is now?" Frances said.

"Had to toss him. That cocky grin of his . . ."

"Not the boot, the . . . person we're looking for—the 'big fellow.'"

Mr. Gangie shook his head. "Been looking for him myself. He's the one been stealing my rats."

Mr. Gangie led them through a series of corridors and down a ladder. The stonework at the bottom looked older than the tunnels near the surface. A spider crawled out of the crack between two stones, and Mr. Gangie plucked it from the wall. He dropped it into a pouch around his waist, then cinched it shut and continued down the tunnel.

"You're probably wondering how a person becomes a sewerman," Mr. Gangie said.

"Actually," Frances cut in, "we just—"

The old man held up a hand to silence her. "I was a boy

once. Like you." He pointed to Frances, who sighed and shook her head. He turned his finger to Luca. "Like you. Didn't have no money, didn't have no food. Was begging on the streets when they caught me. Put me in a cell and told me I couldn't live on their streets for free. Had to contribute."

The tunnel reached another fork and Mr. Gangie turned left without a second thought. The floor sloped down more steeply here, with an inch of water coursing down the middle. Frances had to turn her body sideways and press her back to the wall to keep her balance.

Mr. Gangie went on. "They asked what I could do. I said I couldn't do nothing. Asked me what I knew. Said I didn't know nothing. They thought I was playing them for fools, so they got cross. Told me they had something I could do, even me."

They reached another ladder. Frances peered over the edge into total blackness. Mr. Gangie hooked the lantern to his belt and started his descent. This ladder seemed longer than the first, and the tunnels at the bottom more cramped. Chunks of stonework had crumbled from the peak of the arched ceiling, revealing patches of clay.

"Shouldn't we be going up, not down?" Luca asked.

"Not polite to interrupt an old man whilst he's storytelling," Mr. Gangie said. "Now, where was I . . . Ah. They took me to the mouth of these sewers, put a lantern in my hand, and said there was my new home. I told them I wasn't going down there—didn't like the dark, you see—but they was going to make me. So I struck a deal. I said, 'I'll tend to your tunnels and your filth, but anything I find down there is mine to keep.' One of them laughed and held up his hand and said, 'I do solemnly swear that anything you find in these sewers, whether creature or thing, is yours to keep for ever and ever.'"

Mr. Gangie stopped in front of a large rusty door and pulled out a ring of keys. There must have been hundreds of them. He selected one with a wide square head and inserted it into the keyhole. Then he turned it until the mechanism clanged into place, echoing off the walls and down the corridor.

"He thought he was having a laugh at me," Mr. Gangie said. "But I took the man at his word." With that, he pulled the door open and a wave of torchlight poured into the hall. Frances and Luca looked through the doorway and gasped.

Mr. Gangie chuckled. "Been taking him at his word ever since."

Chapter 27

The Drowned Museum

Typewriters missing keys.

A pillar of automobile tires.

Stacks of newspapers black with mold.

Crisscrossing lines of broken lightbulbs strung across the vaulted ceiling.

In the far corner—a mound of doll parts: arms and legs and heads, marble eyes staring into nothing.

The sewerman's chamber was like a drowned museum filled to bursting with artifacts from across time, flushed and forgotten. It seemed to go on forever.

But the rest of the collection was nothing compared to the rats.

Wooden cages, each two meters wide and half as tall, were stacked into a pyramid at the perimeter of the room. There were thousands of them, each one teeming with rats. The entire pyramid seemed alive with waves of slick brown fur shimmering in the torchlight. The sound of their chattering was deafening, and the smell . . . Frances covered her nose with her sleeve.

"Whoa," Luca said. "Rat Mountain."

"Welcome." Mr. Gangie held a hand up to the rats. "Quiet, little ones, you'll startle the new arrivals."

Frances gaped at a mangled chandelier that hung from the ceiling's peak. "Where did it all come from?"

"I told you," Mr. Gangie said, picking up a tattered bonnet from a pile and turning it over in his hand. "Whatever I find in these tunnels is mine to keep."

"You found all this," Luca said, waving his hand across the room, "in the sewer?"

Mr. Gangie shrugged. "Everything finds its way down here, eventually."

"This is why we didn't see any rats on our way here," Frances said, watching thousands of pink noses and claw-toed feet climbing over each other.

"This and the big fella. Ever since he showed up down here, my traps have been empty. Those are my rats!" He slammed his fist on a table filled with women's shoes, sending several pairs tumbling to the floor. Frances jumped at the sudden noise.

She looked at Luca, who gripped Hobbes's birdcage tighter. *I have a plan*, she mouthed.

"He's not just big," Frances said, taking a step forward. "He's a monster. He ate all the rats on the surface, and he was still hungry so he came down here. He won't stop until he eats every last rat in these sewers." She looked up at the cages. "All of them. We came down here to stop him, but we only have this hose."

Mr. Gangie took the hose and examined it. "Never stop something that big with something like this."

"Will you help us?"

The old man rubbed his hands together, stopping to crack each knuckle in turn. When he finished, a sly glint appeared in his eye. "I've got just the thing."

Frances and Luca followed Mr. Gangie through a door near Rat Mountain. This room was much smaller, and the ceiling sloped more severely on the far end. Frances had noted similar doors on each of the main chamber's walls. *Rooms like this must border it on every side.*

Mr. Gangie pulled at a dingy tarp, revealing a large wooden cage. It was constructed much like the rat cages, but its sides were six feet tall and four feet wide.

"What kind of rat did you build that for?" Luca said.

"Not a rat," Mr. Gangie answered, tugging on the padlock. "A bear."

Luca looked over his shoulder. "There are bears down here, too?"

"Course there are no bears down here, boy. There's a drain at the bottom of the bear pit, you know."

"We've seen it," Frances muttered.

"One day, a great storm flooded the pit. As the water drained, bits of the stone washed away. One of the seven bears noticed the grate was loose and pried it up with his claws. Slid down here and couldn't find his way out."

"Did you catch him?" Luca said.

"Hunted him for days, even built this cage. But the city folk got to him first. Tried to tell them about my deal, that the bear was mine by rights. Said they didn't know about no deal. Said they didn't even know who I was. But I evened the score."

"You said seven," Luca said. "We only saw six bears in the pit."

Mr. Gangie smiled. "Said I evened the score."

Luca turned to Frances, a look of horror on his face. She motioned for him to stay calm.

"We'll help you put this cage to good use," she said. "We just need some bait."

Mr. Gangie whirled around. "You think you're going to use my rats as bait? That why you're here?"

Frances put up her hands. "We won't touch your rats. They're yours."

"Mine by rights," Mr. Gangie muttered.

"Exactly," Frances said. "Besides, we tried that already. I have a different idea."

"You do?" Luca said.

Frances smiled. "I think I've figured out what the monster's been looking for."

Back in the main chamber, Frances and Luca rooted through a pile of tools and gadgets, casting aside a silver shoehorn and a set of measuring cups in the shape of a hollowed-out apple. Frances found an old radio and turned the knobs to test it. It didn't work, so she tossed it, too.

Mr. Gangie looked on, chewing his fingernails. "Careful with that. It's not yours."

"What are we looking for, anyway?" Luca said. He examined a toaster, breathing on it and shining it with his sleeve before setting it back on the pile.

"Something with some charge left in it," Frances said. She pulled a heavy square block from the pile and held it up. A handle and two metal pegs were attached to the top. She smiled. "Something like this."

"What is it?"

"It's a battery, for an automobile." She climbed down from the pile to show Mr. Gangie. "Can we borrow this?"

The old man eyed her suspiciously. "What for?"

Frances set the battery down next to Hobbes's birdcage. "For our bait."

After scavenging around for tools, Frances pulled two wires from the base of Hobbes's neck and stripped the ends with a pair of pliers. She twisted a longer wire to each and wrapped them in leather straps cut from a butcher's apron. She took the other end of the wires and held them up, careful to keep them from touching.

"Think it'll work?" Luca said. He had offered to help Mr. Gangie set the trap out in the corridor, but the odd old man had refused. "Never needed nobody's help with a trap before," he had said. So, Luca sat on the floor next to Frances and asked her questions while she worked.

Frances touched the bare ends of the wires to the two metal knobs on the top of the battery, sending sparks flying.

"Look," Luca said, nodding at Hobbes.

Frances touched the wires to the battery again, and Hobbes's eyes began to glow. They went dark as soon as she pulled the wires away.

"I don't know how long he'll need to charge," Frances said. "We'll have to keep him connected to the battery. Get me some gloves. Leather, if you can find them." Luca scurried off, grateful for something to do. Frances rested her chin on her arms so her eyes were level with Hobbes's. "If this fries your circuits,

I'm sorry. Dad will fix you when he gets home. If he ever gets home."

Luca returned with the gloves. They were made of white leather—or had been until the sewer left them filthy and yellow. Ladies' riding gloves, from the look of them, but they would have to do. If her bare hands touched the battery while the wires were connected, that would be the end of her. Frances slipped them on, took a deep breath, and wrapped the wires around the knobs.

Hobbes's lights flickered on, and his eyelids opened and shut erratically. When he spoke, his voice started slowly and picked up speed until it reached its normal pitch.

"—there is a ladder that should take us to the surface."

"Hobbes!" Luca exclaimed.

Hobbes looked around, attempting to find his bearings. "Luca, Frances. What happened? Where are we?"

"It's a long story," Frances said. "Your battery ran out back in the tunnels. The sewerman found us and brought us here. He's helping us build a trap for the monster."

"It's kind of his thing," Luca added.

Hobbes looked up at Rat Mountain and the hundreds of cages. "What makes you think these rats will lure him any better than the feline?"

"Poor Bernadette . . . ," Luca said.

Frances shook her head. "Do you remember what the shop-keeper said? About the monster, what he took?"

"A propane lamp," Hobbes listed, "a coil of copper wire, a roll of tape."

"Back in the laboratory, when the wall was closing on him, the monster stopped it with his arm. When I saw him later in the alley, that same arm was just hanging at his side."

"Yes," Hobbes said. "I noticed that as well."

"What if the wall damaged something? A propane lamp, a coil of wire, a roll of tape . . ."

Hobbes's eyes glowed blue as he made the connection. "He's trying to repair himself," he said.

Frances nodded and placed Hobbes back into his birdcage. "But he won't be able to do it with a propane lamp."

"I agree. He'll need much more advanced components, components that match the conductivity and craftsmanship of Master Stenzel's. Though, I do not know where he'd find such technology down here."

"Exactly," Frances said. "And do you remember, back in the alley where we set the first trap? He'd already grabbed the rat that spooked Bernadette, but he dropped it when he saw us." She leaned forward so her eyes were level with Hobbes's. "When he saw you."

"That is logical. After all, I am the most advanced synthetic—" Hobbes's mouth clamped shut. He looked up at Frances, finally grasping her plan. "No. Absolutely not. I refuse."

"Hobbes—"

"First, you switch me off without my consent. Then you disassemble me, use my parts for scraps, lock me in this birdcage—which you did not even bother to clean properly—and now you would use me as bait? I refuse. And who is this?"

Frances and Luca looked up to find Mr. Gangie standing over them. "Talking lantern," he said. He shook his head. "Seen a lot of things since I been down here. Can't say I ever seen that."

"A talking lantern," Hobbes sputtered. "The humiliation continues!"

"This is Mr. Gangie," Frances said. "He's helping us."

The sewerman greeted him with an awkward bow. "Indeed I am. Trap's ready, soon as you are."

"We're ready," she said, ignoring Hobbes's glare.

"A little to the left," Luca called, gesturing with his hand.

Frances knelt in the center of a star-shaped room, where five branches of the sewer converged. Mr. Gangie had chosen the spot. According to the sewerman, every major line passed through this junction before feeding into the river downstream, making it the perfect pinch point for a trap. It also boasted ceilings high enough to hang the cage in shadow.

She scooted Hobbes a few centimeters across the muck. "How about now?"

Luca closed one eye and squinted in the torchlight. "Sorry, a little to right," he said, waving her back the other way. Frances sighed and repositioned the birdcage again. When it was just outside the perimeter of the larger cage meant for the monster, Luca put up his hands. "Stop! Perfect. Right there."

"That's exactly where I had him before!"

Hobbes looked on, unamused. "This is not a good plan," he said.

"I've heard that before," Frances replied.

"Yes, usually before something backfires spectacularly."

She set the battery next to his birdcage, threading its cables through the brass wires. After she finished, they extinguished their lanterns, leaving Hobbes's eyes the only source of light. The current was holding steady so far, though she noticed a few intermittent flickers.

"There is a ladder just down this corridor that leads to the surface," Hobbes said. "We can leave and come back when you are thinking clearly."

"No more talking," Frances said. "We don't know how long that battery will last."

She and Luca crouched together behind a turn in one of the corridors, out of sight. Luca held the end of the hose, ready to spring the trap. Frances pulled the wooden case from her pocket and took out the syringe. One more syringe, one more chance.

"Are you sure he's still down here?" Luca said.

"It'll be daylight on the surface. He's down here somewhere. Mr. Gangie will find him."

The sewerman had disappeared into the tunnels, leading a dozen rats on leashes through the muck. The leashes were Frances's idea. Mr. Gangie was reluctant to put his rats in danger, but this way he had some control over their fate, so he agreed. The sight of the old man leading his precious rats ahead of him was almost enough to make her laugh, if it hadn't been so revolting.

"Frances?" Luca said.

It was so dark that, even crouched next to him, she couldn't see him at all. "What is it?"

"We're friends, right?"

"Of course we're friends."

"Good. I wanted to make sure." He paused for a moment. "I know you didn't want me tagging along."

Frances smiled and bumped his shoulder with hers. "I'm glad you're here, Luca."

They were silent for a moment longer, together in the darkness, unable to see each other but grateful for the other's presence, until Luca spoke again.

"Frances?"

"What is it, Luca?"

"I don't want to die."

Frances looked out over Hobbes and the trap she'd helped design. "I don't want to die, either."

Hobbes's eyes flickered off and on again. "I cannot maintain this much longer," he said.

And then, a sound. The terrified squeaking of the rats echoed down the corridor, followed by footsteps. It was Mr. Gangie. He was running.

"Get ready," Frances whispered. Luca gripped the hose.

Hobbes must have heard them, too. His eye lights swept over the approaching rodents, igniting their beady eyes with a spectral glow, as if they were a pack of tiny ghosts. Mr. Gangie was behind them, his face a mixture of determination and fear. He rounded the corner and crouched behind Frances and Luca, wheezing.

"Big fella's on his way," he said.

At first, Frances could only hear the squeaking of the rats and the current of water. Then, footsteps—heavy footsteps that dragged and splashed and squelched in the muck. Hobbes looked at Frances, momentarily blinding her with his eye lights. She waved for him to turn away, and when he did, the darkness was filled with stars, like tiny supernovae bursting across her vision. She could hear the monster's animal grunts. He was getting closer.

"Now?" Luca whispered.

"Wait." Frances squeezed her eyes shut and opened them again, but the stars were still there, blocking her view. The grunting and shuffling grew louder. He must be close, but if she gave the signal too soon, and the cage dropped without the monster inside, they could all be eaten alive. There was a clanging sound, and Hobbes's lights shifted.

"Now, Frances," he shouted. "For God's sake, now!"

"Do it," she said, and Luca let go. She heard the whiz of the hose and the crash of the cage hitting the floor. The creature roared and shook the iron bars.

"Did we get him?" Luca said.

"We got him." Relief flooded through her, even as her heart continued to pound in her ear. It was finally over.

"Frances," Hobbes called.

She could hardly hear him over the monster. His voice was slowing again; his eyes strobed off and back on. The wires connecting him to the battery must have come loose when the cage fell.

"Save your charge," she said, but Hobbes was insistent.

"Look be . . . look be . . . look . . ."

His voice faded away before he could finish, and his lights flickered out.

"He was trying to say something," Luca said. "What was he saying?"

"If I'm not mistaken," Mr. Gangie answered, appearing over her shoulder, "he was saying, 'Look behind you.'"

Frances started to turn, then felt a sharp pain at the back of her head.

Then, nothing.

Chapter 28

A Collection of Cages

"**N**ow I know what Hobbes must feel like," Frances muttered.

She and Luca huddled together in a cage, shivering, their clothes damp from kneeling on the tunnel floor. They had awoken in one of the rooms off the main chamber. There were seven cages, each roughly the same size, and each containing the bones of whomever occupied them before Frances and Luca were added to the sewerman's collection.

"Everything down here is mine," he had said when they came to, a toothless smile stretched across his face. "I told you that. Can't say I didn't."

Now they could hear the monster through the iron door, snarling and pounding on the bars of his cage. Every few seconds, a terrible sound filled the corridors like a hive of angry bees, and the creature howled. He had sounded defiant at first, but each cry grew more desperate.

Luca winced. "What do you think he's doing to him?"

"I don't know," Frances replied.

"He looked so human," Luca said. "The monster, I mean. All this time I thought—I don't know what I thought. He was scary, like you said he'd be, just . . . not what I pictured."

Another howl echoed through the chamber, sending a pang of guilt through Frances's stomach. "We need to focus on getting out of here."

Luca stared at the bones in the other six cages. "They never got out."

"Don't think about them." She looked him in the eye. "We're not going to die down here."

"Okay," he said, taking a deep breath. "So, how do we escape?"

"I've gotten pretty good at picking locks. Fritz taught me." Frances hoped her friend was safe. The intelligence serum would have worn off completely by now. He might not remember where he was or why he was locked up. The pang of guilt became a throb. She shook her head. She needed to concentrate. "Help me find something to pick with."

Her hair pin had fallen out after her tumble into the bear pit. Luca searched his pockets. He pulled out the pocketknife, his whetstone, a ball of lint, and what remained of his peanut butter sandwich. "Can you use any of these?"

The blade of the pocketknife was too wide. As for the other items . . . "No."

Luca shrugged. He unwrapped the sandwich and took a bite. "Knew I was saving this for something," he said, bits of crust tumbling from his lips. He held it out to Frances, who politely declined.

Frances searched her own pockets, confirming what she already suspected: she had only one thing that could pick the lock. Her knapsack lay outside the cage, just within reach of her fingertips. She found the wooden case inside and opened it—the last syringe.

The needle was thin. It might get the job done, but she wouldn't be able to use the sedative on the monster after that. She'd have no way to stop him, no way to get him back to the Manor. She wished Hobbes were here. He could always tell when she was being rash.

He had tried to warn her before Mr. Gangie's betrayal, but of course she didn't listen. Now, he was just another piece in the sewerman's collection.

"Move over," Frances said, brushing her hair from her eyes. Luca slid himself to one side. The cage was clearly not meant for two people—even two children—leaving them with little room to maneuver. She reached through the bars and inserted the needle into the keyhole. She could feel the locking mechanism. There were two cylinders, which meant she'd somehow have to hold one in place while she released the other. She pulled the syringe back into the cage.

"Whetstone," she said, holding out her hand. Luca wiped his hand on his pants and placed the whetstone in her palm. She laid the syringe across the wooden case so the needle hung over the side and used the whetstone to snapped it in half.

"What'd you do that for?" Luca said, his mouth still full of peanut butter.

"I needed a second pick."

Frances took the syringe and the other half of the needle and reached through the bars once more. She used the syringe to hold back the first cylinder, then pushed the second into place using the needle. Something inside the padlock clicked.

"Did you get it?" Luca pressed his face against the bars for a better look.

"I think so." She set the syringe aside and was about to pull open the padlock when the door to the room swung open and in walked Mr. Gangie.

"Big fella's broken, just like you said." He pointed at Frances. "You know how to fix him?"

Frances looked at Luca, then back at Mr. Gangie. "I built him."

"Good." Mr. Gangie pulled the key ring from his pocket and

found a large skeleton key. When he turned it, nothing happened. He knelt down to examine the padlock. "Must've forgot to lock it," he said, yanking it open. "Getting old, I suppose." He pulled back the cage door and grabbed Frances by the collar of her shirt. She clawed at his fingers, which only made him yank harder. Luca scrambled on his hands and knees, but Mr. Gangie slammed the door shut before he could escape.

"Now, look here," he said, holding the key up to the bars. "You didn't think I'd forget twice?" He turned the key inside the padlock, giving it a rattle just to be sure.

"Frances," Luca cried. "What do I do?"

"Stay there," she called over her shoulder. "I'll get you out."

Mr. Gangie chuckled as he dragged her away. "Don't think so, girlie. What's mine stays mine, forever and ever."

Frances grit her teeth. "I will get Luca out. Right after I make sure you never trap another living thing, ever again."

"Down here, you'll do what I tell you to," he said. "And I say fix the big fella."

Then he pulled the iron door shut behind them, leaving Luca alone in the dark.

Frances winced as her eyes adjusted to the torchlight in the main chamber. Mr. Gangie had dragged the monster's cage to the base of Rat Mountain, far enough away to keep his precious rodents out of the creature's reach. The monster was slumped in the corner, head down, wild hair covering his face.

He appeared unconscious. The automobile battery sat nearby, its wires wrapped around a long metal pole.

Frances pulled free of Mr. Gangie's grip. "You were electrocuting him?"

He shrugged. "Figured it worked for your talking lantern."

"Hobbes is a machine! The monster is . . ." She struggled to find the right words. "He's alive. A living creature. You weren't fixing him; you were torturing him."

"I need him working," Mr. Gangie said. He walked over to one of the many piles of junk and sifted through the clutter. "He'll guard my chamber now, make sure nobody ever tries to steal from me again."

Frances examined the monster through the bars. A tangle of loose wires hung from his left arm, where the Manor wall had crushed it. Several wires had been reattached to the wrong circuits, probably by the monster himself in an attempt to repair the damage. So, she'd been right about that. The rest of the mechanical components appeared intact, except those near his back where the electric baton had charred metal and flesh alike. Those would have to be replaced entirely.

Seeing the creature broken and battered, an unexpected feeling rose within her: pity. Nothing deserved to be treated this way, no matter what it was or where it came from. Her mind went to the experiment that brought him to life, to the tentacled machine and the jolt of electricity that knocked out the power to the whole Manor. He couldn't feel that, could he? He was just a lifeless body then—until he wasn't.

The creature lifted his head. Frances startled but composed herself. She feared what Mr. Gangie would do if he knew the monster was awake. He looked at her, his eyes pleading behind thick strands of matted hair. A moan escaped his lips. He swallowed and opened his mouth again as if struggling to form a word. He was trying to speak. Frances leaned in closer.

"Help . . ." His speech was crude and inarticulate, but there was no mistaking it.

Frances looked over her shoulder. Mr. Gangie still rooted through the junk, looking for his tools. She turned back to the monster and met his eyes. After hesitating just a moment, she nodded.

She would need something heavy and blunt. Her eyes darted from pile to pile. There was a lead pipe near the door, but she would never reach it before Mr. Gangie noticed her. She spied a frying pan, a wooden peg that may once have been the rung of a ladder, and countless other potential weapons. Then she saw something gleaming in a pile only a few feet away: a candelabra made of solid gold.

Frances aimed her first strike at the back of Mr. Gangie's knee. The old man went down with a yelp, dropping his tools and clutching his leg.

"You wretched girl," he said, tears forming at the corners of his eyes. "You're mine. You hear me? I'll lock you in that cage so you never see daylight again."

Frances hit him again, in the shoulder this time. Mr. Gangie howled and rolled onto his side, curling himself into a ball. Frances reached down and plucked the key ring from his pocket.

"I don't belong to anyone," she said.

Frances ran to the monster's cage and tried one of the keys. It didn't work. She tried another, then another. She could hear Mr. Gangie moaning behind her. He wouldn't stay down for long. Another key. Another. Mr. Gangie struggled to his feet. The monster looked on, his face twisted in pain and worry. She heard a click and looked down at the padlock. The key turned. The door swung open.

"Come quickly," she said, urging him on. "We have to go."

The monster grabbed one of the bars with his good arm and struggled to his feet before collapsing with a whimper. Frances glanced over her shoulder. Mr. Gangie was standing now. She watched him take a limping step forward.

"Hurry," she said, turning back to the monster. "Please."

The monster rose again, and this time, he stayed upright. Frances called for him to follow, and he stumbled out of the cage, cradling his dead arm.

But he moved so slowly.

Behind her, Mr. Gangie reached the battery and twisted the knob, charging the baton with a hum. He stuck the monster in the ribs and he howled, swinging his good arm at Mr. Gangie, but the old man ducked and shocked him again.

Frances watched helplessly as Mr. Gangie shocked the monster over and over. Each time, he seemed to lose some of his will to fight back. She searched the chamber for something that would turn the tide in his favor, but she knew she would never get close enough to stop the sewerman while he wielded that baton. Then she looked up.

Rat Mountain.

She ran to the base of the pyramid and began to climb, stepping onto one cage and pulling herself up using another while the rats nipped at her fingertips. When she reached the top, she called out to Mr. Gangie, shouting above the hum of the baton. "Hey, sewerman!"

Mr. Gangie looked around until he noticed her standing above him. "What are you doing up there, you wretched girlie?"

"I was just wondering." She placed a finger on her chin. "All your precious rats. When's the last time you let them out to play?"

His eyes went wide as Frances pulled a cage from the pile and the pyramid shuddered and swayed.

"Put that back," he said. "You put it back!"

It was too late. The pyramid leaned, and cages began tumbling down the side, knocking others loose until the entire structure started to collapse. Frances held out her arms to steady herself as she balanced on the avalanche of wood and wire, leaping onto the roof of the monster's empty cage just as the smaller cages splintered against the floor.

For a moment, the chamber was quiet. Then rats poured from beneath the kindling in wave after wave of tails and teeth and claws.

Mr. Gangie gripped his baton, swinging wildly at the oncoming horde. He managed to zap a few of the rats, filling the chamber with the stench of burnt fur, but another wave swarmed over him and dragged him flailing to the ground.

Frances jumped down from the cage and ran to the monster. She kicked the rats off his back and pulled him to his feet. It was a strange feeling, standing eye to eye with the being she'd helped create, the creature she'd tracked throughout the city, the monster whom she'd feared.

"We have to go," she said.

The floor teemed. With every step, rats scurried from her feet like ripples in a flood. One latched on to her pant leg. She pulled the rodent off by the scruff of its neck and flung it aside.

When they reached the door, Frances turned back. "Wait for me outside."

The monster cried out, cradling his arm.

"I have to save my friends," she said, and ran back into the chamber.

Frances found the candelabra and pried open the door to the room where Luca was imprisoned.

"What's going on out there?" Luca said. Then he saw the rats. They tumbled in through the doorway, climbing over each other in a frenzied rush. He scrambled to the back of his cage. "Frances? Frances, please!"

"Stay clear," she said. She brought the candelabra down on the padlock. It didn't break. She struck it again without success.

"You can do it," Luca said. "You're the strongest girl I know."

"I'm the only girl you know." She brought the candelabra down once more, and the lock broke free.

Frances led Luca through the doorway and into the main chamber. Rats were everywhere. The ones who had escaped when the pyramid fell had chewed the others free, so they lined the floor three deep.

"Where's Mr. Gangie?" Luca shouted above the din.

"There." She pointed to a mound of rats, undulating madly. Luca gulped.

They climbed the nearest pile of junk. The rats were fewer up there, and they could leap from pile to pile toward the exit. On the last pile, Frances's foot caught on something. A birdcage.

"Hobbes," she cried. His battery was still dead, but he otherwise looked to be in one piece. "I thought I'd lost you."

When they reached the corridor, the monster was gone. Frances ran her hand along the wall. Her fingers came back slick with blood. "He's headed for the surface."

"That's bad, right?" Luca said.

"Before his battery died, Hobbes said there's a ladder just down the corridor and to the right. We need to find the monster before someone else sees him. It won't be safe for him up there."

Luca took the birdcage. "You go ahead," he said. "There's something I need to do first."

Chapter 29

City of Monsters

F rances grabbed the rungs of the ladder and pulled her hands back warm and slick. More blood. Above her, the manhole cover was off-kilter, leaving a curved sliver of light, like the corona of an eclipse. Her stomach tightened—daylight meant people on the streets.

Fresh snow blanketed the cobblestones on the surface. The cold snap had finally come. Frances gazed up at the swirling flurries, snowflakes alighting on her eyelashes. The last time she felt the snow on her face, she was four years old. . . .

A child's scream punched through the air, muffled and faraway-sounding in the snow. Frances turned as two boys ran past her and huddled at the back of the alley. She hurried to her feet.

"Did you see him?" she asked. The chilled air bit her lungs as she breathed. "Is he chasing you?"

"There," one of the boys cried. He pointed over Frances's shoulder.

A lumbering figure crept into the alley, its form shrouded in snow. Somewhere, a bell tinkled.

"Wait," Frances said, holding up her hand. "You don't have to hurt them. I can still help you!"

The figure continued advancing until it emerged from the snow in a cloud of swirling eddies.

Frances took a step back. The monster had changed. His nose had grown wider, his skin orange. Horns protruded from a mane of scraggly white hair that fell to his waist. He wore a thick gray pelt and goatskin trousers. A bell hung from his belt.

Before Frances could process what she was seeing, another figure appeared. This one was shorter and fatter, with laughing yellow eyes. A grin stretched between two ears pointed like a jackrabbit's. A bell hung from its belt, too.

Frances planted herself between the two figures and the boys. She didn't know who or what they were, but she wouldn't let them hurt the children.

The monsters roared and charged. Frances reached for the fatter one's pelt but slipped and fell onto her back. They were on the boys in an instant, grabbing them with their claws.

"No," she cried.

The boys shrieked and threw something onto the ground, sending the monsters scurrying after them. Coins. One rolled within Frances's reach, and she plucked it from the snow.

"Hey, that's mine," one of the monsters growled, snatching it from her fingers.

"Come on," the other said. They ran into the street. The boys regarded the cold, wet girl on the cobblestones and ran after them, laughing.

Frances struggled to her feet, slipping once more before righting herself. She peered around the mouth of the alley and couldn't believe what she saw.

The streets were filled with monsters.

Hulking creatures with horns and fangs, some with skeletal faces and huge, sunken eyes. Others had coarse beards and bushy eyebrows. They roamed in packs, chasing children house to house.

"What is going on?" Frances said.

"Tschäggättä," answered a voice behind her.

Frances whirled around and found herself face-to-face with another monster. This one had a long nose and a ridiculous grin. Its head was massive, with a red face and black lips.

"Luca?"

Luca removed his mask. His head looked puny atop the thick pelts draped from his shoulders.

"Sorry, Francie. Didn't mean to scare you."

"You didn't scare me." Frances punched his shoulder. "And don't call me Francie!" She turned back to the street. "What's happening out there?"

"It's the first day of the Tschäggättä festival. Remember? Everyone who's not dressed like one of these is getting chased around until they give up a franc or two, or some hot tea if it's a shop." He held up his mask. "This is what I wanted to get so we can walk around without the constable seeing us. I found it in the sewerman's collection. It's not as nice as mine, and it doesn't smell very good, but it's big enough for both of us underneath."

Frances wasn't thrilled at the prospect of being stuck with Luca inside a giant wooden mask but with all the people in the streets, Constable Montavon was sure to be nearby.

"How will we find the creature now?" Frances said.

"Easy. He's the only monster who isn't wearing a mask."

From the outside, Frances and Luca looked like any other Tschäggättä monster. A little short, perhaps, and the birdcage did give them a bit of a potbelly, but so long as no one counted the number of feet beneath their goatskin pelts, they could move about the city without detection.

After a little practice.

"Stop stepping on my toes."

"You're stepping on *my* toes!"

"Shh—look!"

Frances raised her left arm (the other was pinned beneath the costume) and pointed up ahead. One of the constable's deputies patrolled the street, slapping his billy club against the palm of his hand and sneering at the festivities. The second deputy appeared a moment later. They exchanged a few words, then stopped and looked right at them.

"We shouldn't have been staring," Frances whispered.

"They can't know it's us, can they?"

"Let's not stay and find out."

With some effort, Frances and Luca turned themselves around and hurried between the rows of buildings. At the mouth of the alley, Frances stopped abruptly, and they both nearly fell.

Men, women, and children danced down the street to the tune of accordions, snare drums, and trombones. Many wore goatskins and wooden masks; others hawked food and trinkets. She had never seen so many people.

"Footsteps behind us," Luca said.

They turned the mask. The deputies were following them.

"These guys really never give up."

"We can hide in the parade," Frances said.

"But all those people . . . will you be okay?"

"We don't have a choice."

Luca squeezed her fingers under the costume.

They stepped off the curb, and the crowd whisked them forward. Frances thought of the river, how it didn't matter how hard she kicked, how it pulled her under and stole the breath from her lungs. She gasped.

"It's okay," Luca said. "I'm right here with you. Stay under the mask, and you'll be fine."

They pushed through the throngs, using the mask to wedge between bodies until they hit something solid. It was the back of a float, a replica of the wilderness where the city of Bern now stood. Actors dressed as Duke Berthold and the great bear battled with wooden spears.

"We're trapped," Luca said.

Frances pictured the deputies wading through the crowd in their wake, shoving families and vendors aside to reach them. She scanned the parade, searching for a way out.

That's when she saw him, through one of the eye holes, at the edge of her vision. The monster—her monster—was stumbling along with the parade, a tangle of pain, confusion, and fear on his face.

Without thinking, Frances ducked beneath the mask and out from under the pelts.

"Wait," Luca cried. "They'll see you!"

She climbed aboard the float and darted between papier-mâché trees, sliding on her knees as the Duke and the bear crossed spears over her head. She cupped her hands over her mouth and called to the monster.

He turned, searching for the source of her voice. Their eyes found each other just as another voice boomed over the crowd.

"Stop!" Constable Montavon stood at the edge of the street, his eyes fixed on Frances. He waved to his deputies. "Grab her, you fools!"

Frances leaped from the float and waded toward the monster, hips and hands and knees knocking her this way and that. With each step, the crowd seemed to constrict around her. She called for Luca, but her voice was swallowed up. Someone shoved her from behind, and she fell to her knees. A foot came down hard on her back. She hit the cobblestones and tried to crawl, but her shoulder was pinned, then her leg. A boot came down on her injured ankle, and she screamed.

A woman her mother's age reached out to pull her to her feet, but the parade's current carried her away and the crowd closed over Frances again. Bodies blotted out the sky. Her vision faded. She was certain she was dying, and though she was afraid, she had the strangest feeling she'd been here once before.

A familiar voice surfaced through the ringing in her ear. It was Luca, trying to clear the people away while they ignored him because he was just a filthy kid who smelled of sewage. She decided to give into the fading world and fade away with it. There was something peaceful about it. Like crawling under the covers of her bed and feeling the fabric and smelling the smells that reminded her of rest and sleep and dreams.

The last thing she saw was the sky as the bodies suddenly cleared away. An arm wrapped around her waist, and a hand gripped her side. Not Luca's hand; it was much too large. The sky was darkened again by the silhouette of a figure with a broad face and wild hair, and Frances felt herself being lifted off the ground and carried away until she could no longer hear Luca calling her name.

Chapter 30

Grimme

When the world came back into focus, the cobblestones were gone, replaced by snowy hills and red flowers tipped with white. Frances blinked and looked around. To her left was a row of rosebushes, and beyond that a small copse of trees. To her right—

—she crawled backward on her hands and feet; her breath caught in her throat.

The monster made no move to follow. He looked up at her, then closed his eyes. His breathing was shallow and labored. He was in pain, she realized. The sewerman must have injured him worse than she thought.

Frances hesitated. The monster had plenty of opportunities to hurt her—in Mr. Gangie's chambers, on the street back in the city, even while she lay unconscious here in the snow. She stood, slowly, not wanting to startle him, and took a tentative step forward. The creature's eyes opened, and he gripped the grass with both hands. *He's afraid of me.*

"It's okay." She knelt down beside him, where she could hear his heart pounding in his barrel chest. It felt so strange to feel fear coming from something so strong and terrible. She reached her hand up and pulled back her hair, revealing her scar.

The monster studied the scar, then her eyes. He raised his hand but quickly pulled it back again.

"Go ahead," she said, leaning closer.

He reached up and traced the line of rough, marred skin that ran from just behind her temple to the base of her neck. When he finished, he propped himself up against the hillside and brushed aside his hair, just as she had done. Then he took her hand in his and pressed her fingers to his own scars.

Frances smiled. But when she reached for his damaged arm, the monster recoiled.

"I can fix it," she said. "I can help."

"Help . . ." Weak as he was, his voice still sounded volatile; combustible, like a distant thunderstorm, or a locomotive.

Frances nodded her head. "Yes, help. But I need to get you to the laboratory. Will you come back with me?"

All the time she'd spent tracking the creature, poring over

her great-grandfather's journal, devising plans, setting traps, and here she was, less than a kilometer from the Manor, asking him to return with her.

The monster hesitated, searching her eyes.

He nodded.

"Okay," Frances said, exhaling. She stood up and took his hand, helping him to his feet. "But we'll have to find you a name. We can't keep calling you 'the monster.'" Frances thought for a moment. "How about we name you after your creator?"

The monster gave her a puzzled look.

"No, not me. Albrecht Grimme." She crinkled her nose. "Not Albrecht, though. How about 'Al'?"

"Al . . . ?"

Frances laughed. "Okay, what about 'Grimme'?"

The monster smiled. He pointed to his chest. "Grimme."

"Grimme it is, then," she said, and then she was smiling, too.

When she looked back at the city, its towers and archways ghostly and indistinct through the haze, her smile faltered. Luca was still down there, somewhere, and Fritz. And poor Hobbes. *If anything happens to them . . .*

She took a deep breath. They would be okay. They had to be. Luca would escape and she would find him, and they would deal with the constable together. But first, there was something she had to make right. "Come on, Grimme. Let's get you home."

● ● ●

The clouds had begun to clear and the sun was high overhead by the time Frances and Grimme crested the hills above the rose garden. The gray shingled spires came into view first, followed by the arch of her bedroom window, and the boxwood dragon, draped in snow.

She was home.

A black automobile was parked in front of the Manor, its doors ajar, as if someone had left in a hurry. The Manor's front door hung open, as well. Frances's mind raced. Had someone found out about what she'd done? Had the constable called the government authorities?

Then she saw the suitcases. Joy and relief and a terrible anticipation bubbled up in her chest and caused tears to well up in her eyes. Her parents were okay. They were home.

They were going to kill her.

"Just a little farther," Frances said. The walk had been long, and Grimme had grown heavy on her arm. He had begun to slow half a kilometer back, his limp deepening. His breathing was labored and hoarse. He managed a few more steps before his eyes rolled back in his head, and he slipped, collapsing onto the drive.

"Grimme!" Frances knelt over him, putting a hand on the leathery skin of his cheek. "Hold on. I'm going to get help."

She ran past the black automobile and bounded up the front

steps, ignoring the pain in her legs and neck. When she reached the door, she almost collided with her mother and father as they rushed out to meet her.

"Frances!" Victor and Mary threw their arms around their daughter, nearly crushing her in their relief.

"You had us so worried," Victor said. "We saw the lab and we . . . we feared the worst."

"What is that smell?" said Mr. Byron, joining them on the porch. His driver, Braun, followed close behind.

"I'll explain everything," Frances said, wriggling free of her parents' embrace, "but first I need your help."

Frances led them to Grimme. They each took a step back when they saw him. Victor gasped. Even Braun flinched.

Mary put a hand to her mouth. "Oh my God," she whispered.

"Is this—" Victor said. "Did you— But how—"

"Yes, yes, and it's a long story," Frances said.

Victor looked from her to Grimme and back again, his tongue useless.

"Don't just stand there," she said. She pushed past them and fell to her knees beside Grimme. "Help him."

Mary knelt beside Grimme and pressed two fingers to his neck. "His pulse is irregular."

"Everything about him is irregular," Mr. Byron said.

Grimme let out a groan, and Frances told the adults to back

up—she didn't want him to feel threatened when he came to. It looked like he was going to try to sit, but he collapsed and let his head loll to one side.

"Positively remarkable," Mr. Byron said. He stood over the body, rubbing his hands together. "More so than I ever imagined."

Victor held up one of Grimme's arms. He ran his fingers across a braid of wires that led from his shoulder to his elbow. "Ingenious. The nervous system was the problem we could never solve. Grandfather nearly went mad trying to figure out how to get signals to travel through the body." He smiled and shook his head. "We never considered a mechanical solution."

His expression turned from one of nostalgia and pride to something darker as a realization dawned across his face. "Frances, where did you get these components?"

She hesitated. "I had some help from Hobbes."

"I didn't program him to . . . Wait." He narrowed his eyes. "Where is Hobbes now?"

"He's fine. Mostly. He will be fine. Look, I'll explain everything after we get Grimme to the lab. I think he's dying."

Mary nodded in agreement. "I'm afraid she's right. He's badly damaged."

Victor took Grimme by the ankles while Braun lifted him by the arms. They only managed to drag him a short distance before setting him down next to the automobile to rest. Even

Braun seemed to strain under his weight.

"A creature of his size and strength," Mr. Byron mused, as much to himself as anyone. "What could have done this to him?"

"I can only take credit for the broken arm," Frances said.

Mr. Byron smiled. "Aren't you full of surprises, child."

Frances paused, lifting her head. She could swear she heard someone calling her name. There it was again.

"Frances!"

She looked through the snow to find Luca huffing and puffing up the hill, dragging the birdcage at his side and waving his arm in the air.

"Who is that?" Mary said. "And what does he have in that birdcage?"

Frances ignored them and ran to meet Luca. She pulled his arm around her shoulder to help him up the drive. When they reached the others, he sat down, panting and clutching his chest. "Hi," he said, holding out a hand to Victor. "I'm Luca. Luca Frick."

"Victor Stenzel," Frances's father said, shaking the boy's hand. He turned to Frances. "Who is this?"

"He's . . ." Frances found she didn't know what to call him. After all they had gone through together, nothing seemed to fit. "He's my best friend," she said at last.

Mary and Victor looked at each other in surprise. "A friend,"

Mary said. She glided to Luca's side, taking his hand in both of hers. "It is very nice to meet you, Luca."

Luca stared at Mary as if he had never seen a woman so beautiful until Frances elbowed him under his ribs.

"Frances," Victor said. He picked up the birdcage. "Why is the disembodied head of my greatest technological achievement locked inside a filthy cage?"

"I can explain—" she began.

Luca shook his head. "There's no time. You have to go."

"Go? Go where?"

"Anywhere," he replied. There was fear in his eyes. "Frances, he's coming."

"Who's coming?" asked Mary.

"The constable. And he's bringing the whole city with him."

Chapter 31

Pitchforks and Torches

Frances once read a book by a famous explorer. He described being alone at the edge of the Sahara and feeling the ground rumble under his feet. When he looked toward the horizon, a cloud appeared in the distance. Dust. Moments later, dozens of elephants bore down on him, passing on either side as he struggled to keep his footing on the quaking earth.

That was the image that came to mind when she saw them—hundreds of people, row after row, marching ten abreast and spilling over the edges of the street. As they got closer, she recognized the baker who kicked her off his front stoop, Helga the shopkeeper and her attaché of men. Most of them she'd never seen before, carrying rakes and pitchforks and brooms as if they were swords and spears. A few still wore their Tschäggättä masks. To Frances, their sneering mouths and bulbous, fiendish eyes were only an exaggeration of the faces that marched beside them; reflections in a broken mirror. Constable Montavon and his deputies led the way, billy clubs at the ready, pistols strapped to their hips.

As the constable approached, Victor and Mary pulled Frances between them, placing their hands on her shoulders. Behind them, Grimme groaned and struggled to sit up against the door of the automobile.

"Stay there," Frances whispered.

The constable raised his arm, and the mob fell silent. A woman peeked out from behind him, looking more scared than outraged. Ms. Frick. Frances still couldn't believe that woman was Luca's mother.

"You've reached the end of the road, Frances," Montavon said. He gestured to the Manor behind her and the mob blocking the drive. "There is nowhere left to run."

"What is the meaning of this?" Victor said, taking a step toward the constable.

"You must be the parents." He tipped his hat at Mary. "Ma'am. Tell me, while you were sitting in your house on the hill, high above the rest of us, did you wonder what your daughter might be doing? What trouble she might be causing among the common folk?"

Mary looked down at her daughter. "What is he talking about, Frances?"

"You've been out to get me since the moment we met," Frances cried, pointing at the constable. She turned to the crowd. "I was trying to protect you."

Shouting erupted from the mob before the constable lifted his arm to quiet them again.

"The girl says she was trying to protect us. Were you trying to protect us when you brought that abomination down upon our city?"

"I didn't mean for any of this—"

"Enough," bellowed Montavon. "Enough of your excuses. Your lies. I have the truth." He reached behind his back and held up her great-grandfather's journal.

"Oh my God . . . ," Victor whispered. Beyond them, a spark appeared in Mr. Byron's eyes. He turned to his driver, who nodded.

"In this book, I have seen things that would haunt your dreams. It is filled with strange symbols, demonic writing, and ideas that only the most twisted of minds could conjure. Ideas that defy the very laws of nature. With this book, these . . . *heretics* would take life and death into their own hands. You've all read that other book, the Good Book." The crowd murmured in agreement. "It says one day the righteous who have died will be raised again. Tell me"—he pointed to the monster—"where does it say we come back like that?"

The mob surged, shouting curses and waving their makeshift weapons in the air. They began to chant, "Kill it! Kill it! Kill the monster!"

"It doesn't matter who you are or what family you come from," Montavon went on. "No one can escape justice. Hand over the monster."

"No," Frances said, squaring her shoulders.

"Frances—" Mary began.

But she had already made up her mind. "I *said* no."

Montavon laughed. "You misunderstand me." He gestured to the mob seething behind him. "I am not giving you a choice, girl."

Frances ignored him, taking a step forward and addressing the crowd instead. "Grimme didn't ask to be the way he is. You look at him and see a monster. That's what I saw, too, at first. I was going to kill him. But the longer I chased him, the more I realized there was more to him than I first thought. He had every opportunity to hurt people, but he never did, not even when they hurt him. He hid from us, not to lie in wait, but because he was afraid of us and what we would think if we saw him. He was alone, injured, with no idea what to do. He was just trying to survive. How is that any different from any of us?"

The crowd fell quiet. A few hushed voices spoke, then a few more. Soon they were all speaking at once, mulling over Frances's words.

"What happens," Montavon said, shouting over them, "when survival is no longer good enough? What happens when that thing decides it no longer fears us? What then?" He had regained the mob's attention, and he was reveling in it. "Are you willing to take that risk? Because I am not." He turned to his deputies. "Arrest the abomination."

The deputies advanced on the monster, clubs out. They tread cautiously, their faces slick with sweat, even in the cold. Frances could see their hands shaking.

Grimme grabbed the door handle and pulled himself up with a grunt. The deputies planted their feet, trading nervous glances.

"Stay there, Grimme," Frances said.

This time, he didn't listen. He took a step forward, swaying with the effort. Then he took another, steadier this time, stronger. He curled his lip and snarled at the deputies.

"Don't," Frances cried. "They'll hurt you."

The deputies hesitated, but the constable urged them on. "Take him," he barked.

One of them rushed Grimme and pinned his injured arm to his side, while the other clubbed the back of his knee. Grimme howled in pain, grabbing the officer by the neck before he could land a second blow. He might have been a rag doll the way he tumbled through the air. He hit the crowd sideways, taking out six or seven people on his way down.

Grimme hooked an arm around the second deputy's waist as he tried to flee. Then, ignoring Frances's pleas for him to stop, he lifted him high over his head and threw him to the ground. Standing over the cowering officer, Grimme tilted back his head and roared. It was a terrible sound, filling the air and rolling down the hillside like thunder. Until it was silenced by a sound even louder and more terrible.

Grimme staggered back, looking around for the source of the blow. Montavon stood with his pistol raised, a tendril of smoke rising from the barrel. He fired again, and Grimme doubled over.

"No," Frances cried. She broke free of her parents' grasp and ran between Grimme and the constable, putting up her hand. "Stop!"

Frances felt the bullet enter her chest before she even heard the blast.

Her ear rang with the sound of it. Her mother screamed, somewhere, but her voice was swallowed in the crowd's panic. A moment ago, they were a single organism acting with a common mind and a common fear. Now that organism split into hundreds, running in every direction at once. Frances watched them drop away, then the tops of the trees, and finally the sky as the back of her head hit the cobblestones.

Victor and Mary rushed to their daughter's side and gathered her in their arms. Luca, too, though he wouldn't get close for fear of hurting her.

"It'll be okay, Frankie" Victor said, brushing her hair from her eyes. He forced himself to smile. "Just hang in there. We'll get you all patched up."

Mary turned to the constable with fury in her eyes. "What have you done?"

Montavon held his pistol out in front of him like he had never seen it before. "I'm sorry," he said. "She shouldn't have . . . Why would she defend such a creature?"

The taller deputy picked himself up off the ground and backed away, his mouth twisted in shock. He helped the other officer to his feet without a word. Neither took their eyes off Constable Montavon.

"She wasn't supposed to be there," he said.

Mr. Byron cleared his throat and addressed the constable. "I believe it's time for you to leave."

At a nod from his employer, Braun took a step forward, arms folded behind his back.

Montavon didn't seem to notice either of them. He could only stare at Frances and the red stain spreading beneath her in the snow. Finally, his deputies took him by his arms and led him away. "It had to be stopped," Frances heard him say as they disappeared over the hill.

She drifted off for a moment. When she came back, her father and Mr. Byron were arguing.

". . . This is about the well-being of the subject," Mr. Byron was saying. "The well-being of everyone. The potential is simply too great to—"

"My daughter's well-being is my only concern at the moment," Victor snapped. "If you can't stop thinking about money for long enough to . . ."

Frances closed her eyes and let her head fall to the side. When she opened them again, Grimme was there, lying next to her. His breathing was labored. Tears gathered at the corners of his eyes. He was watching her.

"Looks like we're both pretty banged up," she said. It hurt to speak, but everything hurt, so she spoke anyway.

"Frances," he said. His voice was hoarse and thick. "Frances help."

She smiled. "We helped each other."

Grimme's breathing slowed further, and his eyes rolled back in his head. Frances reached out to him, but he was too far away.

"Someone help him," she said. Her voice came out thin and frail. "He's dying."

Mary and Victor looked at one another, unsure what to do. Neither wanted to leave their daughter's side.

"Help him," she shouted, wincing with the effort. Mary let Frances go and crawled to Grimme. She examined his eyes, then checked his pulse and put her ear to his chest. She didn't have to say anything; Frances could see it in her eyes. Grimme was gone.

"No," she cried. "Bring him back." She looked up at her father. "You have to bring him back. I can show you how." Victor tried to calm her, but she shook her head and found Luca on his knees a few feet away. "Luca, tell them." But he was crying too hard to speak.

"We can bring him back," she said.

And then she died.

Chapter 32
The Girl in the Snow

Frances bounced in the back seat of an automobile, watching the lamps and storefronts flick by like pictures on a screen as the wind whipped in through a crack in the window and tousled her hair. There was a loose spring that poked her through the leather seats. She looked down to find it.

Her mother gasped, and the brakes squealed. She looked up as her body rose into the air. As she flew, she realized she wasn't a child anymore, that the twinkling glass was gone. It had been gone for years. She braced herself for what came next, what always came next. She raised her arm to shield her eyes, but the light passed right through it. Someone called her name.

"Frances."

She sat up with a start, gasping and blinking under the light.

"It's okay, Frances. You're home." It was her father. His shirt was wrinkled, and his appearance even more disheveled than usual.

"The constable—"

Victor stroked her hair. "He's gone. You have nothing to fear."

She was in her own room, lying in her bed. A heavy blanket was pulled up under her arms, but she couldn't stop shivering. A tube ran from her wrist up to a bag of clear fluid hanging from a pole. How did she get here? The last thing she remembered was the constable pointing his pistol at Grimme. . . .

"Where's Grimme?" She asked. "Is he okay?"

"I'm sorry, Frankie. He's gone. The mechanical enhancements were a stroke of genius, but it was only a temporary solution. His body was too degraded. The injuries he sustained—from the constable, and it looked like he was electrocuted at some point?—it was all too much." Victor bit his lip and breathed in through his nose. "The procedure never seemed to take as well with him as . . . well, as—"

"As it did for me," Frances said.

Victor blinked. "Frances, you—"

"It's okay," she said. "I think I figured it out a while ago. I just wasn't ready to admit it. But the accident . . ." She looked up at her father. "There are still things I don't understand about that night."

Victor was quiet for a long time. Frances listened to the wind whistling against the window and the steady drip of her IV.

"I'm afraid it's a rather long story," he said finally.

"I'm not going anywhere."

Victor smiled. "True enough." He took a deep breath and let it out slowly.

Then he began.

"The year was 1929. We had lived in the Manor for about eleven months by then. I don't know if I've ever told you this, but I didn't want to come back here. Too many ghosts. Too many memories."

"Of your grandfather?"

Victor nodded. "It was your mother's idea. She insisted, truth be told. You know how she can be. Our work had out-grown the university and we needed a lab of our own. We moved in, updated the lab with new instruments, and that was that.

"It was everything we could have needed. But it was such a big house. So many empty rooms. We decided to start a family. We tried and tried. For three years. It just wasn't to be."

Frances opened her mouth to speak, but Victor held up a hand. "We were heartbroken. I wanted to keep trying, but the disappointment was too much for your mother. I think she blamed herself. Either way, we gave up. As our hope faded, the ghosts returned. I began taking long walks in the city just to get away.

"I was setting out on one such walk when it started to snow. Mary begged me to stay, but it was only a light flurry. By the time I reached the city, I couldn't see the tip of my nose. I found shelter under an arcade and decided to wait it out.

"I heard a crash, then another . . . the sound of breaking glass. I pulled my scarf up around my face and went to investigate. A car was stalled in the middle of the road, its fender torn off and the door on one side crushed. Two men were leaning in through the window, helping pull the driver free. I wondered what he could have hit.

"Then I saw the other car. It had rolled before coming to a stop on its side. The roof was mangled, the windshield blown out. Damaged almost beyond recognition.

"I was the first to reach it. I peered in through the window and found the driver and his passenger—his wife, I imagine. They were dead. Probably on impact."

Victor's eyes misted over.

"I almost didn't see her. She was so small. The smallest thing I'd ever seen." He smiled. "She was breathing. Her injuries were severe, but she was alive. I kicked open the door and pulled her out as carefully as I could. I wrapped my coat around her and held her. What else could I do?

"She woke up. Just for a moment. I wiped the blood from

her face with my scarf, and she looked up at me. When our eyes met, I . . ."

Victor sniffed. He was crying. Frances wiped tears from her own eyes.

"She called me 'Papa.' She said, 'My tummy hurts, Papa.'" He held up his hands. "What could I do? So, I told her not to worry, that I was here, that everything would be okay. She died a few minutes later.

"People were starting to gather, but no one noticed us through the snow. I held her, this child who died in my arms. I couldn't let her go. We had a moment together. Just a moment. But already, I loved her. More than anything else I'd ever known.

"I carried her back to the Manor. Two kilometers against the wind. By the time we reached the front door, her skin was cold and blue."

Frances's shoulders shook with sobs. Victor put his hand on hers and squeezed.

"Mary was reading by the fireplace. When I burst inside, the wind snuffed the flame right out. I couldn't explain what I'd done. I hadn't thought any of it through. All I knew was that if I could just get the girl to the laboratory, I could help her—I had seen it happen once before.

"Poor Mary. She thought I'd gone mad. I never talked

about my time with my grandfather. Not even to her. When we reached Albrecht's old lab and passed beyond the false wall, I could see her working it out in that brilliant mind of hers. Nothing gets past her, as you know." He thought for a moment. "It was one of the few times I've ever seen her afraid.

"I found his journal—the one the constable took from you—but I didn't need it. Every step of the procedure, every compound, every instrument; it all came back like it was yesterday. Of all the memories that haunted me in this place, the day your great-grandfather and I performed that procedure was the most terrible.

"Yet, out of that memory came the first day of your new life. Your life with us. We found no record of kin beyond the couple who perished in the accident—your parents."

Your parents. The words sounded unnatural, formed by unwilling lips.

"For months, our hearts stopped at every knock at the door, every ring of the telephone, knowing—fearing—it might be a distant aunt, calling to take you away. Over time, the fear subsided. You had become our daughter, and that would forever be true."

Frances was silent for several minutes. Victor waited patiently, holding her hand and giving her the time she needed. She tried to process what her father had said. No, not her father. Her father died in a car crash seven years ago. Along with her mother and . . .

"All this time," she said. "I've been like—like him."

"The procedures were similar, yes. It never really took with him, with Grimme, as you called him. I suspect that, even if the constable hadn't killed him, he wouldn't have lasted much longer. I'm not sure what makes you different, but you are."

Frances thought about Grimme's injured arm, the sewerman's electrified baton, and how weak he had looked when they sat together in the garden. "He was trying to repair himself."

Victor raised his eyebrows. "Really? Fascinating."

"People all over the world die every day," she said, fighting back tears. "How is it fair that I should get so many chances when everyone else gets only one?"

"My sweet girl," Victor said. "If I could bottle the procedure and send it to every corner of the earth, I would. I'm sure Mr. Byron would be pleased to charge for it. But every other subject we tested failed. Apart from you, Grimme was the most successful, thanks to the components you took from Hobbes. You were the only one who thrived. Even then, we had to be careful."

"That's why you never let me leave the house."

Victor nodded. "We couldn't bear to lose you." He smiled. "Perhaps you've proven us overly cautious."

"I released a monster into the city, then got us both killed." She laughed, but it came out broken. She sniffed and dried her cheeks.

Victor looked down at her. "You connected with him, didn't you?"

Frances nodded, tears returning to her eyes.

"I'm very sorry he's gone, Frances."

"Me too."

Chapter 33

Everything You Could Ever Need

Frances's recovery surprised even her father. After a week of monitoring, he declared her fit to rejoin the family. Instead, she shut herself in her great-grandfather's workshop.

She spent her time transcribing the journal from memory. It had disappeared after the incident with the constable. Mr. Byron said he would look into everyone who might have an interest in Albrecht Grimme's work—a long list, he said—but so far, no one had been able to tell him anything.

Reproducing her great-grandfather's notes was painstaking work. The pages were seared into her mind—she suspected she had the intelligence serum to thank for that—but much of what she could recall was still a mystery. She was searching for clues that might tell her something, anything, about what she'd become. She pored over every diagram and decoded every word. When she'd cataloged all she could remember, she started again.

Her only companion was Fritz, who had been released once Constable Montavon failed to report to the station after the events at the Manor. Her parents wanted to put the chimpanzee back in his cage, but Frances wouldn't have it. Not after what he had done for her.

To Frances's great surprise and joy, many of the missing animals were discovered during the cleanup of the Manor, having fled the Zoo the night Grimme first awoke. Lourdes and Shelley were found burrowed in the laundry hamper. The yellow-crested cockatoo roosted in the Great Room (her birdcage having been occupied). The snake turned up later that week, when he was found coiled around the showerhead by a very wet, very unamused Mary Stenzel.

Despite her mother's displeasure with the improprietous reptile, Frances managed to convince her and her father to cease all experimentation on animals. Fritz volunteered to act as their caretaker. All agreed he was the perfect choice.

Days later, there was a knock at the workshop door. When Frances didn't respond, the door opened and Hobbes stuck his head inside. His head, which was once again attached to the rest of his body. The damage to his systems had been so extensive that Victor was forced to reboot him. When he came back online, many of his memories were missing or corrupt, effectively deleting their adventures from his mind. As a result, he was back to his rigid, overbearing self.

"He may recover some of those memories with time," Victor had said. "Have patience."

She said she'd try but found herself avoiding him anyway. It was too painful—her memories were still there, even if his weren't.

Hobbes stepped into the lab. He regarded the trays of uneaten food stacked near the door and frowned. "You have to eat," he said.

"Do I?" Frances replied. "I've been thinking about it. Do I need food? Have I ever?"

"At this rate," Hobbes said, "it appears we shall soon find out. In the meantime, you have a visitor."

Frances turned back to her work. "I'm not in the mood."

"I can come back later . . . ," called a soft voice from the hall.

Frances spun on her stool to find Luca peeking nervously around the door.

"No," she said. "Come in. I thought it was— I didn't know it was you."

"Do you require anything further from me?" Hobbes said.

"Um, no. Thanks," she replied, and he marched out of the room, closing the door behind him.

"He looks taller," Luca said.

Frances laughed. She wondered if it was the first time she'd laughed since returning home.

"Sorry I didn't visit sooner. My mum wasn't too happy with me. Says you're a dangerous influence. She doesn't know I'm here."

"I'm glad you came."

"Here." Luca held out a vial of purplish liquid. "Melina says hi."

Frances held the vial up to the light. A tiny plant floated inside, its roots still intact. "What is it?"

"She says it'll help your scars. Something about your 'condition'? She said you'd know what she meant."

"My condition?" Melina couldn't have heard about the procedure. Not even Luca knew. At least, not fully. She thought back to that night at the apothecary. Soon, understanding dawned across her face. "She must have figured it out when she treated my leg. That's why she asked about my accident."

"What do you mean?" asked Luca. "Figured what out?"

Frances told Luca everything that had happened, everything her father told her. The accident, the procedure, everything, holding nothing back.

"I always knew there was something spooky about you," he said when she finished. She tossed a rag at him, which he failed to dodge. "Just kidding! Mostly."

His smile faded. He looked down, toeing at the stone floor.

Frances could see he wanted to ask her something.

"You don't have to be scared of me," she said. "I'm the same as I was. At least, I think I am." She picked up the notebook. "That's what I've been trying to figure out."

"Actually, I was kind of scared of you before." Luca paused, chewing his bottom lip. "What did you see when you, when you were—"

"Dead?"

He nodded.

"Honestly? I don't remember. I was on the ground; then I was in my bed. It was like falling into a dreamless sleep and waking up the next day like nothing happened."

His face fell. "Does that mean there's no heaven?"

Frances thought about his father, and how much Luca must want to see him again. She thought about her own parents. Her real parents, who had died in the accident.

"I don't think it means anything. Maybe I don't remember because it was something so . . . so *other* that my mind couldn't hold on to it."

Luca considered this. "Maybe we're not allowed to remember," he said, "because, if we did, we'd want to go back so badly we couldn't be happy here anymore."

Frances smiled. "Maybe."

"Still, it'd be nice to know for sure, wouldn't it?"

"It would," she agreed. "But it'll have to stay a mystery for now."

Luca picked up a tool from the table and looked it over. "There are all sorts of mysteries out there, I guess. But if anyone can solve them, you can."

Frances thought about how it felt to wake Grimme—the excitement, the pride, the sense of discovery. Then she thought about how it all turned out. "I don't know if that's a good idea."

"Why not? You're a scientist. I thought that's what you do."

"It's what my great-grandfather did." She turned back a few pages in the notebook and held it out for Luca to see. "I've been able to decipher more of his notes. The ones I can remember. I thought it would be formulas, new hypotheses, exciting discoveries. But you know what it is?"

Luca shook his head.

"Regrets," she said. "Listen to this one:

"'With Melina's departure, I am alone. How long until I begin talking to my subjects? What would we have to discuss apart from my work? Yet, they are my work. Perhaps it is better they cannot yet talk back.'"

"That's depressing," Luca said.

Frances flipped to a new page. "Here's another:

"'Perhaps there is no need to continue the experiment. I have failed to wake the subject—instead I have become him.'"

Frances finished reading and closed the notebook.

"You're not him," Luca said.

She sighed. "I don't know what I am."

"You're you! Everybody has stuff that makes them different. I like playing with dolls—"

"Luca, I shouldn't have called them that. I'm sorry."

"I'm glad you did. I'm okay with it." He grinned. "You dress like a boy, I play with dolls. It kind of works."

Frances smiled. "I guess it does."

"So, you died," Luca continued, shrugging his shoulders.

"Twice," she corrected him.

"Okay, you died twice. That's not so weird. Everybody dies; you've just had more practice than the rest of us."

"But it was my great-grandfather's work that brought me back."

"So? Who you are hasn't changed. You're Frances Victoria Stenzel, the smartest, strongest, bravest girl I know."

"The only girl you know," she reminded him.

"Frances Victoria Stenzel, the only girl I know."

They laughed together. Luca stood up and held out his hand. "Come on. Your parents said I could stay for lunch. Maybe you don't eat anymore, but I'm starving. The lab will still be here when we're done."

Frances looked around the room, at the instruments and

tools, the specimens and research. She took Luca's hand. "Okay," she said. "I'm ready."

Frances told Luca to wait in the Great Room and went upstairs for a fresh change of clothes. She pulled a white shirt and gray pants from the wardrobe, along with her trusty green suspenders. As she tied her bow tie, she saw something scuttle across the corner of her vision. She whirled around. It was the spider. She found the glass jar on her dressing table where she'd left it a lifetime ago and crept toward the creature. With one swift movement, she trapped it inside.

"What am I going to do with you?" she said, giving the glass a gentle tap.

The spider huddled against far side of the jar as Frances slid a sheet of paper underneath. Its leg looked healthy. The splint was gone. She brought the jar to her window and pushed it open with her shoulder.

"You won't bite me this time, will you?"

Not wanting to take any chances, Frances removed the sheet of paper and picked the spider up from behind, keeping her fingers away from its fangs.

"I bet you think the Manor's a pretty big place," she said, sitting on the windowsill. "Everything you could ever need." She hooked her heels under the window seat and stretched her full length, just far enough to reach the top branch of a tree outside. She set the spider down.

"Go. Be free. There's an entire world out there."

The spider hesitated, gripping the bark like an eight-fingered hand as the branch swayed in the breeze. Then it crawled toward the trunk of the tree and disappeared among the leaves.

Frances finished dressing and straightened her tie in the mirror. She looked at herself for the first time since she came back and frowned. Her hair had grown. It swept across her shoulders, now, curling up at the ends. She found a pair of scissors in the drawer with her hairbrush and pins, and a smile spread across her face. Perhaps it was time to make a change.

Downstairs, Luca and her parents were already seated around the kitchen table.

"Hi," Frances said. Victor, Mary, and Luca looked up from their food and the room fell silent. Her parents stared at her, their jaws nearly on the table.

"Your beautiful hair . . . ," Mary said. She sounded as if she might cry.

"Your beautiful face," Victor said, smiling.

Luca cocked his head to one side. "Did you do something different with your tie?"

Frances smiled and passed her fingers through her hair. It felt so light and cool. She was glad to get it out of her eyes and off her face. She wasn't going to hide anymore.

Hobbes set a plate of food in front of her, and she sat down to join her family, scars and all.

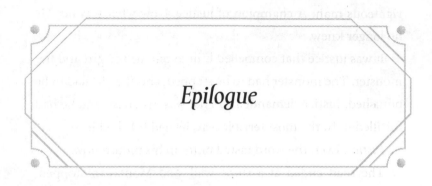

Epilogue

Constable Willermus Montavon trailed behind his deputies, head hung low, arms limp at his sides. When they entered the station, he did not. He continued on instead, ignoring their calls. The sun set fire to the sky and extinguished, leaving Bern in darkness. Still, he walked.

To a shopkeeper locking her doors, or a nurse drawing the shutters for the night, the constable's course might have appeared wandering, random. Montavon himself might have thought the same, at first. But his destination had been set before he entered the city, perhaps at the moment he pulled the trigger and watched, helpless, as his bullet missed its mark.

The spires of the Basel Minster loomed in the distance. He had spent many nights in its sanctuary, kneeling in the mottled glow of stained glass. Each window depicted a martyr's righteous end. Willermus Montavon had considered himself a righteous man. A champion of justice. Now what was he? He no longer knew.

It was justice that compelled him to pursue the girl and her monster. The monster had to be stopped, and the girl had to be punished. Justice demanded it. That was his quest, and he had fulfilled it. In the most terrible way, he had fulfilled it.

Justice. Even the word tasted bitter in his mouth now.

The road ended at a stone wall, and Montavon stopped. Beyond it, he heard the soft roar of the Aare river. Snow melting in the mountains quickened its course, sending it surging against its banks. He unclasped the badge from his vest and set it on the ledge, then did the same with his cap and club. He would tender his official resignation in the morning, but already the uniform felt wrong, like it had grown heavier, stifling. His pistol he pulled from its holster and held out in front of him. The moonlight seemed not to touch it; it was a black scar across his hands. He opened the chamber and let the three remaining bullets clatter to the ground. The weapon, he dropped into the river. Its splash was lost to the rushing currents.

From his vest, Montavon drew the leather-bound book he had taken from the girl. Its contents were alien to him, but he remembered her eyes when she saw it in his hands. *That look* he could read.

This book held secrets. Secrets she was terrified to see revealed.

Yet, when he fired on the creature—born, no doubt from these very pages—she leaped to save him. *Why? Why would she sacrifice herself for a monster?*

The image of that fateful moment flooded his mind, unfolding before him again and again until a weight settled onto his chest, catching his breath in his throat.

Montavon loosened his collar and looked out over the water. If he cast the book into the river, could he be certain it would be destroyed? The Stenzel girl wreaked so much havoc, and she was only a child! Men far more wicked than she walked the earth. Men with resources, armies. He didn't dare imagine the horrors such men might devise with its knowledge.

The weight bore down harder, pressing now from all sides, like a serpent coiling around his chest. He reached to brace himself against the wall, but a sharp pain beneath his ribs stopped him short. The book fell from his hands, and he slid to the ground.

Across the street, two figures emerged from the darkness and stepped into the lamplight.

"Help me," he called.

The men crossed the empty street in silence, their faces still masked in shadow. One of them tossed his scarf behind his back and leaned over Montavon. Face-to-face, he could see the man was smiling. A thin mustache stretched across his lip.

I've seen this man before, Montavon realized, *with the girl's family. He was there when I—* Pain seized his chest and splintered down his left arm.

"My, my," Mr. Byron said. "Aren't you in a state?" He extended his hand, but when Montavon reached to grasp it, Mr. Byron ignored him and plucked the book from the ground instead.

"No!" Montavon cried. He lunged for the book. Mr. Byron snatched it away and watched, amused, as he collapsed against the cobblestones.

"I'll admit we did plan to kill you," Mr. Byron said. "Loose ends and all that. However, it appears your own heart may save us the trouble." He studied Montavon's face. "Guilt, perhaps? All its crushing force bearing down on you? The conscience is a powerful thing. That's why I got rid of mine many years ago." With a wink, he smoothed his trousers and turned to his companion. "Wait until he's finished, then collect the body. I'll be in the automobile."

The body? Montavon's mind raced. *What does he want with my body?*

Mr. Byron looked back over his shoulder and smirked. "Have no fear, Constable. We won't let you go to waste." Then he crossed the street and disappeared once more into the darkness.

Montavon struggled to prop himself against the stone wall.

The weight was merciless now, squeezing the air from his lungs. He could no longer hear the river.

The man called Braun stood over him, expressionless.

Waiting for me to die.

Montavon remembered a sketch on one of the book's pages, a man laid out on a gurney, tubes protruding from his neck and arms. At once, he understood what they had planned.

He was too weak to call for help, and he would never beg. So when his heart seized like a clenched fist and his vision began to fade, he could only reflect on fate's cruel poetry: it was the girl's heart his bullet struck, and his own heart that failed him now.

At the end, a single word was left drifting through his mind.

Justice.

Acknowledgments

Well, you finished the book. Out of all the stories in the world, you picked this one and stuck with it to the end. For that, you get the first and most important thank-you. I sincerely hope you enjoyed every word.

Of course, before *you* could finish this book, *I* had to finish this book. A lot of people helped me do that. The remaining thank-yous are for them.

Thank you to Susan for her support, creativity, and unyielding honesty.

To the rest of my family and friends for all the big and little ways they made it possible for me to write. (For all the big and little ways they made it *im*possible for me to write, they are hereby absolved.)

To Alice Jerman for seeing this story's potential and helping shape it into what it is today.

To Marlo Berliner for finding the perfect home for Frances and her friends.

To Clare Vaughn, Jacqueline Hornberger, Alexandra Rakaczki, Catherine Lee, and everyone else on my HarperCollins team for lending their skill and creativity to this project.

To Brandon Dorman for bringing Frances's world to life with his spectacular illustrations.

To Shannon Roberts for helping me "kill my darlings," Kristyn Benton and Liz Farrell for believing *Frances and the Monster* was a story worth completing when it was only a few pages long, and Ruby—beta reader extraordinaire—for her insights and excitement.

And to my Swiss readers: thank you for your patience as I've tried to faithfully render your capital city as it was in 1939. I should also ask your forgiveness for the creative liberties I took along the way—most glaringly, relocating the Tschäggättä festival from February in Lötschental to September in Bern.

With that said, all historical events related to the outbreak of the Second World War have been reproduced as accurately as possible, right down to the radio broadcast in Chapter Four, which was taken word-for-word from the English-language transcripts of Switzerland's Swiss Short Wave Service archived at swissinfo.ch. Any inaccuracies are entirely accidental and entirely my fault.